A NEW BEGINNING

"Sidra, I can't stay," Cameron said quietly. "I won't spend my life in a cage. Live or die, I'm leaving the biosphere."

She knew that nothing else she could say would change him. "I'll help you," she said at last. "I'll press the buttons for the doors."

He stood in the docking chamber, looking lost and alone as she pressed the button to trigger both doors in a timed sequence. The outside glass door wouldn't open until the inside biome door was sealed. The stainless steel panel was already closing. In one moment, he'd be lost from her vision and from her life. In three minutes, the docking door would open and he would step Outside.

She followed the heavy door as it closed, moved with it, her eyes holding him to her.

"I love you," he said when the door was almost closed. "Remember that."

It was the only truth she had ever wanted to hear.

Without hesitation, Sidra stepped inside the docking chamber. The steel doors sealed with a loud mechanical click. And she was there beside him.

They watched the glass door of the biosphere lift and open. The first true breeze of their lives moved over them. Together, they walked free and stepped Outside. . . .

PINNACLE BOOKS HAS
SOMETHING FOR EVERYONE—

MAGICIANS, EXPLORERS, WITCHES AND CATS

THE HANDYMAN   (377-3, $3.95/$4.95)
He is a magician who likes hands. He likes their comfortable shape and weight and size. He likes the portability of the hands once they are severed from the rest of the ponderous body. Detective Lanark must discover who The Handyman is before more handless bodies appear.

PASSAGE TO EDEN   (538-5, $4.95/$5.95)
Set in a world of prehistoric beauty, here is the epic story of a courageous seafarer whose wanderings lead him to the ends of the old world—and to the discovery of a new world in the rugged, untamed wilderness of northwestern America.

BLACK BODY   (505-9, $5.95/$6.95)
An extraordinary chronicle, this is the diary of a witch, a journal of the secrets of her race kept in return for not being burned for her "sin." It is the story of Alba, that rarest of creatures, a white witch: beautiful and able to walk in the human world undetected.

THE WHITE PUMA   (532-6, $4.95/NCR)
The white puma has recognized the men who deprived him of his family. Now, like other predators before him, he has become a man-hater. This story is a fitting tribute to this magnificent animal that stands for all living creatures that have become, through man's carelessness, close to disappearing forever from the face of the earth.

BEYOND EDEN

J.M. MORGAN

PINNACLE BOOKS
WINDSOR PUBLISHING CORP.

To my mother, Juanette Hobbs Fields,
who gave me everything she had — her love.

PINNACLE BOOKS

are published by

Windsor Publishing Corp.
475 Park Avenue South
New York, NY 10016

Copyright © 1992 by J.M. Morgan

First printing: April, 1992

Printed in the United States of America

Prologue

And it came to pass, two years before the dawn of the third millennium — the year 2000 — a terrible wailing was heard across the face of the land. A scourge created by the hand of man was loosed upon the Earth. Like a field that is harvested, one by one the people fell. One by one the sickness came to each. To all. Soon, only the animals were left free to graze unchecked on farmlands, to feed along rows of planted corn, to glean the bounty of fallen fruit from abandoned gardens.

In those days, Earth was silent of human voices . . . but for a scattered few.

Chapter One

The boy's back was broken. Wind savaged the grassy Montana plains. The harsh, warning days before winter had come like clawing wildcats, tearing great clumps of earth and gouges from the land. It was a northern wind, holding cold, killing the last of the growing season. Killing the boy.

The child was nearly ten. He was thrown from his horse when the shearing blast spooked the animal. Falling, he heard his spine snap when he hit the ground . . . then heard nothing more until he awoke hours later, shivering in the fierce talons of howling death — alone. Dark swelled up around him. His name was Cody, youngest son of the Inuit man, John Katelo. And he was dying.

Through the long night, tunnels of freezing cold swept over the boy, stealing the breath from his lungs, the life from his body. His thin voice called again and again to his father, to his mother, but was hidden in the loud and constant wailing of the blizzard. With the honey-colored morning, the child's voice was silenced.

"What's that over there?" eighteen-year-old Seth Katelo asked his one-year-younger brother, Jonathan.

He pointed to a small, snow-dusted mound less than fifty feet from where their horses stood, the animals blowing heavily in the icy air. They had been searching since before dawn.

Their father had gone out the night before, in the worst of the storm, looking for Cody. When Seth and Jonathan had left home in the dark before morning, neither Cody nor their father had returned yet. In terror of losing not only her youngest boy, but also her husband and two more of her sons, their mother, Salena, had pleaded with them not to go.

"I've given two children to this land." She spoke of the death of two babies between Cody, and her youngest child, four-year-old Noelle. "Much as I love Cody, we have to face the fact that he may be lost to us, already." She hadn't cried. Her face was hard-set as stone. Her eyes dry and terrible.

"The storm may hit us again before nightfall. Don't make me live through losing you and Jonathan, too. I'd lose my mind then, Seth. I would. What would become of the rest of them?" she'd asked, drawing her hand toward the three girls and one boy standing behind her.

It had been painful, watching his mother's tearless grieving. Seth's eyes had begun to fill, burning in hurt for her. Still, he knew that if his little brother Cody had survived the freezing night, he would be in desperate need by now, perhaps near death, and couldn't make it home without help. Determined to find the boy, he'd torn himself from the desperate clutch of his mother's fingers with the blunt words, "I won't leave Cody out there to die alone."

Jonathan had said nothing, but saddled his horse. They'd ridden out together. Now, hours later, the sky carried a ceiling of woven clouds, thickening with a weight of dark even as they watched.

Their horses snuffed the ground, furrowing trenches in the soft snow with their muzzles, and cropping grass. "I'll have a look." Jonathan urged the chestnut mare forward.

"No, we both will." Seth gave a nudge with his knees to the dance-footed black. The horse gave up the sweet grass reluctantly, and trotted across the drifted plain, toward the snow-covered mound.

Seth was hard-pressed to believe it, even when he saw the familiar white rawhide fringe on Cody's jacket. The twisted angle wasn't right for the shape of a human . . . for the shape of a little boy. The body was bent back like a V, legs and arms pointing in different directions.

"His back's broke." Jonathan got down from his mount. He walked the few steps to the body and brushed the powdering of snow clear from the child's face.

Seth needed air. A squeezing fist held his chest so tightly he couldn't breathe. He was looking down at Cody's face, but everything he knew of Cody was gone from it. The curled-lip mask staring back at him was a cruel image of his brother. The boy's brown eyes were open, but they were dull and unmoving. No life to them.

Jonathan stood beside the body, waiting for a minute. When Seth didn't dismount, he began pulling the boy's legs into a straight line with the torso. The sound was like the slow splintering of a tree branch from its trunk.

"Stop that! What do you think you're doing?" Seth shouted, swinging his booted foot over the back of the horse and jumping down. "You're hurting him!"

"It's all right." Jonathan straightened up from his task. His eyes were glistening with unshed tears. "He can't feel nothin', Seth. We'll take him home to

Mama . . . but not like he was. Not like that."

Seth bent down onto one knee, closer to Cody's body. His hand moved gently over his brother's hands and face, lingering with a scared, light touch. They were small hands, a small face. Just a little boy. Too young to die. Too young to die alone, like this.

"You did the right thing," he said to Jonathan. "You knew what was needed, when I didn't. Come on." He slid his hands beneath Cody's shoulders. "Help me lift him onto the saddle."

They rode slowly back to the house. There was no hurry now. Neither of them was anxious to break the news to their mother. Seth propped Cody's body against his own, sitting up on the saddle. He wouldn't sling the boy over the horse's flanks like a camp blanket. Holding one arm around his brother's chest to keep him from falling, they made their way home.

John Katelo always spoke of the time when the sickness had come as the year of bad spirits. He had seen the ghostly faces in the skies above his campfires that first winter—after he had broken out of the research station in Siberia, Biosphere Four and fled across the frozen tundra. He had seen the spirits of hunters, the old ones, young wives, and children. He had heard the torment of their cries as they walked the Earth, unable to find a way back into their world.

They had followed him, for he was alive, and life was what they wanted. If any man knew about bad spirits, it was John Katelo. He had been completely alone, except for a kind of brotherhood with the little pup, Kip, and he had seen the ghosts of the dead. He had asked their forgiveness, for surviving when they had not. He had hidden his fear, and spoken to them as Brother and as Sister. The old ones, he called Uncle, or

10

Aunt. Respectfully, he honored them with burial caches of their goods, with prayers to the Great Father, and with the songs of a Chukchi hunter. But, he would not take shelter in their houses of death.

That first winter he had worked hard to build shelters of his own as he made his way south, to teach the young dog to hunt, and to endure the winds of the tundra. For many days, he had heard nothing but the sound of those winds, blowing against the cave-of-ice igloo. In the sound were the voices of those spirits who had gone before him. He had heard them clearly, their cries beating against the outside of his shelter—the joined blocks of snow. From within, he had listened, and was afraid. Only the companionship of the dog had kept him sane.

Thoughts came to him now of the old dog. Kip had been gone five years this winter. In those days, he had been Katelo's only friend in that first turning of the seasons after the death of the world, and had saved his life twice since then, earning a place of warmth and ease in his old age at the Inuit's hearth.

Now, with the death of his youngest son, John Katelo knew that the boy, too, had heard the keening cries in the wind. Alone, the child had been surrounded by the hungry voices, and his spirit stolen.

More than any other thing he had endured in the twenty years since the virus created in Biosphere Four had escaped the glass dome and spread itself like a blanket of death around the Earth, John Katelo felt this loss of his son as a personal wound, lacerating him. He carried the injury of this child's death as an amulet of grief within himself. No one, not his wife, not the family he loved, could take it from him. No man should live among spirits of the dead; no child should die alone.

The hurt was still fresh, therefore, when his eldest

11

son, Seth, came to him and told him the longing of his heart.

"Jonathan and I will leave this valley," Seth said without apology. For his mother the boy would have eased the words, but for his father he said them openly. It was the way between men. Katelo understood this. He did not ask why.

"Where would you go?" he asked, instead. He knew well enough that both Seth and Jonathan were men now, and could not be contained within their father's circle of family forever. The land in this valley had been good to them, plentiful with grass and planted seed. Here, Katelo, and Salena Cross, the woman he had found in the north country, had waited out the winter on their long trek down from Canada. Here, six sons had been born to them, and three daughters.

The valley was a hollow between the mountains, protected from the worst of winter, and high enough to keep the cattle in grass all summer. They had stayed, finding a place of peace in this sheltered basin, beside a lake of blue water. Their house faced away from the past, toward the beauty of that lake. Behind them lay the spears of gray-black mountains, and the world of bitter cold.

"We'll go south," said Seth, "in the hope that we will find others."

Katelo knew they would be looking for wives. In his heart, he hated to see his children go away from him into the unknown, but to insist that they stay would only insure their loneliness. In the twenty years that he and Salena had lived in this valley, they had seen no other living soul but that which they had made of their own flesh.

To see his first two sons leave home was a weight added to his heart, along with the grief he carried over the death of his youngest boy. It burdened Katelo and he felt the power of this burden pull him down, but said nothing. He had lived through forty-three winters. By that spring he felt the great cost of every day of those years.

More terrible than his own sense of loss, John Katelo worried about how the leaving of her two eldest sons would affect Salena. Cody's death had brought a mournful silence to her. She moved through her days without words, turned inward to a quietness his voice could not touch.

"We will say nothing of this to your mother until you are ready to leave," he told his sons.

But to his surprise, Salena knew and had readied belongings for the boys to take with them on their journey. Katelo watched as her fingers moved over the clothes she had made for Seth and Jonathan to wear, smoothing the fabric and laying the shirts, pants, and warm coats into satchels for each boy. He watched, his heart twisted into a tight knot at the sight.

"When you have found what you are looking for," she said to each of them, "you must come back to us. Bring your wives, your families, and return. This place is your home. Remember.

"Your father is no longer a young man. He will need your help in years to come. You must give me your promise now, before you step one foot from this place where you began," she charged first Seth, then Jonathan. "Promise," she demanded of her firstborn.

Seth was openly weeping, his will to leave visibly broken by his mother's words. "Keep me in your heart, Mother," he said, "and I will come home."

She turned to Jonathan. "Promise."

Katelo watched in breathless hurt.

Jonathan was like him, more Inuit than Seth, or any of the other children. His eyes were clear, and his voice steady. "If there is life beyond this place," he said

13

gently, taking his mother's hands in his own, "I will find it, and I will come here to tell you."

"Then go with your mother's blessing," she said to them, kissing each, and holding these two sons one last time in her arms.

Chapter Two

A gray-clouded wind pushed at the Outside day. From within the dome, through Biosphere Seven's thick triangles of sealed glass, Cameron Nathan observed the contrast of his own too tranquil world. Beyond the protective wall was movement, wild and harsh. The sands of the high Texas desert blew in billowing sails along the land, lifting skyward into a vortex of swirling pillars of dust and sounding cracks of blue-white lightning.

There was no lightning in Cameron's world. The land of the Insiders was a halcyon place, five hundred acres of productive farmland in a totally self-contained environment, its climate controlled in all elements of temperature, oxygen, humidity—and calm. It knew no storms or rages against its unblemished peace. For the heart of a seventeen-year-old boy, it was as monotonous and blunt as an unsharpened knife which could draw no blood.

"Cameron! There you are." A few months older than Cameron, Sidra Innis gave him a look of mothering disapproval. "Jessica's been looking everywhere for you. Something important's happened. She's making an announcement to the whole colony—and waiting for you." She moved closer to him. "Why do you want to sit out here, anyway? It only makes you sad."

She had the distinctive Indian looks of her father, Outsider, Josiah Gray Wolf—a long, narrow face with high cheekbones, wings of black eyebrows, and straight black hair. She also had her mother's green eyes, and skin tone only a shade darker than Cameron's.

"What's it like out there, do you think?" He stared beyond the walls of glass. "What's it like to feel the wind? See that?" He pointed to a swirling cloud of sand and brush kicked up by the storm. "Imagine standing there and letting all that power brush against you. Imagine hard rain and snow, Sidra. Being outside, in a blizzard. They know what it's like." He watched two of the people from the colony of Outsiders who lived near the biosphere. They moved freely in the open space, unrestrained by the confines of any protective walls.

"You're wrong to envy them, Cam. They don't have a shelter like ours to shield them from cold or heat. Do you think they want to be in the storms? Their lives are a struggle just to survive. Look at their faces the next time you're dreaming of Outside. They're exhausted. Each of them has backbreaking work to draw anything from the earth, and then there's a storm or days of scorching heat, and it destroys all their efforts. Don't wish you were out there, Cameron. They deserve your pity."

He wasn't sure he believed that. Everything she'd said might be true—he'd seen as much for himself—except, the Outsiders were free. He wasn't.

He'd been born within the glass sanctuary of Biosphere Seven—the research station in the high Texas desert—and could never leave its boundaries . . . not if he wanted to go on living. Outside, was the manmade virus that had spread across the earth three years before he was born, destroying all human life, except for a few survivors who'd possessed an inherited immunity to it. They were the colony of Outsiders living beyond Biosphere Seven's glass beehive-shaped dome.

"We're late for Meeting. Come on," Sidra urged him, taking his hand. When he didn't move, she added, "Stop letting it tear at you. It's not for us, out there. Life is desperate in that world. The virus is still—"

"The virus!" he stormed. "I don't want to hear about the virus anymore. It controls everything. All our lives! It keeps me caged behind this barrier."

"Be grateful to be inside the sphere," she answered his fury. "The others have no choice. Nothing protects them. Any one of them might trade places with you, to have the comforts we've been given. It's savage out there. Packs of wild dogs attack them. Is that what you want? Many of them become sick, with fevers, with ulcers on their legs and arms, and no medicines to do anything about it. Their babies are born and quickly die of the virus. Only a few of their children inherit the immunity and live."

She stepped closer. "Can't you be satisfied here, Cam? We're safe inside the dome. It's a protected world. Can't you find a way to be happy in it?" Her fingers touched his arm.

He wanted to reassure her, wanted to take that worried look from her eyes—beautiful eyes. He wanted to reassure his mother, Jessica, too. But, he couldn't. The life offered here wasn't enough, not when he knew there was an open Earth beyond Biosphere Seven's sealed dome. As much as he loved and respected his mother—and in a very different way, Sidra—it wasn't enough. It never would be.

"I'm not ready to stop hoping." He knew his words hurt her. "Maybe everyone else within the sphere is ready to spend his entire life here, but I'm not. Someday, I'm going out."

Her glance shifted away from him and she stared at the ground. Cameron had grown up with Sidra and knew beyond any doubt that she loved him. She had never said as much and they hadn't yet been together as man and woman, but he knew.

His feelings were like the blackening clouds, a storm of emotions. Part of him wanted to pull Sidra to him, say the words he knew she wanted to hear, that everything would be all right, kiss her soft mouth and lie with her in his arms. Part of him longed for that. But an equal part, one that he could not deny, said he would never be satisfied with a life contained within the isolated world of Biosphere Seven.

"You're right about one thing; we'd better go to Meeting," he told her. "I don't want to be responsible for both of us being late."

They left the observation window, walked through the savannah biome, and headed for the habitat wing. His mother, Jessica Nathan, would be speaking to the entire assembly. Cameron knew she expected him to attend.

"Don't worry." He matched his step to Sidra's shorter stride. "There's nothing I can do right now about leaving. You're stuck with me for a while longer."

She smiled, and he wanted to kiss her for the love in it. But the love she felt hurt him, too. He knew that one day it might trap him.

"Come on," he said too roughly. "Let's get going before being so close to you makes me forget everything I want Outside.

They walked a short distance, then he stopped and turned to her once more, his voice angry and hard. "I'm not going to let the dream go, Sidra, not for anyone. Don't make the mistake of believing that I will."

She didn't answer with words, but her eyes spoke. They said he had hurt her, that he would always hurt her, and that she would go on loving him. She walked past him, toward the habitat buildings and the Meeting.

Sick with longing and regret, Cameron followed.

Chapter Three

March 2018: We have begun a new year with news from the Outside. It is a beginning, and a hope that we sorely need. Our families are in good health, and the sphere remains our protection from the virus still active beyond the glass walls of the dome.

The children are my greatest concern. As they mature into men and women, what hope will they find within the boundaries of these walls? Have we done too little to save ourselves? Is it possible that we haven't risked enough?

So much is at stake within this biosphere, among the lives of these children. We know of only a few survivors living on the Outside. Beyond them, we of Biosphere Seven, and perhaps a very few more in one or two of the other spheres, may be all that remains of the human race. Knowing that, any risk may be too great.

Exiting her computer journal, Jessica hurried from the room. The people were waiting, and she had a lot to tell them.

Jessica Nathan, a slim attractive woman of fifty-two, stood at the podium ready to address the gathered family of Biosphere Seven. As their acknowledged leader for the last twenty years, she looked out on the faces of the young. These were the children conceived and born within the enclosed world of this sphere. She also saw her peers, five of the original team members of the habitat, and remembered how it had been in the beginning. . . .

Life within the glass walls of the Crystal Kingdom had seemed a noble thing twenty years ago when Jessica Nathan, Quinn Kelsey, and eight other young scientists had entered the completely enclosed, totally self-sustaining habitat of Biosphere Seven. The biosphere, one of six habitat domes scattered around the Earth, had been an experimental prototype for future manned stations in space.

The stations, constructed of glass and steel-framed walls, were sealed against atmospheric contamination from Outside — just as they would have been in space, or on another planet. Each unit contained individual biomes, or ecospheres, of preselected environments and agricultural land. Each biome housed its own rich variety of life: animal, plant, insect, fish, and human.

Biosphere Seven, the largest of the six prototypes in the project, had been designed as far more than a Noah's Ark. It not only housed life, but was the nurturing source of its own existence. Because Biosphere Seven maintained an independent system of air and water, it could grow crops in the fields of its farming biomes, raise livestock within the enclosed space of that shelter, and provide fish from its sea — all without outside influence from its source planet.

It had been an honorable venture, an interval of

gained knowledge to improve the threatened environment of Earth. It had begun as an opportunity to learn a system of maintenance for the planet, to expand the possibility of future satellite stations in space, and to prove man's adaptability to survive in a detached and isolated world.

A noble venture. Those five men and five women had become the players in this drama of a new Earth, a new life. Jessica Nathan had been chosen as the team leader of the fellowship of ten. She had left behind her the real world, and a husband whom she loved—Brad McGhee.

Brad had been chosen as Spokesman for Biosphere Seven, and had remained on the Outside to act as the communications representative with the public. With his blessing and hope for their future, Jessica Nathan had entered the glass-domed world of the biosphere as a neophyte, a wide-eyed child full of wonder and awe. They were creating a new society, these ten. A new future. They were the positive hope of mankind.

And then . . . it had all gone wrong.

An experimental virus created in the remote outpost of Biosphere Four, the Siberian unit, escaped the confines of that glass dome and began a legacy of death, starting with those scientists within the satellite station, and spiraling out into the world beyond. A pandemic, the likes of which the human race had never known, scourged man from the face of the Earth. With few exceptions—people living within the remaining biospheres, persons with an inherited immunity to the virus, and fewer still, individuals who contracted the virus but amazingly survived—except for these, all mankind perished.

And we're what's left, thought Jessica, *this scattering. Seeds cast by the hand of an unseen God.*

For twenty years they had survived, six of the original team members and their children born within the shelter of the sphere. They were the Insiders, for life within their world was only possible inside the encasing glass walls of the habitat.

Two of the original team had died within the dome. Two more had risked the Outside—one, only to die a few days later of the virus. The other, Josiah Gray Wolf, to venture alone into the heart of the land and gather the few remaining outside survivors to himself—those men and women left in the United States, a final gleaning of the race of man—and bringing them back to this place of refuge just beyond the walls of the domed city. Now, he led them as a kind of patriarch, or chief.

They called themselves the Outsiders, ten survivors of the great pandemic and the children born into their camp in the years since the time of devastation. Josiah Gray Wolf was their leader. And Brad McGhee, the husband Jessica had left behind in the old world, had become their prophet.

A change had come to them all. A transfiguration. Human life, where it still existed, had been irrevocably altered. The old Earth they had known was gone.

Jessica stared out into the sea of faces. Children. Friends. Family. It was the children whom she held in her thoughts. They were the hope of humanity's future. Eighteen new lives had begun under the protective shelter of Biosphere Seven, encompassing in total the genetic heritage of every member of the original team, with the exception of Piper Robinson, who had died sacrificing her life to defend the satellite from a break-in by the man who had financed its development, Jordan Talbot Exeter. He had died trying to join them by opening the sphere, an act which would have meant exposure to the virus for them all. Piper Robinson had protected them with her life.

Because the inhabitants could not select partners from beyond the walls of the dome, it had become vital that the genetic pool remain as diverse as possible. To achieve that larger potential, each woman had been asked to bear children on a rotating basis to each of the men within the unit.

These unions were not considered a marital link — not in the way Jessica and Quinn had remained steadfast partners throughout their years within the dome, as had Cathe and Daniel — but a plan for genetic preservation. It was a system Jessica and Quinn had suggested to the others after the first biosphere-born generation had begun inside the sphere. With three women and three men remaining from the original ten, it had been the only practical way to prevent inbreeding.

Even with such purposeful intention, the scant number of genetic possibilities available within their enclosed world would seriously limit the choice of partners among these children. The oldest Insiders — the catch-name the children called themselves — among the biosphere-born were now reaching adulthood. How much longer would it be, Jessica wondered, before they realized the full scope of the problem? She tried to dismiss the tangled thoughts from her mind, concentrating instead on the unexpected good news of the day.

She spoke to the families gathered before her. "In the twenty years since Biosphere Seven first opened its doors to our small colony of man, cataclysmic changes have come to the inhabitants of old Earth. As all of us know, it was twenty years ago that a virus created in the Siberian laboratory of our sister station, Biosphere

Four, escaped through the sealant of that unit, releasing a new and unchecked plague upon the human race. Bioengineered to only affect people, the virus quickly swept its scythe of death through small cities and whole continents. In a matter of weeks, the greater population of mankind was gone. In months, only a few remained."

It was a history lesson which all the adults and older children knew. Her message was primarily directed toward the younger audience, the children who had no memory of this, and as a reminder to them all of the disastrous consequences of unscrupulous scientific experimentation. It also served as a platform from which to announce her news.

"Of the six original biosphere domes, Two through Seven, our community of Biosphere Seven has had knowledge of only one other habitat which might still exist. Biosphere Four, in Siberia, we know was devastated by the virus. Biosphere Six, we learned from Brad McGhee, was destroyed by the surrounding population in China, as an act of outrage against the creators of that unit. Our communication systems have indicated that the seals of Biospheres Three and Five were also breached. Beyond our uncertain knowledge of these outposts, we at Biosphere Seven have received no communication from the single remaining satellite . . . until now."

A hushed excitement hummed a raw current through the room, expanding and contracting in a living rhythm. She waited for the assembly to fall silent again. As she paused, she glanced across the chamber at Quinn Kelsey and felt the calm assurance of his steady influence flow toward her. He was the rock she had held to all these years. Without him, she might have become like Diana.

The room quieted again and Jessica gave them the message they had all waited so long to hear. "Last night, after twenty years of radio silence, a lengthy communication came from Biosphere Two, our sister station in north Wales."

Loud cheering built from the adults at the back of the room, cascading in a sounding wave toward her. She laughed with the sheer joy of it. The younger children applauded something they had heard only as a fairy tale—the story of another glass city, with farms and families like their own, shielded from the virus by the protective walls of a biosphere dome. It was a fantasy they had heard stories about since the cradle, and now were asked to believe had come true.

"The leader of Biosphere Two, Paul Schefield, spoke to me last night. He and eight others of the initial Bio Two team have survived. Like us, they have had children born into their isolated world." Another round of cheering followed this announcement.

"I believe he was as excited to hear from us, as I was to hear his voice after so long a silence. He told me that they were completely cut off from the world, isolated on a northwest island off the coast of Wales. In all this time, no Outside survivor ever ventured across the stormy barrier of the Atlantic to verify that they were still alive. For them, they were all that was left of the world."

Jessica could see the strong emotional effect her words had on them, especially on those old enough to remember what it had been like to believe themselves totally alone. She continued. "It was only a week ago, after two men crossed that ocean channel in a small boat, that Paul Schefield and the people of Bio Two learned there were other survivors.

"Like our own Outsiders, a remnant of the population of the British Isles have endured the ravages of the virus and have maintained a stronghold of courage in the midst of despair. Those two survivors from the boat were able to reestablish a connection to the computer satellite and reopen Biosphere Two's link with our enclosed world."

This news was greeted with awed silence from the separate clusters within the hall. They were loosely divided into matrilineal groupings: the Nathan family, Jessica's six children—two each by the three available fathers, plus her adopted son, Trinity, child of Maggie Adair; the Innis family, Cathe's eight children—the product of four individual paternities, as Josiah Gray Wolf had fathered Cathe's daughter Sidra before he left the biosphere; and the Hunt family, Diana's three daughters—one fathered by each of the three men.

Standing alone and apart from these strictly female clusters, were the three adult males of the biosphere complex, Quinn Kelsey, Griffin Llewellyn, and Daniel Urquidez.

"This news is a confirmation of our hope that at least one remaining biosphere besides our own may have survived. And there is an additional tantalizing reward. We now have strong reason to believe that there are other pockets of outside survivors living in isolated groups throughout the world.

"The family of man has been severely damaged," she emphasized, looking at these eighteen children, the last hope of their world, "scattered and restructured," tight emotion played havoc with her voice, "but before God . . . not annihilated."

The community stood and applauded. Her own children, five sons and two daughters—Trinity, Cameron, Roarke, Bram, Meredith, Rachel, and Matthew—were cheering loudest of all. In this moment of

27

happiness, Jessica rejoiced in all her children and wanted to believe that she loved them equally, but knew her heart had a mother's preference for the son and daughter she had borne to Quinn Kelsey—Cameron and Rachel. They alone among her six birth children had been conceived of love.

"Jessica, how does this knowledge help us?" Diana Hunt stood and spoke from the center of the room. "They're alive, yes, but we can't reach them; they can't reach us. Does knowing they exist make anything better?"

The eyes of Diana's three daughters, Cassandra, Alix, and Lara, mirrored their mother's expression of doubt.

Damn the woman! Diana had always been the dissenter. Couldn't she let it alone, just once? It had been that way since Diana realized she could never leave the biosphere. None of them could leave the unit and survive for more than a few days in the virus-polluted atmosphere of Outside. Diana had stayed. There hadn't been any choice, but she hadn't made it easy for the rest of them. Her actions let them know, always. She was here against her will.

Jessica directed her answer to the children in this assembly. "Knowing that there are other survivors does help. It tells us we aren't alone. There are other communities, maybe many of them, struggling to find the answer of how to live with the virus, or a way to destroy it."

She spoke directly to Diana's three daughters. "Our survival as a species depends on us thinking of ourselves not as an isolated colony, but as the family of mankind. One life spared from anywhere in the world enriches all of us. That one life may be the catalyst for discovering our freedom."

28

The room resounded in applause. Diana sat down, her needle of doubt brushed aside by Jessica's clear insistence on hope.

The children still believed in their future, Jessica realized. Their faces reflected their trust in her, and in the parents who'd brought them into this world. They were innocent of doubt. They believe we will go on, she told herself, gladdened by their spirit.

But, will we? In the secret valleys of her mind, she wondered. *Will we?*

Chapter Four

"When the virus came," it was said among the Outsiders, "the Earth stopped spinning for a time and let the people off."

That was how it seemed to many, as if the world they'd known had vanished, replaced by this harsher land of intimidating loneliness. The challenge of living every day, of simply not dying like the rest of the world, exhausted many. They were alive. They had been spared, but life was desperately hard . . . and for what?

For some, like Brad McGhee, the answer wasn't to be found in any explanation of physical law. Nature couldn't answer for his survival. Nature hadn't protected him, any more than it had millions of others. Like ninety-nine percent of the old world's population, he'd had no immunity. There had been nothing to prepare him for the only real challenge to mankind in the Twentieth Century — a new and deadly virus.

When it happened, his body had yielded easily to the illness. Nature hadn't saved him. It couldn't. Like the others, he had been left to die. He had stumbled down the banks of the riverbed, blind, almost deaf, and weak to the point of total collapse.

But he had lived.

That was twenty years ago, and still Brad—or Prophet, as he was now called by the colony of Outsiders, as their spiritual guide—could recall the sense he'd felt of the Lady who had lifted him from the place of death and brought him back into the world of the living. That he had lived was her will, her decision. How he had lived, since that day, was his.

The People called him Prophet. He was known to have visions, to see a certain light of future . . . and the People came to him. For the Lady's sake, he would not turn them away. He wasn't a religious man, not a priest, rabbi, or minister, but for some he served that function. His belief was in the spirit.

He was, by his own understanding, the spoke of a far greater celestial wheel, a kind of channel. He was a single voice for the messages of God. And he was one voice, carrying the prayers of man. Brad, the Prophet, was still a spokesman for his people, but now he was the messenger between heaven and Earth.

At fifty-three, Prophet had remained unattached to any woman. He had avoided relationships, beyond the strong feelings of love he still carried for the wife of his youth, Jessica Nathan—who for the past twenty years had lived as the wife of Quinn Kelsey, within the separated world of Biosphere Seven. Time had changed the man called Prophet, but it had not lessened his love for Jessica. The commitment to this woman was as strong as the one he bore to the faith which sustained him.

Each of them, he was certain, had something of great importance to accomplish. Jessica, in leading the survivors within the city of glass, and in sustaining a hope in their future. He, in reminding the People of the Outside colony that there *was* a merciful God, that this God knew of their plight and had spared them. Without Prophet's sure belief, many might have given up and chosen to die.

"It doesn't take a vision to tell me you're not with us."

Prophet turned and saw the leader of the camp standing behind him. A lay of dark clouds outlined the man; wind swept through the long strands of his hair, and the first drops of hard rain beat at his face.

"Your body's sitting on the boulder, but your mind's somewhere else, locked within that glass cage."

Josiah Gray Wolf was the one other person in this Outsider's colony whom Prophet had known from the beginning, since the start of the Biosphere Seven project. Josiah had once lived inside the dome, as one of the original team members.

God had chosen Josiah, and not the other way around. This man's life had been saved for a purpose: to gather the lost ones to himself and bring them to this place of refuge in the wilderness, the high Texas desert. If Prophet was the colony's spiritual messenger, then Josiah was their patriarch. The children called him Sagamore, an honorary Indian address meaning wise man or chief.

Prophet looked closely at the man, noting how little Josiah had changed over the years. He was still as straight of back as he had been when he was thirty, and his hair almost as dark. His body had a strength that belied his years.

"I was wondering how they reacted to the news about contact with Biosphere Two." Prophet stood and turned his back on the beehive dome. He kept any other thoughts he might have had—about Jessica, about the dream of holding her in his arms again—to himself.

"About the same as our group did, I imagine." Josiah walked the few steps to join him.

"I'm not so sure. We can imagine that colony in Wales becoming part of our lives. It wouldn't be easy, but it is possible. With those inside the dome, there isn't a chance of that happening."

"Unless one of us learns to navigate a ship or pilot a plane," Josiah reminded him, "we've got about as much shot at it as they have."

"You're a good man for not whitewashing truth."

"I look at things straight on. Which brings me back to what you're doing out here, sitting on a rock, staring down at the biosphere."

Brad didn't answer.

"You're still in love with Jessica, and I know that can't be easy. You've been a strength for everyone else. I just wanted . . ." Josiah let the words fall away, then started again. "I'm always there for you if you need to talk. That's all I wanted to say."

"Thanks. I'll remember." What Prophet needed was more than words. What he needed was faith. The fact was, he was losing his.

"I'll see you back at camp? The storm will be worse before nightfall." Josiah's eyes showed more than a little concern.

"Give me a few minutes. I'll be there soon."

Josiah left him then. Turning back, Prophet stared at the glass dome nearly hidden in the dark of lowering clouds. *Can I go on? How much longer?* He was so alone.

Waiting for the healing dark, he watched the pale corona of sun fade behind the muted angles of the dome. It had been like this on that first day, over twenty years ago, when Jessica had entered Biosphere Seven and left him behind. He had sat on this same hill that day, lost in the colors of the sunset. Later, he had called her from the media headquarters next door to the sphere.

"I miss you," she'd told him.

"After one day?" He'd made as if to laugh it off,

then hadn't. "I miss you, too. Are we going to get through this? I mean — "

"We'll get through," she'd promised. "And when it's finished, we'll start our family."

That was what she'd said and what he'd hoped for . . . but it hadn't come true.

Forcing himself to turn away from the memory of his wife, just as he'd had to turn away from the world which was lost, Prophet descended the hill, returning to the only home that was left to him — the colony of Outsiders.

Jessica Nathan sat on the damp earth of the rain forest and thought of her seven children. Would this enclosed world be enough for them? Was it enough for Cameron?

The gentle slope of the rain forest formed a hill overlooking the agricultural fields to the south. Where the earth retained the coolness of the forest, an orchard of fruit-bearing trees, orange, apple, pear, and lemon, seeded the ground in rows of green leaf and pale pink and white blossoms. The rain forest itself was home to the more tropical varieties: banana, pineapple, papaya, and mango. In the warmer biomes, they grew kiwi and grapes. The salt marsh nearby gave them cranberries.

Some form of fruit trees and berry bushes bore year-round in this temperature-controlled environment. There were only two seasons; they were the continuous pair of planting and of harvest. There was a sameness to the land, and to the small world it nourished. It was a sameness Jessica had grown to feel a peace with, but would her children? What need to escape these confines did they already feel?

She thought of Cameron again, and the look she

had seen in his eyes more than once during these last few weeks.

Cameron wanted a freedom he couldn't find in this sealed world. He wanted to be free of any cage, any walls which bound him to one place. She knew. She had always known. She'd felt it, too. Cameron was the son of her spirit, and she understood his heart as well as she did her own. And now, she knew he would risk anything for this freedom. That was the certainty and the fear which had brought her to this place.

Chapter Five

Of the original team of ten Biosphere Seven members, only six remained, three women and three men: Jessica Nathan, team leader; Catherine Innis, biologist; Diana Hunt, botanist and geochemist; Quinn Kelsey, computer analyst; Daniel Urquidez, hydroponics analyst; and Griffin Llewellyn, entomologist.

Three of those first ten had died: Maggie Adair, Piper Robinson, and Mike York. The fourth was Josiah Gray Wolf.

Josiah Gray Wolf was among the rarest people of old Earth, those with an inborn immunity to the virus. Not long after the catastrophe—the manmade virus loosed upon the Earth—he had been trapped outside and forced to breathe the contaminated air. Unlike the millions of other humans who died from the sickness, Josiah had proved able to live in this changed and hostile world, leading his band of survivors as they brought a renewal of life to the desert, and held it against all odds.

The union between Josiah Gray Wolf and Elizabeth Cunningham—Beth, as he called her—had produced seven children. Their four sons and three daughters were strong, intelligent young people, each with an individuality of character which marked them as distinctive.

36

The eldest, a tall, dark-haired girl, eighteen-year-old Willow, was the recognized leader of the troop of children in the camp. She herded these younger ones like a sleek, watchful collie, from her own brothers and sisters, to all the other children who were old enough to race across the high dune grass.

She had been named for the mourning of the world, for the willow tree which bends its branches down in sorrow, yet endures. Like the tree, Willow was a blend of such spirits. She was old enough to remember the early years of the camp, when the grief-stricken husband and father, T. J. Parker, had left the colony.

T. J. Parker had been one of the ten survivors her father had found after the virus swept the world almost bare of human life. He was one of the original ten to have begun this colony, nearly twenty years before.

Willow could remember the way he looked. Almost. He had been a large man, strong and quiet. Always quiet. That was what she remembered most about him, that he had kept apart from everyone. And his eyes, she remembered the sadness in them. It was the only image she could bring to mind of his face, blue eyes full of sorrow.

She hadn't known it then, not as a little child, but later she had been told that it was his grief over the death of his wife and three sons which haunted him. They had died in the first weeks of the virus, and he had lived. For that, he had not forgiven himself, or forgotten.

Living among other survivors had only made the loneliness worse for Parker. He had stayed with them for six years, never really becoming part of the colony. None of the children born into the camp during that time were his; none of the women lived with him. He kept himself alone, and the distance of that grief grew wider and wider, until he couldn't be near people at all.

Willow remembered the day he left. She had been five that year, the oldest child born in the camp. She had stood beside her parents, watching with the other survivors as Parker turned and walked away.

She remembered the sight of his back, how she had stared after him for miles as he crossed the hard, broken ground of the high desert. She had watched until her mother told her there was nothing more to see, but still she had imagined she could see him — the broad, dark blue shirt of his back, moving away from her and into the face of the morning sun.

Sometimes in the night she still dreamed of him, and saw again the wide, square image of his back. It was only when he turned around that she grew afraid, when she saw his eyes and knew his pain. It was the dream that had followed her childhood, waking her from sleep with tears even the comfort of her mother's arms could not ease.

That man's leaving them had shocked her. What he had done was like a willful death. She had been taught by her parents that life was a blessing. She had seen babies die of the virus, when only days old from their mother's womb. She had cried at these deaths, as had many of the grown men and women, for the loss of such children was a loss to them all.

Life was a gift, Willow knew. To waste such a gift was the worst tragedy she could imagine. Not only had Parker endangered his own life by such an act, but he had taken with him a strength which rightfully belonged to the People. His leaving had stolen a life from them, as well. That, she had not understood.

It was easier not to think of such things, to bear only gladness in her heart during this month of awakening life. Willow's mother called it March, but no one among the young called it that. To them it was the

Mother's Moon, that season early in the year when the first spears of new grass thrust their way up through the winter-hardened earth. Now, the seeds of vegetables could be planted into the yielding ground. A warm sun released them from the cold of winter and gentle rains watered the earth, bringing forth a regeneration of life.

This was a busy time, for the men must dig deep into the ground to turn the heavy soil. The women bent their backs to drop tiny seeds into row upon row of the waiting gardens. The high desert held its sun until late in the year, and would give forth a harvest of root vegetables, vines of snap beans and peas, dark green plants of tomatoes, peppers, and cucumbers, berries and fruits of the vine. This was the first planting. Later, they would seed the earth for a second harvest of squash, sweet potatoes, turnips, beets, onions, and other crops.

Late in the year, the children—their bodies closer to the earth—would crawl beneath the trees and fill sacks of walnuts, pecans, and hickory nuts. Clumps of peanuts grew willingly beneath the shallow ground, and it would be left to the bigger boys to shovel them free. The little ones would pick the peanut pods off the roots and carry them in cloths to the storage building.

The lush green rows of trees were a bounty not usually given to the desert. It was Willow's father, Sagamore, who had brought them here. When she was small, four or five, he had taken the van and driven alone into the deserted cities looking for fruit trees, berry bushes, and nut trees to bring back to the camp. Willow didn't remember a time without such things, but she knew the elders did, and that it was her father who had risked his life to bring these gifts to the People.

There were terrible things in the empty cities. The

People said Sagamore had been brave to go there alone. She'd heard them talk of it when the elders had thought she was asleep, or when the women gathered to do the wash and believed she paid no attention to their words. She had heard them talk of corpses littering the ground, of wild dogs chasing through the abandoned roads, and of the spirits of the dead following after her father's van. She had heard the terrible words and knew her father to have been a true leader to have dared so much for them.

The colony did not have apples, bananas, or pears. The ground was neither cold enough nor wet enough to grow such things. Willow had heard the names, but had never tasted the sweetness of these exotic fruits.

There were strawberries in the warm weather, and sheltered arbors of grapes. Most wonderful of all were the orange and lemon trees. The oranges grew just across the river, along one bank, making a lovely grove. In the late fall when the trees ran sweet with sugar, Willow loved to sit beneath their still green boughs, squeezing the tangy juice from the ripe fruit into her mouth, and breathing in the tart and honeyed fragrance of the orange and the sour sharpness of the lemon. Now in spring their tiny white blossoms scented the air.

Through the winter, each tree was covered with thick blankets to protect it from the bitter cold. Even with their efforts, each year some trees died. Winters could be hard in the high desert, and despite the insulation of blankets and layers of dried grass packed high around their root beds, many of the beautiful orange trees had been lost.

Willow's mother, Elizabeth, was the teacher to the many children of their camp. She taught the younger ones to read, to write their names and do simple arithmetic. With the older ones, she told stories of geography and history. It was clear to Willow that these were only stories, but her mother told them well. None of the children really believed there were places where houses grew as tall as hilltops, or water that stretched so wide you could not see the end of it. She and the other firstborns listened politely, but no one—she was sure—considered such things true.

As Sagamore's eldest child it was Willow's responsibility to watch the youngest ones when the men, women, and older children worked in the fields. On this day, the seven littlest of their camp were beside her, nestled on blankets at her feet, crawling on the soft earth before the adobe shelter of sun-dried brick, or carried in the warm cradle of her arms.

The baby she held was the youngest child of Emily Pinola and Stephen Wyse. The couple had four other children, three boys and a six-year-old daughter. They were paired, as were Willow's mother and father. The same was true of Merry Logan and Skeet Hallinger. Each couple had remained a separate unit within the larger family of the People. Crystal Rivers lived alone, as did Natalie Peters, Rosalina Santos, and Prophet.

Feeling the baby stretch and move, Willow brushed a kiss on the newborn's forehead. The child's skin was warm and smooth, a scent of earthiness rising from it like fresh-cut grass in spring, after the season's first rain. She nuzzled the infant closer and breathed the child's name into its small ear.

"Alyssa," she whispered. "The day is broken open like an egg, little sister, with gold and blue, and white clouds to shield your tiny eyes. Open them and look."

Sagamore had taught Willow to speak a newborn's name in this way, as a soft wind into its ear. The child should hear the sound like a play of music in the breeze. Then for all its life she would know that the Earth was home, for here she was first called by name.

She would always remain with the People and not travel back into the hidden skies of death, to that other land where none could follow or find her.

The baby's eyes were brown berries, thistled with twin stripes of dark lashes. Her hair was fine-wisped and lightly reddish, the color of a sorrel mare. Awake, the small mouth moved in the act of hunger. Her lips drew and released . . . once, twice, three times . . . drew again and then trembled, crinkling as if ready to cry.

"Shh, little sister. Be still. Listen to the fluttering wings of birds on the air, and the song of the crickets in the tall grass. Hush," she lulled the child, raising the infant to her shoulder and standing to walk with it, "your mother will be here soon."

Standing alone in the deserted village, but for the seven babies with her, Willow looked toward the riverbanks where the men and women worked the fields. She saw no sign of anyone coming. The baby would have to pull its fierce hunger inside like a tight fist, and wait.

A spur of sudden dark stabbed at the pale sky behind her. She turned, staring in wonder at this swirl of ashen cloud twisting in the wind and spinning toward them. She had never seen such a cloud. Holding Alyssa closer, she watched fascinated as it danced the sky and touched along the ground.

Only when it shattered the walnut tree and flung the splintered chips into the air did she know there was danger.

"Father!" she screamed, but the sound of the wind had grown into a deafening roar, covering her voice.

Young trees ripped from the earth, torn into the mouth of this wind. It was coming straight at her, at the babies, ripping everything from its path. Where it touched, the ground exploded, sending dirt and rock and grass in a powdered froth into the sky.

As she stared in terror, the adobe storage house at the end of the line of trees burst open and spun into the tight circle of this cloud. Where it had stood, there was nothing.

There was nowhere to run. The dark cloud lay a path twice as wide as the village, flattening the hillside of grape trellises and skipping along the ground in a reckless fury. It claimed shelter after shelter. The remaining harvest of last season disappeared, scattered on the dust of the wind.

The babies screamed.

Willow glanced again toward the river, toward the distant fields where the People were sowing the ground. They were too far away for her to see them working, but someone there must have noticed the cloud. The land between them was stark and empty. She was alone.

No, not alone, she thought. Seven infants were with her. She couldn't carry them all. Even if she might have done so, the size of the wind stretched farther than she could run before the rage would be upon then. There was no escape.

With the newborn still in her arms, Willow rushed for the adobe house, scooping up a second infant at the doorway, the four-month-old son of Merry Logan. Laying the two babies on the reed-covered floor, she struggled back to the others.

The cloud was tearing at the earth, curtains of dust rising from the ground only a few feet from her. Daylight had grown black, a thick swirl of grinding sand and rock blocking everything from sight. She crawled, spinning clods of dirt and pebble graveling her face. Blindly groping, patting the ground, her hand felt the roundness of a child's leg and pulled the infant to her.

That was three. There were four more still outside.

43

Where are you. . . ? Where? her mind screamed. She could not speak. Nothing could speak in the face of this wind.

Again she reached out her arms, stretching her body full length on the ground, searching for the children. One arm brushed against something hard, a child's head. With her other hand she touched a leg. One was far away from the other. Without trying to see, she dragged them both behind her, pushing them into the shelter.

Two more.

Incredibly, she heard a sound, the gurgle of a strangled cry. It was just ahead but she couldn't crawl. Each time she moved the air reached beneath her, lifting, threatening to pull her into it. She would be taken, lost in that swirling cloud. No one would ever find her.

The small cry came again, this time sounding weaker. And she moved. Dragging herself along the shuddering ground, Willow clawed at the earth, her fingers digging clumps of clay and sand. Pulling. Reaching.

She couldn't see them but felt two babies huddled together, their bodies tangled in a jumble of legs and arms. She grabbed a limb in each hand and scooted back, hoping she had both children in her grasp. The wind drew at them, threatening to snatch the infants from her fingers, but she held on. Back into the doorway. Back into the adobe house. There, she gathered the seven babies beneath her and stretched her body over them.

A terrible silence struck. In that instant Willow heard the shrieking cries of the babies. *Were they dying? Smothering?* She was afraid to look up . . . afraid to see what might be above her . . . what might snatch her up into the dark, whirling heart of that cloud.

44

Red dust fell from the adobe bricks as the house vibrated. The earth beneath her trembled and she was shaking, too.

She felt an intense pressure, heard a loud pop . . . and the curved roof exploded, tearing away into the cone of dark wind . . . carrying Willow with it.

Chapter Six

The whirlwind spun a crooked path across the high desert, shifting direction with the abruptness of an unexplainable whim. It passed in a clean line through the village, destroying the vineyard, several trees, two storage shelters, and the house where Willow and the children had been, but leaving all else untouched. To the People, it was as if a destroying hand had struck through the length of the village on sudden impulse and then moved on.

To Josiah, it was much more. His daughter was missing. The roof of the adobe which had sheltered the young woman and the infants, was a gaping wound. A cracked seam had cleanly severed the earthen bricks, sanding the remaining core smooth with the fierce rush of the wind.

The seven babies had been found safe within the adobe ring. Incredibly, other than minor scratches, they seemed unhurt. It was clear to Josiah that Willow had placed them there together. But what had happened to her? They searched the land until nightfall, but no one found the girl.

Josiah was not counted among the searchers. To him, it was as though his child had been taken up by the hand of a trickster God, and stolen. He sat in the dust of the broken adobe and would not rise. Every strength in him was drawn away. He could neither speak nor listen, but was pulled into a shell within himself, closing out all others.

This eldest among his children with Elizabeth had been his favorite. Like him in the way she saw the world, Willow's clear vision was enriched with hopefulness and promise. To her, he had taught the lessons of the Indian people, and the harder lessons he had learned when sent out to gather the few inheritors of this land. She was the child of his soul, and as such, he grieved for her as he would have grieved for the loss of his mind or his heart.

Through this long night of mourning, Josiah prayed in the ancient way of his family, the Indian people. His consciousness severed itself from all connection with these Outsiders, lifting to a separate plane. He was alone. With only the voice of the wind to guide him, he sat unmoving, yet traveled to a place of pure spirit within himself.

Through the night he prayed and watched behind closed eyes.

At the first light of morning he stood and left the boundary of the earthen ring. The children whispered that Sagamore had aged in those hours within the shattered circle, but he moved among them once again as their chief, shepherd of the survivors, and father to this family of man.

Quinn Kelsey monitored the computer panels in Biosphere Seven's systems control room. His awareness was finely tuned to any notable shift in the structural security of the glass walls and dome housing the five-hundred-acre community. He had supervised the analysis of these same readouts for the last twenty years, and knew with quick certainty what evaluation to make of this systems check. Everything was fine. Which was incredible, considering the fact that a tornado had passed within a mile of them one day ago.

"How are we?" asked Jessica, slipping quietly into the room and taking a chair beside him.

He leaned across and gave her a quick kiss hello. "You look tired. What time did you come back to bed last night? Or did you?"

She smiled an acknowledgment of being caught red-handed, or in this case, red-eyed. "I don't think any of us slept much." Then, more seriously, "Do we have a better damage assessment than the one available last night?"

She was referring to the initial stress figures and temperature readouts recorded during the first hours after the tornado struck ground. A primary visual assessment was the earliest evaluation, combined with temperature core readings and a structural integrity analysis. Through the night, the computer had worked up a more detailed compilation.

Quinn looked up from the monitor. It had been a long night for both of them. This was the second tornado the biosphere had withstood. The first, almost twenty years earlier, had nearly destroyed them. Luckily, this one had been different.

"It's as if a jet plane made a crash landing, skidded on the ground for over a mile, taking out everything in its path, but left whatever lay outside that line of destruction untouched. We lost one of the external wind generators on the beacon hill range, but Josiah can put that right. Overall, I'd say it missed us completely."

She rested her head in the cradle formed of both hands. "We were lucky . . . this time." Her eyes closed and for a minute Quinn could see how much the concern over this had cost her.

"Come on," he said gently, stroking her arm, "it's not as bad as that." He wanted to comfort her, draw her into his arms and make all the worry go away.

Her eyes were dark shells, patterned with deeper lines of color. "I'm not afraid for us, but for the children. Have we brought them into the world only to let them die when a storm tears a break in the seal? How much longer can it go on without an accident . . . without some defect to the dome's integrity? It's going to happen, Quinn. It's only a matter of time. We have to do something to protect them."

The tone and pitch of her voice were verging on desperation. Clearly, this was something more than just the storm. It was a fear that had been building in her for a long while.

He tried to soothe her anxiety. "Jessie, we've done as much as we can do for them."

"And it's not enough! We can't just wait for it to happen. That tornado could have cracked a single glass in the dome shield. *A single glass,* Quinn. That's all it would take. The virus would enter our atmosphere and those children would die. Everything we've tried to do here, it would all have been wasted."

She didn't cry, that hadn't been Jessica's way of releasing tension for a long time—not since she had made her final choice between Quinn and Brad—but there was exhaustion in her voice and in her eyes. Nothing she'd said was new, but there was an urgency in her words, not there before.

"Is this about the contact with Bio Two? Is that what's really behind your reaction?" he asked. "You know there may be other survivors, like Josiah and Outsiders, and you want to be with them?"

"No! It's not about them, it's—"

"Are you sure, Jess?" He loved her, but he never soft-pedaled what he thought to be the truth. They had an honesty between them that they both trusted. He wouldn't break that, even if it meant hurting her.

"It isn't that." She was calm again, but the deep worry had not left her eyes. "Quinn, we're going to lose these children. Can't you see? If we don't find a way out, and soon, we're going to lose them all."

He had no answer for her fears. They had lived with the threat of contamination by the virus since 1998. Now, in the year 2018, the threat hadn't changed. If any of them left the protection of the domed city . . . or if the seal should break and the outside atmosphere penetrate the sphere . . . all of them would die. It was as simple as that, and there was nothing anyone could do about it.

"The virus may mutate. That's our hope." It was the only optimistic possibility he had to offer.

"It's not enough. I'm not going to stand back and watch them die. Whatever the risk, we have to act now. Otherwise, we might as well have died with the rest of our world. We were given a chance, Quinn. We have to take it."

Jessica stood and walked from the room, leaving him wondering just how much of a risk she was willing to take. And would it endanger all their lives?

A warning signal began to throb at the back of Quinn's mind.

Was what he'd heard just a temporary overreaction to the stress caused by the tornado? Or did it mean something far more dangerous?

He turned back to the blank computer screen, the face of worry and fear reflected in his own image on the darkened glass.

Willow's head felt pulpy as a cottonwood branch. Her forehead gave when she pressed her fingers against it, and was puffed with a swell of fluid beneath the tight skin.

Opening her eyes, she saw a flat and unfamiliar landscape. The ground was a rough crust of desert, broken and dry as scabs on the earth. In the distance was the mesquite-studded savannah, and shading her face was a wide Tasajillo cactus. She could see its two-inch thorns standing out from the dry husks. Her eye was only a finger's width away from one of the needles.

Reacting in panic, she jerked backward . . . and felt a broad belt of pain lash every muscle of her back. Twisting in this sudden torment, she tried to rise to her knees but crumpled when the pain slammed into her head, too.

Had she screamed? There was a sound. For one instant, all that Willow saw before her was a sea of brilliant red stretched over the desert sand. It seemed to waver like shimmering heat on the horizon. And then, when the red glaze cracked . . . everything went dark.

Chapter Seven

The river beneath them was a white-water torrent. Seth held onto the saddle pommel and leaned out, gazing down at the churning chaos one hundred feet below. Whole trunks of trees hurtled through the watercourse, their green boughs catching the light before plunging under the raging froth again.

Jonathan's mare stepped closer to the edge of the rock plateau. He looked down. "We try to cross here, we're dead."

Seth pulled the left rein of the stallion, turning the horse away from the cliff's edge. The water was like this unforgiving land, wild and dangerous. "Better follow the river downstream a ways, try to make an easier crossing there."

They moved back from the steep drop, but Seth still felt the fall of it within him. It was the nature of this journey and this land, a fall into threat and risk. The threat was real, in the distance of each day's travel from home. Alone, there was nothing standing between them and danger but their own courage.

Yet, they had risked all. It wasn't fear that had driven them from their home, but longing. In Seth, that longing had been a space of noise within him that could not be quieted. It hummed like a voice, strange and enticing, drawing him away from all that he knew. He feared it, but feared more the awful silence that would come if he stopped listening.

They rode along the crest overlooking the river for most of the morning. When the sun was high overhead, Jonathan found a wide sloping path down the face of the steep canyon, leading to the water's edge.

They stared at the graded drop, knowing that a slip could cost them their lives.

"I'll go down alone," said Jonathan. "If I make it, you follow."

Seth shook his head. "No. We'll go together."

Their horses' forelegs sank into the soft earth of the nearly vertical trail, struggling with each step and pitching forward. Loose shale slid beneath the animals' hooves and clattered to the rocks below. Twice, the black slipped and thudded to its chest in the powder-fine ground.

"Hang on!" Jonathan shouted.

Seth didn't need to be told. He hung onto the pommel, locked his legs around the horse's girth, and pulled his feet free of the stirrups. If the black started falling, Seth would push himself free and jump clear.

Jonathan's mare whinnied in terror, but both she and the stallion made it down the scraped track of the canyon. Their hooves pawed the solid earth at the bottom of the cliff as they stood and blew, and their muscles trembled.

"We'll stop here," said Seth.

They dismounted, standing on their own fear-weakened legs, then watered and rested the horses.

They'd been riding four days, and had seen no one.

With the first light of morning, they began to

cross the river. The short-bodied mare swam against the cold, fast-moving current with seeming ease. Jonathan wrapped his legs around her neck, high over her shoulders, and twined his fingers into the mare's copper mane. She pulled them both across the river's trace, with the thick muscles of her short legs and the great heart beneath the small, barrel chest.

The stallion showed his fear of the river. He snorted and shied at Seth's urging to step into the churning watercourse. Seth kneed the horse, kicked, and finally had to quirt the animal into the rushing water. At the first touch of the river's heart-stopping cold, the black reared up on his strong back legs in terror, nearly throwing Seth from the saddle.

"Lay flat along his back!" Jonathan shouted, his voice carrying over the thunderous rush of the river and the shrill whinnying screams of the stallion.

Seth grabbed two fistsful of mane, as he had seen Jonathan do, and pressed his face against the stallion's back. He could feel fear tremble in the flanks and along the strong, dark neck.

He laid his face close to the horse's right ear and spoke softly. "Easy now," he said in a calming voice, trying his best to soothe the animal. His life depended on finding the stallion's courage. "That'a boy. Go on. Go on, Smoke," he urged, calling his pet name for the stallion since it had been a foal. In this way, with Seth leaning close and promising the black they would make it, the two crossed their first river together.

On the bank of dry earth past the river's edge, Seth slipped off the black and pulled a fistful of dry grass from a nearby scruff of ground, rubbing and rubbing the wet from the stallion's neck and flanks, until the horse's trembling stopped.

"He'll do better on the next crossing," said Jonathan, stepping close fo the blowing stallion. "He knows what moving water is, now. That was his fear."

The next crossing, thought Seth. Had his own terror of the river bled itself into the horse? Had Smoke felt his rider's panic?

A tight nod showed he'd heard what his brother had said. There were no words in him to pull his own feelings to the light. What did it matter if Jonathan knew how afraid he was; would that change anything? They would go on.

"It took courage back there." Jonathan eased a gentling hand over the black's muzzle. "It took a strong heart and a steady nerve. That will get us through the worst of it, Seth. We're going to be all right."

It wasn't clear if Jonathan was talking about the horse, or Seth himself. If his brother had seen his fear, if Jonathan knew that he was weak, that he wasn't sure about this trip or leaving home, or . . .

"I remember Mama telling us of a long stretch of flat land past the river crossing."

Seth didn't get it.

"From the time she came north with that man, Jack Quaid."

He remembered then. They had both heard the stories of their mother's journey—before she'd met their father—up from the south country with the man named Quaid, both of them running from the sickness that was sweeping over the land.

"She said there were long days of walking before they came to the river's head and into the grass valleys. She called it the Missouri. Guess that's its name, that stretch of river we just crossed." Jonathan's gaze lingered on the water.

To Seth, the name meant nothing. His mother's story meant nothing. It had no connection to him. What did mean something, was what Jonathan had said. If their mother's memory was right, it might be days before they needed to ford another river. Holding on to that slim hope, Seth knew that at least for a few more days, he could go on. His fear wouldn't make him quit Jonathan yet. If he was lucky his brother might never have to know how much that fear had cost him . . . how much Seth had wanted to turn and run.

John Katelo, the Inuit, had told his children, "In the days before man vanished from the Earth, people were too many. They carved their mark on their world's land and water and sky. Like a disease, they ate away at all that was good, and covered the rich valleys where grass fields and forests once grew with buildings and concrete, blocking all hope of life from the land."

Seth and Jonathan had not seen much of what their father had meant, not in the days before this journey, but now they saw well what his words described. They had lived in the sheltered valley by the lake, surrounded by mountains and trees and grass. They had known the dying winds of fall, the cold of winter, the rich smell of spring, and the hard bright heat of summer. But they had not known cities.

A city was a place of man smothering the land, covering the living ground with stiff, dead rivers of black road, houses rising up like warts on the earth's skin, and buildings taller than trees . . . taking their places . . . giving nothing back.

Cities were an experience they were glad they had missed as children.

The horses were shy about these places. The two Katelo brothers were shy of them, too. Cities felt strange and distant from all the things they understood. In the twenty years since the virus, cities had remained fixed as places separate and apart from the living world they knew. In an odd way, those buildings had become the tombstones of man.

"You ever think what this must have been like?" Seth asked.

Jonathan shook his head.

"Look at it," Seth went on, staring in a kind of repulsed fascination, "nothing but stone boxes for man to live in and work, and hard roads to get from one city to another. The land is buried beneath what they left. It'll take forever for it to come back . . . for it to be trees and grass and rivers again."

"Come on," said Jonathan, insisting. "We don't belong here."

But the cities were wide and many. The spaces of green earth between them became narrower and fewer. Until the mountains rose up again and forced the cities out. The mountains . . . they were glad of them.

"I'm grateful we've never known that kind of life," said Seth, letting the black have his head along the high mountain pass. "People who lived like that . . . I don't feel sorry for them, that they died. I don't," he said, hotly defending himself from the dark judgment in Jonathan's eyes. "Look at all the hurt they caused. We're better off without them. I mean it. The whole world's better off."

"Our mother was one of them; did you forget that?" Jonathan said. "She lived in these kinds of cities, and maybe she was just like the rest of them. Would you be better off with her dead, too?"

"I didn't mean that. You know I didn't! It's just that I can't breathe in those places. I start feeling trapped and scared. Don't they make you feel scared?"

"They make me feel sad. That's all. Come on," said Jonathan, urging his horse ahead, "let's move away from here."

The night was blacker than a closed box. It sealed around him, dark buried beneath dark, buried beneath more dark. There were no clouds visible, no stars, no moon. It seemed to Jonathan as though the sky had lain flat and pressed out all brightness and color.

They had camped in this small valley between two mountain ranges. In the last rose-glow of twilight it had seemed a peaceful place, quiet and restful. But now in this fixed blindness, it seemed there was nothing beyond the thick barrier of this uneasy night.

Seth slept close enough to the fire for Jonathan to clearly see his brother's features against the snapping flames. In sleep, Seth's face was eased of the tightly drawn lines of worry and the hard-pressed mouth of fear. For a long time now, Jonathan had known about Seth's unspoken terror, understood it, and said nothing. He was absolutely sure Seth would not want either his sympathy or encouragement. Seth would want nothing from him but his companionship. They needed that from each other. The world was an empty place. Too empty to be alone.

Still, he needed time away from Seth. Jonathan

had come into his manhood on this journey, a sense of being free of his parents and living on his own will, his own strength. He needed time alone to winnow through his feelings like new grain. And so he stood, leaving the campfire, and walked alone into the close and solitary dark.

In his life, Jonathan had never experienced a need for prayer. His existence had been the reality of living each day: food, clothing, shelter. It had been little more. He had never understood the complicated system of his father's beliefs. Never had any faith in the spirits of water . . . of trees, animals, or rock. He had never imagined a soul in soft brown earth, or in the rain which fell upon him, or in the growing things of the field. These had been his father's truths, not his.

On this journey he had changed. More and more, he found himself thinking about his father's trek across Siberia and the faraway plains of ice and snow. He thought of the single kayak crossing the neck of sea that separated the two great lands, and the solitary man moving steadily forward, toward finding other life. As a child, Jonathan had listened to his father's stories of this trek, but had never really thought of them till now.

How alone his father must have been. How afraid. Jonathan walked deeper into the swimming dark, holding these thoughts to him. It was as though he were stepping into the silence of that time, an emptiness. He and Seth had each other; his father'd had no one.

He remembered now how that image had frightened him as a boy—one man completely alone in the world. For him, this reality had been as close to one part of his mother's religion as anything could have ever been. Her God was far different from his father's. Her beliefs, too. She'd talked of souls and angels, heaven, and a place of constant torment called hell. It had seemed so clear to Jonathan as a child. His father's lonely trek had been that hell.

Now, he wasn't sure.

Jonathan moved farther away from the light of the fire. It was the dark he sought. It was solitude. An echo of the aloneness his father had known.

"I heard their voices," John Katelo had said to the young boy beside him. Jonathan had been ten when his father told him. They had been alone. He remembered the words and the look on his father's face when he spoke of that time. It was the look of a man he hadn't known before, a stranger in his father's skin. That look had frightened him as much as the haunting words.

"I heard their cries on the wind, high unending wails. They called to me," John Katelo, had said, "the voices of the dead. They were the Lost Ones, wandering spirits of the earth, searching for the lives that were taken from them. They followed me like hungry wolves. I was what they sought. I had escaped from that place called Biosphere Four and I was all there was of human life."

Jonathan remembered his father's words—here in this place of unbroken silence—and listened again.

What he heard were not the voices of the dead, but the sounds of the living earth. The air breathed its whisper to him, weightless and hushed. The water of the nearby stream moved to the sound of inhuman music. The ground called up from the depths of its ancient core, a pulse he could feel like a living body, and the sound of it beat through him . . . alive . . . alive . . . alive.

He heard the earth, and not the voices of the dead. They were gone.

Something in him, some spirit flame that had been kindled in this night, hoped they had found their way, these Lost Ones. They were no longer of the Earth, or of man. Their voices had been silenced. Jonathan knelt in the dark on the yielding ground and said the first real prayer of his life . . . for them.

Chapter Eight

Willow Gray Wolf was more than just another child to the gathering of Outsiders; she was Sagamore's daughter. He had other daughters — children by Elizabeth Cunningham, and Sidra, daughter of Catherine Innis — but Willow was one of the People, the eldest child to have been born of their community.

It was through these firstborn, children with unique bloodlines, that the Outsiders had learned to see themselves as a separate people, a true race of survivors. Something special in them had allowed their lives to continue when all others had died.

Through Willow, and the other children born into the colony of those few survivors gleaned from the deadly harvest of their world, their gathering had become far more than a group of victims, a strong and proud nation of people. It was through their children that they saw their continuance, their uniqueness, and the worth of their lives. Most of all, it was through Willow, eldest of these firstborn. She had been the symbol for all the others — tall, strong, a quiet presence among them whose very being spoke of the renewal of life.

To the Outsiders, to lose such a child was much

more than the death of one of the elders; it was counted among them as a death of the future of the People.

For this reason, Willow was greatly mourned.

The high plains of Texas had in its geological past pushed up from the rich soup of the Gulf of Mexico. Within the basin formed by the blue-shadowed mountains were hills of cedar, an ocean of sighing grass, limestone plateaus, scattered playa lakes, and a constant, punishing wind.

A hot sun burned the face of the land, scorching ground and rock. It did not warm but blazed a driving heat into the earth, searing the sloping scarp and flat mesa. There was no kindness to this place. Here, only the strong survived.

In the ages which followed the surfacing of the plains from the great inland sea, course after course of life succeeded on this new ground. Herds of dinosaur roamed the rich coastal valleys, building mud nests by the rivers and swamps. Numerous as the buffalo which would later follow, the dinosaur knew the language of these riverbanks and fertile bogs, and made its home on the wide stretch of blowing grass beneath a burning sky.

Through the Earth's history they came, animals and man, striving against the hard boundaries of life pulled from this unforgiving land. Horse and camel, mastodon and three-toed sloth, they thrived on the rolling hills beneath a screen of cedar forest, and on a flinty scarp. The same night sky sealed in the ancient dark. The same close press of stars shone above them.

And man, too, found a time of survival here.

From the ice-bound regions of the north, he followed the track of game to the swelling green of this country and died in great numbers from its relentless winnowing of the weak from the strong. Those who lived hunted the rich game of this broad-backed plain. Man hunted the mastodon and great beasts of the Ice Age.

Beyond those days, when the ice had receded, he followed the track of buffalo and the longhorn cattle up from Mexico. He lived with the fear of mountain lion and bear, rattler and water moccasin, centipedes and scorpions with two-inch stingers. Black tarantulas moved as a sea across the prairie, a horde of one hundred thousand strong, their backs glistening in the sun.

These were the companions given those who existed in this hard space. Coming into life was a miracle. Death was an agony. And in between, survival was a constant challenge. They were truly the people of the new Earth, for this was a place far removed from the river deltas and green forests where mankind first began.

In its way, it was a new world, and in it once again, mankind was tested.

The man lived in a cave at the base of the mountain. He kept no record of time and did not know how long he'd been there. The toll of years meant nothing to him. He did note the change of seasons—the color of trees in autumn, the first stems of spring flowers pushing through the snow—but he neither sowed nor harvested. He planted no garden, and killed no animal for meat or fur. The simplicity of his life did not require these efforts. The cave provided him with food and warmth. It was enough.

He was perfectly alone, except for his wife and children, whom he spoke to in long conversations each day as though they were still beside him. He didn't answer their parts, but waited for them to respond, as if hearing their voices.

The clothes he'd worn when he first came to this place had torn, become threadbare, and fallen into pieces long ago. He'd never thought of replacing them. The cave kept him warm, even through the heaviest snows of winter. Deep within its long chambers, the temperature never varied.

The land was now in spring, and he could go beyond the outer boundary of the concrete tunnel and sit in the open meadow, letting the sun's heat warm his back. There, he could see wildflowers budding on the hillsides and the pale green grass. He saw the slate-colored mountains that encircled him, and the blue haven of sky. He watched the changing patterns of clouds and color, seeing the beauty of each gentle day.

His nakedness no longer disturbed him. He had grown used to it and there was no one to notice his unclothed body, no reason to cover himself. He could feel every breath of wind against his skin. And rain. He stood now in a warm spring rain, face upturned to the cleansing sky.

There was no need to hunt or labor at putting an ease to his hunger. In the deep storerooms of the cave—it went for miles beneath the mountain—he had found case after case of dried and preserved food. He was surrounded by a wealth of sustenance: powdered milk, coffee, cans of tuna, macaroni noodles, tins of fruit and vegetables, provisions set within this shelter as if intended especially for him.

On this abundant provender, the man had lived.

The face of the sky grayed to the tint of ashes in a cold fire. The man watched the heavens change, knowing the rain would go on through the night. A wind had joined the cloudburst, colder than the healing water. It was a storm from the north, bringing the last breath of winter to the waking land.

He shuddered against the chill.

"You see, Jamie," he said to his youngest son, the three-year-old with blond baby curls and cheeks as round as a summer moon, "Mother Winter isn't done with us, yet. She holds on, that old hex, mad as sin that we made it through to spring. You never put your trust in a spring day, Jamie. It can turn on you fast."

He turned now to his eldest son. At ten, the boy was becoming tall and lanky, with legs and arms too long for the rest of his body. He had his mother's face, her strong image stamped onto the bony angles of his cheeks and jaw, and Sara's eyes, too, blue as two jays spread-winged on the breeze. The man had to look hard to see anything of himself in the child, as though she had made this first one wholly out of her own nature.

"Keith, go and help your mother bring the clothes in off the line. This storm won't pass us by lightly. And don't give me that look. Helping your mother is as much a farm chore as anything else I might ask you to do. You're nearly as strong as she is already, and as tall." He could see the boy liked these words. He had an ego, young Keith, and was discovering what it was to become a man.

"Go on, now. Help your mother while I put the tractor in the shed."

The man watched the scenes hurry by him . . . six-year-old Michael chasing the chickens into the hen coop . . . Scrap, their dog, barking at the gale as it hammered the shingles on the white clapboard house . . . Sara rushing for the porch, carrying a mound of folded sheets in her arms.

He watched the dream figures move around him but never stirred from the place where he sat. If he moved he might lose them from his mind . . . from his memories. The fear of losing all remembrance of his wife and sons had driven the man away from contact with those few people of the new world, and brought him here. It had kept him in this self-imposed isolation, where he found a thin border of peace and lived it as a shrine within him.

The sky thundered and the rain washed the images away. It was harder for him to see them at night. In the dark he saw other things, images of death, and people driven mad by grief and suffering.

At night, he saw his children shaking with fever, crying in terrible pain to a father who could bring them no relief. First Keith, then Michael . . . they had lived through days of agony, the yellow pustules, the choking cough, and the sickness which ate at them, making them cry out. "Daddy! Help me, Daddy!"

In the end, the virus killed them. First, it killed Sara, and then the two boys. But not Jamie. The man hadn't let it take the three-year-old. Couldn't watch that happen. Not to the baby. He had smothered Jamie. Placed a pillow on that small, round face while the child slept. He had smothered the boy, his youngest . . . to protect him.

And that was why the images would never go away.

"God, oh God!" he cried. Rocking, rocking, tearing at his hair as the truth came at him. The world had died—his wife, his sons—the world had died, and he was still alive.

The screams went on. Through the cold. Through the rain. The torment of the man rose up from hell and found him as it did . . . as it always did.

When the silence came, he stood and walked back toward the cave. Toward the fifteen-foot cyclone fence. Past the blue wooden sign, reading: Cheyenne Mountain Complex. And the other one over the gate: NORAD, Combat Operations Center.

At first, the girl wasn't sure she had opened her eyes; it was so dark. Her head and back felt savaged, but she managed to sit up when she heard something scurrying in the tangle of cactus brush just ahead of her. Rats liked cactus to hide under. And snakes.

Sitting up was only slightly better. The sky and land had blended into a solid black and the earth held no shapes to claim her. She could see nothing but flat, empty space.

The scratching sound came again. In this well of dark, she feared it more than the covering night.

I want to go home, she thought. But which way was home?

She stood, feeling the weight of pain stretch the length of her body as each muscle trembled and worked to keep her upright. Fat tears rolled from the corners of her eyes, but she brushed them away, needing to see as clearly as she could.

There was no light. The stars were dulled beneath a blanket of clouds; the sliver of moon was hidden, too. *Which way?*

The scuttling sound rushed at her and she stumbled back, turned, and ran. Anything could be before her, anything behind her. She ran across the hard, unyielding ground of the high desert. Ran, dark terror in her heart. Ran, until she felt a hand reach out and stop her.

No, not a hand . . . exactly. What she felt was her own mind acting as a whole being, blocking her from going another step. And a terrible certainty that what lay only inches in front of her was a far worse danger than what she had left behind.

Her legs would no longer support her and she dropped to her knees. One hand reached out, probing into the seething dark—then drew back, afraid. How she knew it, Willow could not explain, but on the other side of her was emptiness. She sat at the edge of the chasm and waited for the dawn.

Chapter Nine

"Sagamore, will you come with me today?" Nine-year-old Shepherd Hallinger stood waiting for his answer.

Josiah sat overlooking the scarp, a jagged cut of land which broke the upper plains from the lower desert. From where he could see, the ground dropped away, protecting the fertile plateau from the encroachment of sand and erosion.

"Sagamore? You promised you would show me how to hunt pronghorn when I was old enough. Today, I'm nine."

Josiah turned away from the lonely desert and looked at the child. The boy was a smaller likeness of Merry Logan, his mother—dark hair, finely chiseled bones, and shining brown eyes. Josiah was impressed with the courage this young boy had shown in exacting the fulfillment of a promise from his chief.

"Pronghorn are not as easy to hunt as rabbits," he told the child.

"I know how to hunt rabbits." The boy's features became a stubborn square. "I've been bringing my mother rabbit meat since I was six. I'm nine. I need to learn to hunt the animals a man brings to his family."

It was a long speech for a little boy. Josiah held his smile inside him, not wanting to offend this show of pride with his own amusement. He had nerve, this one, and desire. Such things were catching, like the energy the People felt after a spring rain had soaked the land and brought up the smell of growing earth. It was a force of life.

"Go tell your mother you will hunt with me tomorrow," said Josiah. He stood and felt a strength return to his legs, his arms.

"Will we be gone all night?" There was a visible longing in the child's eyes. To a boy his age, the hunt represented coming into manhood. Josiah knew this and was careful of his words.

"It may take more than a single day to find pronghorn. They aren't easy for any hunter," he added, making much of them to this boy. "Ask your mother to make a packet of one night's food. We'll find whatever else we need on the land. Bring warm clothes. We'll leave in the morning, before the sun is up."

Shepherd hurried away, running with an energy and excitement that Josiah had forgotten how to feel. How long ago had he been young? How long ago had there been anything worth running for?

Life was a deep valley of sameness to him—each morning falling into its recognized place, each sunset casting shadows. It was the shadows that he clung to, a remembrance of what the world had once been. Somehow, life was brighter in that dark.

* * *

Willow watched the sun climb above the edge of the cliff where she sat. She had waited through the hollow fear of night, knowing something had stopped her from taking another step. Something had wrapped around her mind and held her back.

Now, as dawn lightened the sky, she saw that she was at the crumbling edge of a high cliff, overlooking a sheer drop and a river canyon three hundred feet below.

The white-gold of the sun was painful as it lifted higher, meeting the level of her eyes. She drew back from the blinding brightness, turned, and crawled some distance away. Only then could she see the broken plateau she had run through in the night.

It was a flat stretch of limestone marked with so many canyons and deep pits it looked like fragile lace. One wrong step could have been her death. But she had not been meant to die. Not in the tornado. And not last night. Something . . . a warning that had slammed up against her like a wall, had wanted her to live. Had something protected her within the terror of the funnel cloud, too?

Her head still hurt. The pain wasn't as bad as it had been last night, but it was a steady throb, like the pulse of her blood. When she stood, the blood hammered. Watching where she placed each step, she walked across the limestone shelf and back to the hard earth of the high desert.

Fear left her. She grew strong in the comfort of a knowledge that was not one of vision or circumstance, but another kind of awareness. It was a sight from within her mind, not her eyes. It was a voice which spoke to her mind, not her ears. And it was a hand which had closed around her and held her safe from the savage fury of the whirling cloud.

When she was a little girl, her father had told her stories of Indian shamans who spoke to spirit animals, of drumming circles and journeys, and of following the hidden paths to the upper and the lower worlds. The stories had been like dreams she had known while awake.

All these years, her father's words had stayed inside her, little memories woven into one beautiful image. And she could see it now. She could hear the drumming, see the spirit animal, and know her first step on the journey.

The sun warmed her back as she walked. In the silence of the great desert, Willow heard the soft voice of her own spirit, guiding her, leading her home.

"Shepherd, what do you see before you?"

The sun was high overhead and a fresh scent rose from the wide sweep of spring wildflowers and new grass covering the uneven tableland. A bright sky hung overhead and a soft breeze moved through the air.

"I don't see anything, Sagamore. No pronghorn could live in such an empty place, only rocks and grass," the child said in a fretful voice.

Josiah was sure the nine-year-old was tired. The land had been climbing all morning, easy slopes at first, then harder ones to test their courage and their strength. Maybe he had pushed the boy too hard.

"Let's sit and rest for a minute on that rock

ledge," he suggested. When they had been there for a while, he spoke to the young hunter again. "Look at the ground through an animal's eyes, the way they would see it."

Shepherd bent nearer to the ripe and yielding earth. "There's still nothing here. It's just dirt and grass, and some flowers."

"Closer." Josiah slipped onto his knees, then stretched out full length on the ground. He lay with the squared base of his chin against the tiny points of stiff grass.

Shepherd moved next to him and did the same.

"What do you see?" Josiah asked again.

"Nothing. I don't see—" Shepherd started, then the words caught, broke free, and tumbled out again in a new excitement. "I can see tracks, Sagamore! Something stepped there and crushed the grass. And there, too. I can see where it walked. I can see tracks."

The ground gave up a rich scent of clean grass, yeasty earth, and the delicate fragrance of wildflowers. Josiah closed his eyes and breathed in the smell of life, seeded and growing once again from this ancient land.

"The stalker must see through the eyes of the one he hunts," he said to the boy. "For that time, he must become the rabbit, or the pronghorn, or the bear. He must know the heart of the other and belong to it."

Shepherd was on his feet. "Where do the tracks go? Are they pronghorn?"

Josiah kept his eyes closed, unwilling to rise from the earthen bed that claimed him. His body seemed to sink into the ground which was the Old

One his people had once called The Mother. Had his daughter become a part of the land? A part of The Mother?

He turned onto the harder surface of his back and looked up into the cloudless wash of blue. Father Sky and Mother Earth. Those were the names his people had given their creators. These two were the source of all life. But something of that life had died within Josiah. Since Willow's death, the private world within his spirit was a stark and empty desert.

He heard Shepherd run ahead, following the press of tracks along the floor of new grass. He didn't try to rise but stayed where he was, knowing what the boy would find. It was the first hunt and the child must do this himself.

"Here, Sagamore! Come and see. I found *two* fawns!"

Now, Josiah made himself get up and follow the sound of the boy's excited shouts. He moved to a sharp rise of stone jutting out like a jagged bone from the earth's crust. There, in a slash on the rock's face, he found both Shepherd and the two antelope fawns.

The young were huddled together in the narrow cut between the rock. Their wet brown eyes stared up at Josiah as he neared. Beautifully marked, they couldn't have been more than two or three weeks old. One opened its long, narrow mouth and bleated in fear.

"Don't kill them," Shepherd cried, and pushed himself between Josiah and the twin fawns. "Sagamore, please don't."

The boy's eyes were more fearful than those of

75

the deer. Josiah watched him, and knew his struggle. Shepherd had come as a hunter looking for game—and had found life.

It was a good thing for the boy to know the value of the living creatures who shared his world. This time, it was more important than bringing home a kill from the hunt. The fawns looked healthy and fat. The doe would be somewhere nearby.

"Come, we'll leave them here," Josiah said to him, and moved away from the small den.

Shepherd followed, relief flooding over the worried lines of his face. They walked for a time, then he asked, "Where was their mother?"

"She's here somewhere, watching us."

"I'm glad we didn't kill them, Sagamore. They were so small. They wouldn't have given much meat."

It was clear the boy was making excuses for his emotional reaction back at the den. Josiah wanted him to understand exactly what had happened and not see it in a false way. "Maybe we should have taken them back with us, fed them until they were big enough, and then killed them."

"No," Shepherd said quickly. "That wouldn't be right. They're wild things. That would be terrible, like stealing their lives. No, we couldn't do that."

"Why not? In the old days of Earth, people used to pen animals like cattle and sheep, chickens and other farm animals. They kept them for food. They were born, lived, and died because of man. Why should those fawns be different?" It was a hard question for a nine-year-old, but Josiah wanted to

76

know how the boy thought, and how much he could understand of what had just happened.

"But those farm animals weren't born wild," Shepherd said, trying to explain his new and complicated feelings. "Maybe they had been with man a long time. Maybe they didn't know how to take care of themselves anymore. But those fawns . . . they belong out here, and free."

"All animals have the right to be free," said Josiah. "That's why we have no pens or cages in our camp. The animals of Earth don't belong to us. We share our world with them."

Shepherd nodded, agreeing with this.

"Then, do we ever have a right to kill them?" Josiah asked, still testing the boy. The answer would tell him a lot about the mind of this young man.

"The right? You mean, is it right for us to hunt them? I don't think so. We kill them so that we can live," Shepherd struggled with this new concept, "but no," he decided, "we never really have the right."

Josiah felt himself respond to the boy's words. It was a gift to his spirit and lightened the weight of his heart.

"Will we go home now?" Shepherd asked.

"No. Not yet. We came to teach you how to hunt pronghorn. That's what we'll do. There's more to hunting than killing. There's learning to track, and to see through the animal's eyes. A hunter must learn those things, too."

They walked in silence for a time, the boy quiet and holding his thoughts within him. Josiah could see he was still troubled. He waited, knowing Shepherd would ask his question when he was ready.

At last, the child's words spilled forth like a break of rushing water. "What will my father say when we come back without the pronghorn? Will he be angry? Will he say I was afraid, Sagamore? Was I wrong not to kill them? Will the others say I was afraid?"

"Josiah's first instinct was to tell Shepherd not to worry about such things, that he would make everything all right, but that would have made light of the boy's feelings and of the importance of his decision.

"What you did today, Shepherd, was to make the decision of a man. It was your heart which spoke to you and told you what was right. You listened to it, but now you're afraid. The decisions of a man aren't easy. They test you, understand?"

Shepherd nodded. He was listening to Josiah as if the balance of his life hung on the words.

"Your father's a good man, but he may not understand what you did. He may think you were foolish. He may even be ashamed of your actions."

Shepherd's head lowered and he stared at the ground.

"Your friends may call you afraid, too. I can't promise you they won't. Not everyone will understand what happened when you saw the fawns — happened, inside you. But remember, they weren't there. You were. And I was."

As if regaining a strength that he had lost, Shepherd lifted his head and stared up into Josiah's eyes. He was no longer the boy, proud and daring, knowing he would find a kill. He was the blossoming of a man, with a youth's first understanding of what it was to be a man. To hold to what he knew

78

was right, when everyone else might think him wrong.

"Do you think I was right, Sagamore?" It was a simple question and deserved the truth.

"I think you were brave and strong. I was proud of you today."

"I was afraid," Shepherd didn't look away, "but I'm not as much afraid now."

They walked on, and didn't speak of it again.

Chapter Ten

The night hatched above them, breaking in dark seams and cracks, and spread itself softly over the sky and land. The pale vault of heaven was hidden from their eyes, and the soothing black claimed them. It was the dark of the seed within the ground, of the child within its mother's womb, and the dark of dreams. It covered, healed, and nurtured both the man and the child.

Josiah built a fire, and beside it he and the boy sat like father and son. We could be any father and son, he thought, from any time since the beginning of man. The fire was their protection and their home. It shielded them from the night's terror, warmed them from the cold, and captured their imaginations in its dancing light.

It had been an important day. Josiah wanted to fill the boy's head and heart with memories of this time. He took a stick and pushed the burning branches of the fire circle closer together. The flames leapt higher, fingers of heat, crackling with power.

"Stories live in the flames of a campfire. My father and my grandfather used to tell me what they saw in the night's circle of heated rock and burning firewood. They could see into the flames."

"What do you see, Sagamore? Is there a story in our fire?"

Josiah smiled at the boy's eagerness. Today had been good. It had given Josiah a son of his own spirit to replace the daughter he had lost. Nothing would ever replace the love he held for Willow in his heart, but this boy was like him in the way he saw the world. There was a bond in that, too.

"Look into the flames, Shepherd. Watch them move. I'll tell you the story that I see."

The boy hunched forward, elbows on knees, leaning his chin into the pointed cup of his hands.

"It's a night of cold wind — like this one, but colder still. A boy not much older than you leans close to the dancing fire. A deerskin is wrapped loosely around his thin shoulders, and he huddles closer to the flames for warmth.

"He's alone," said Josiah.

"Is it here, at this fire? Why is he wrapped in deerskin, Sagamore? Why is he alone? What's his name?"

"Be quiet, little squirrel. You'll learn nothing with your many questions. Look back into the flames and find your answers."

He waited while the boy became the watcher once again.

Then Josiah began softly, like the first faint draw of smoke and small glow when fire sticks are rubbed together to catch a spark. His words became the living voice of the fire.

"The boy of the story is here, in this place, but it is the time of the long ago grandmothers and grandfathers. Icy cold grips the land like a hard fist."

Josiah threw a twig onto the burning brands, and a snapping tongue of orange blaze shot out into the heavy black of the night, leaving a trail of singed air on the breath of wind.

"This boy follows the herd of deer."

"Like me!"

"Yes, like you. He is a hunter. He has not eaten in two days, and needs the flesh of the deer to stay alive."

"But, why is he by himself? Where are his people?"

Josiah gave him a look.

Shepherd pulled back into silence.

"His name is Loki. His people followed the great herds of deer and elk down from the north country. Once, there were five men in his camp. Now, Loki is the eldest hunter."

Shepherd started to speak, then closed his mouth and turned back to the images moving in the flames.

"This night, Loki thinks about his mother and his small sister. Always, his mother has found food for her family. After his father died it was she who brought rabbit, birds, and other small game to her children. She knew where to dig the roots they could eat, and where the berries hid among the bushes. She had kept them alive.

"Now, the cold has found its way into her spirit and she is too sick to—"

"I don't want her to be dying," interrupted Shepherd.

"It's only a story," said Josiah.

"I know. It's a story, but . . . maybe she's not dying."

"I can only tell you the story that is in the fire," said Josiah. "Should I stop?"

There was worry in Shepherd's eyes, but he answered, "No, Sagamore. Don't stop. Tell me what happens."

"Loki, the eldest hunter of his camp, sits alone by the fire. He hears something moving in the distant dark. It is far away still, but his ears are those of a young boy, sharp and true. He listens and waits.

"By his side is a lance. It is his father's, a weapon which once brought down a great bear. Loki's fingers find their hold around the wooden shaft, knowing danger draws closer."

A wind stirred the fire, sending long slashes of orange-red knives high against the night-blackened sky. Josiah felt a shiver travel through him with the cold of that sudden gust. Far more than a chill, it was a sense of warning.

"What's wrong, Sagamore? Why did you stop?"

He couldn't explain the feeling. He had known it once before . . . in the days when he'd wandered Earth alone. It was in that time when he'd driven across the country looking for other survivors, and had found no one yet. He had felt it then, that sense of portent, a preknowledge of something about to happen.

"Sagamore? Was it a bear? Did Loki throw his father's lance at a bear?"

For a second, Josiah didn't know what the boy

83

meant. Realizing, he tried to clear his mind of this other thought and go on with the story. Branches snapped and dropped with a hiss into the center of the fire circle as the live flames consumed them.

"Out of the hiding black of this night comes a figure. It is tall as a bear and makes a dragging sound when it moves, like the draw of a heavy tail. It lives still in that secret light of shadow, not quite seen. And the light of the fire cannot catch it."

"Sagamore."

"It waits at the edge of the dark, sensed but not seen."

"Sagamore . . ."

"Loki stands, holding his father's lance. He raises it high, aiming for the dark spot where he feels the spirit closing to him, where he watches the dark messenger stepping over—"

"Sagamore, listen! Don't you hear that? Something's out there."

Josiah stopped. It wasn't a sound; it was an awareness. He *felt* the change Shepherd had noticed as sound.

The wind came again, lifting the skirt of fire from the circle of stones and shattering the flames into tiny sparks, live above their heads. The sparks showered down, raining slivers of light over them.

And she was there.

Josiah saw her, before the boy spoke again. He saw her standing on the other side of the flame, her long hair swept back by the wind, her face illuminated by the shooting twists of light. She stood in the perfect stillness of a spirit, captured in the dancing fire.

"Willow?" his breath was caught by lungs which would not draw air, his body as still as hers. Had she come to him from the shadows of the other world? His child.

The wind dropped, and the bright fan of light descended with the lowering flames. In that instant, she was gone. He lost her to the sudden dark.

"Willow!" Josiah leapt to his feet, the imprisoned voice booming from him in hard bursts. Like gunfire, it felt . . . firing with explosive force from the center of his chest . . . from his throat, his lungs, his heart. "Don't go!" Behind him, he heard the boy cry out in fear. Josiah was not Sagamore now. He was a father who had lost his child, found her for an instant, and was losing her again.

Her voice, when it came, was small and chipped with frailty. "Is it really you? Father . . . I'm so tired."

And then she fell. Her legs folded beneath her and she dropped. Before Josiah could reach her, before his arms could stop it from happening, the palm of Willow's left hand grazed the hot stones of the fire circle and lay flat against the burning wood.

Shepherd screamed.

No cry or sound crossed Willow's lips. Lifted from the fire and carried in the shelter of her father's arms, her spirit had gone from them . . . back into the healing shadows of the other world.

Chapter Eleven

Trinity Adair knew Cameron better than anyone else within the enclosed world of Biosphere Seven. Trinity was Cameron's older brother, adopted by Jessica Nathan and Quinn Kelsey after the death of his birth mother, Maggie Adair. Trinity's biological father, Mike York, had been the last person from the biosphere to have attempted living outside the glass dome. Trinity had a vague memory of himself as a little child, waving goodbye to this man. That dim recollection was all there was. Mike York had died three days later of the virus, and with that death, all connection with his natural parents had stopped.

For the rest of Trinity's life, Jessica Nathan and Quinn Kelsey had been his parents. He was the eldest child in the family, but not their eldest child — that was Cameron's place. After Cameron's birth, Trinity had always known he could never be what Cameron was to them.

Still, he knew Cameron better than anyone else in the family did. He understood his brother's need to leave this place and recognized that the need was real.

In physical appearance the two were different.

Where Cameron had the dark coloring of Jessica Nathan, Trinity had the fair skin and blue eyes of his mother, and the rugged good looks of his father. Standing together, Trinity and Cameron were a vivid contrast, like opposite ends of a color spectrum. On one side there was the sun; on the other, the night.

Yet, they were brothers. For whatever reason, Trinity had always felt it was his place to protect Cameron if he could. It was a sense he had long ago learned to keep to himself, never quite understanding the source of it and knowing he could never have explained his feelings to anyone else.

In effect, he was his brother's keeper. And so it was Trinity who knew before anyone else exactly what Cameron was planning.

Cameron was going to leave the biosphere.

Days ago, on an afternoon when Trinity had been walking alone by the desert biome, he'd overheard two voices coming from behind the cluster of rocks up ahead. One, he recognized as Cameron's. The other voice took him longer to place; it was the man the Outsiders called Prophet.

Trinity had never spoken to this religious mystic. He knew that Brad McGhee, or Prophet as he was called now, had once been married to Cameron's mother. McGhee had become sick with the virus years ago, and felt that he had been saved by some spiritual force. It was this belief that had caused him to become known as Prophet. When Trinity overheard Cameron saying this man's name, he knew something important was taking place.

"What you're suggesting would mean your

death," he'd heard Prophet say. "You expect me to help you kill yourself?"

"I'm leaving, whether you help me or not. This way, if you do what I ask, you'll give me a better chance of surviving."

"I could tell your mother what you're planning. That might stop you. It's suicide, Cameron. Don't you understand that? The virus is still active. It's destroyed the human race. What makes you think you could survive it?"

"You did."

Prophet's voice became lower, harder for Trinity to hear. "Yes. I'm alive. My life was spared for some purpose, God knows what. I lost everything that was known to me of that other world: my strength, my wife, even my name."

"But you lived."

Prophet's voice grew louder, coming through the intercom in the glass. "Listen to me! You don't want this, Cameron. You mustn't think of doing it."

"You would have been my father. I think of that sometimes. We would have lived with those Outside and I would have been your son. Have you ever thought . . . ?"

"Yes. I've thought about it. About you. And your mother. In the beginning, I thought of little else. I still . . ." His voice dropped lower, as if he had turned away from that thought. "It doesn't help anyone to let such thoughts hold you to the past."

"Don't turn away from me now," said Cameron. "Please, I need your help. You have an immunity to the virus. You had the sickness, and lived. Prophet, if things had been different, I might have been your son and shared the immunity of your blood. I'm asking you to share that blood with me now."

"You're asking me to kill you! I can't do that to your mother. Have you thought about what your death would do to her? You want me to be a part of this?" he stormed. "My blood! You don't know what you're saying. I could never hurt her. Not even for you."

Trinity knew what Cameron would say next, even before the words sounded on the motionless air.

"My mother told me once that she still loves you. She loves my father, but she said in some part of her that's locked away, she's your wife . . . and will be until the day she dies. If you ever loved her, help me."

"Don't—"

"I'm leaving the dome, with or without a blood transfusion from you to protect me from the virus. I've made up my mind. I don't want to live at all, if it means living here. You might have been my father. If you'll do nothing else for me, I'm asking you to keep my secret."

Trinity waited. There was a long silence.

"What blood type are you?" asked Prophet.

"AB," said Cameron. "I'm a universal recipient."

"All right, but you'll have to get me the equipment. We have nothing to—"

"I can get everything we need in Diana Hunt's lab."

Trinity heard Prophet's deep sigh. "God help us,

89

what are we doing? What have you started?"

"My freedom," said Cameron. "And the rest of my life."

Trinity had moved away then. It wasn't the time to let Cameron know that anyone had overheard his plans. If it became necessary, Trinity would tell him later. For now, he would only watch and find whatever ways he could to protect his brother.

One thought remained and terrified Trinity Adair. It wasn't that he feared Cameron would die on the Outside. Or that Prophet's blood would contaminate everyone else within the sphere. The thought which tormented him was a worse fear. If Cameron left their world . . . Trinity would be alone.

It was that dream which haunted him day and night. Like a spirit who could not rise to its eternity, he lingered in the thought, and was afraid.

Jessica Nathan had kept her wedding ring—the one from her marriage to Brad McGhee. She never wore it anymore. The ring had been put into a box long ago, with the pictures and the memories of that love. Today, she climbed on a chair, reached high onto a closet shelf, and brought down the box. The ring lay on top of the pictures of her and Brad. She picked it up, and the memories came flooding back.

April 9th, their anniversary. She held the ring in the palm of her hand, closed her fingers around it into a tight fist and felt the gold circle bite into her flesh.

She was Quinn's wife.

Her fist opened like a flower whose petals were fingers. She stared again at the ring. It was as though she were a widow. Only, Brad wasn't dead.

How many years had it been? She knew. Didn't have to count. Twenty-five years today. Dear God, a milestone.

Quinn had stopped asking her if she still thought of Brad. Stopped, years ago. She was sure he'd never stopped wondering, but he had stopped asking. Because, she supposed, he knew the truth.

A soft knock at the door gave Jessica time to put the ring and pictures back into the box and replace the lid before calling, "Come in."

Her younger sons, Rourke and Bram, came into the room. Children of different fathers, these half-brothers might have been twins. Like Cameron, they had Jessica's dark hair and eyes, high foreheads, long narrow faces and soft mouths. They were handsome in a way she would have called ethnic. In Rourke and Bram, she saw the faces of her father and grandfather. In their veins were the ancient Jewish people, born again through her.

She looked at these two sons and felt a tender pang of guilt for having, in some hard to define way, betrayed them and Quinn by her memories of another love. Quickly, she put the box of memories back on the shelf.

"Is there something . . . ?" She heard the slight quaver in her voice. Would they notice?

"We wondered," said fifteen-year-old Rourke, always the leader of the two, "we were just thinking . . . how long has it been since the last person left the biosphere? Since anyone tried to survive Outside. We thought . . . maybe it was time someone tried again."

She was stunned. "How can you ask that? Do you know what kind of fear you've given me? Putting that kind of worry in my mind? You must never consider going Outside. Never! Do you understand? There's nothing there for you but certain and painful death."

Bram was the first to submit. "We didn't mean to scare you. We just wanted to see what it's like out there. Don't look like that. We won't go. We won't even think of it anymore. We promise, don't we Rourke?"

"Okay, sure. Don't get upset, Mom. We think about stuff sometimes, that's all."

"Not that. Don't think about that," she said.

She put one hand on each boy's cheek. Her father's eyes looked back at her. Her grandfather's eyes. Oh, God. Would they live and die in this glass world? They wanted to be free. Wasn't that their right? How long could she keep them safe? How long before the next crisis, the next tornado, the next thought of escape?

"I'm sorry to have yelled at you," she said. "I know you think about Outside and that other life beyond this dome. I think of it, too." She didn't look at the box on the shelf.

"We saw a wild horse today. It was walking along the edge of a steep cliff, in those hills behind the waterfall biome," said Bram. His voice was hushed when he spoke of the horse, and his eyes bright with a kind of awe of it.

"A horse? What color was it?" she asked, wanting to draw out this sense of wonder in him.

"Brown—a stallion, I think. He stood there a long time and looked down at me, at least that's what it seemed like. He wanted me to come after him. Do you think he was trying to tell me that?"

"Don't be stupid," said Rourke. "It's too far away. He couldn't see you through the glass."

Bram reacted as if struck. "He could too! He saw me. He was watching and asking me to come out. He could see me, couldn't he, Mom?" Bram's eyes were wide circles of hurt and outrage.

The mother's heart in her wanted to break at this small tragedy. The truth was, the animal *was* too far away to have seen through the glass. Bram would have had no way of knowing this; he'd never been Outside. He didn't understand the distance.

"Oh Bram, I'm sure the horse—"

"Jessica!" Cathe Innis's voice was loud and sharp with fear. "Jessica, come with me. Quick, it's Matthew. For God's sake, hurry!"

Chapter Twelve

Hurrying hadn't mattered. Matthew had been dead even before Cathe Innis had called for Jessica. He'd been dying while his mother had held the wedding ring in her hand, while she'd been looking at the old pictures of her and Brad in the box from the shelf. He'd been already dead, even as she was remembering that other love, that other life. She'd lost her child during those moments, and hadn't even felt it.

After, that was what hurt her the most. She was his mother. She should have felt him dying. She should have known that he'd needed her.

The ring had stopped that knowing.

It was a private torment she couldn't share with Quinn. How could she tell him of this secret pain that fed her heart with an agony of guilt? It was more than grieving for her dead child. It was knowing that she was at fault for his death. She should have been with him. He was too young to have been left alone. Even here, within the sphere. He was too young. . . .

Matthew had been climbing on the feed bins . . . a six-year-old boy towering at the topmost edge of a metal storage silo. He had been looking down into the colorful patterns of grain at the top of the tank. And he had slipped and fallen into the bin. Headfirst. The loose grain had swallowed him, sucking him into its depths like pebbled quicksand.

One of the other children had seen him fall—Diana's youngest daughter, Lara. She'd brought help. While some of them were still trying to reach him, Cathe had run for Jessica. But it had been too late. Matthew was dead when they pulled him out, suffocated by the dust of the grain. His eyes were packed with it, his ears, his mouth.

Matthew had been the youngest of Jessica's children. His genetic father had been Griffin Llewellyn, and while Griffin was visibly saddened by the boy's loss, it was Quinn who openly mourned the child.

In all but biological blueprint, Matthew had been Quinn's son. All of Jessica's children had been brought up as Quinn's, no matter which of the three men of Biosphere Seven had been their biological father. Paternity had always seemed to be a state of mind to Quinn. And so Jessica knew he hadn't been able to understand her remoteness and silence toward him, following Matthew's death. She had closed him out, keeping her grief locked within her, a secret sorrow.

"Jessica, for God's sake, talk to me. Matt was my son, too. We need to help each other get through this. Jessie, what can I do . . . ?"

Quinn had tried to reach her, but she was numb, cold with a kind of remorse which could not be touched, even by his love.

The truth was, Jessica couldn't find a way to explain to him this sense of responsibility she felt over her son's death. Not to Quinn. Not to anyone. She was as much trapped by her feelings of shame and guilt as her son had been trapped by the shifting grain.

Only Matthew was dead; Jessica had to go on living.

It was in this cold lull after Matthew's death that she fixed on a plan to free the children of Biosphere Seven. She would watch no more of their sons and daughters die. She would take whatever steps necessary to save them. Her first act toward this goal would be another pregnancy—only this time the biological father would not be one of the three men within the biosphere dome, but an Outsider.

There was no doubt in Jessica's mind who the father must be.

For the sake of them all, it must be Brad's child.

The eldest daughter of Diana Hunt had always been different from the other children of Biosphere Seven. During Cassandra's first couple of years Diana had thought the girl was deaf, for the toddler had seemed unaware of sound and had not spoken a single word by the time she was two.

It hadn't troubled the mother, this silence in the child. Diana Hunt had alienated herself from the others in the biosphere long ago, and was used to the solitude of her own mind by the time her daughter was born. She never urged Cassandra to speak, or seemed disturbed that the little girl might be flawed in some way. They were alike, Diana and this small, quiet child, easy confederates in the fragmented world they shared.

The others had whispered that Cassandra was

damaged, that Diana—being a chemist—had formulated and taken mind-altering drugs during her pregnancy, and that as a result of this the mind of the sweet-faced, dark-haired little girl may have been damaged. Over the next years, both Jessica and Cathe had tried many times to urge the girl to speak, worrying when Cassandra would turn away, ignoring their words and their fears.

Diana never seemed concerned about it, or their worry. She knew that nothing she had taken during pregnancy had caused her daughter's indifference to the boundaries of this world. Cassandra Hunt had simply detached herself from the suffocating, enclosed refuge of Biosphere Seven, just as her mother had in the year before the child was born. In this, mother and daughter were of one mind. They were *in* the sphere, but they were not *of* it.

It was later, at the age of about three-and-a-half, that the girl's strange behavior became too peculiar to be ignored any longer, and the label autistic was placed on Cassandra. From that point on, it was as though Diana's eldest daughter had been excommunicated from the other children, from the adults, from the organized colony of Biosphere Seven. She was accepted as different. And therefore, ignored.

In a world of urgency and voices, the silent girl was lost.

She had grown up in that world, unnoticed by the others.

But she had noticed everything.

Cassandra was the watcher, a vibration of the feelings of each member of the biosphere. She knew their longings and their hurts. She knew that Cameron was ready to risk anything in order to leave

97

the sphere. She knew that Sidra loved him and would rather die than live in a world without him. And she knew that Trinity loved Sidra . . . but that Sidra never saw his love.

Cassandra knew other things, too. Not just about people. She knew about the sphere, things no one else noticed. She saw the biosphere as a living being like herself, and *felt* its presence. She knew its moods, its hurts and longings. The places where it flourished. The places where it failed. Cassandra saw the beating heart of the sphere—within her mind, she saw it—and understood something the others never considered.

The biosphere did not want them to leave.

A consciousness had lifted from the soul of this world's Earth, from the water of its sea and its small rivers. The air of the biosphere tingled with that budding sense. It was a living being, a replication of old Earth, awakened within this glass womb.

And it was possessive of all that it held.

Cassandra knew. It would never let them go.

"What is it you see out there, Cassi?" Trinity asked.

They were in the rain forest. It was darkening, the vivid colors of life lowering into the dim recesses of night. He didn't wait for an answer but went right on, speaking as though she hadn't heard him.

"This place is like a green dream, isn't it? I mean, you can feel things growing . . . as if they were part of you. Weird, huh? So, Cassi-girl, what do you think about? Or do you think about anything? Is it just . . . processing going on inside your head? I wonder. Your eyes don't look numb. That's what they say you are, kind of numb. I don't believe it.

98

Your eyes look . . ."

He pulled back, as if he'd seen something unexpected.

He started walking away, without saying good-bye, then stopped and turned around, as if reminding himself that she was there. That she was real.

"Don't stay in the rain forest too long. The bugs come out after dark, and they bite." He seemed to be considering something, and then as if suddenly decided, added, "You have pretty eyes, Cassi. Blue as the sky."

He left her, after that.

She tested the words in her mind, sizing them and sorting each a separate one into a holding point within her. There was *don't* and *bugs* and *dark* and *bite*. She felt them moving in their places, wriggling for her attention. But one word she lingered over, coming back to it again and again. *Pretty.*

Prophet hadn't seen his wife in all the years since the virus had claimed their world. Not seen her up close, anyway. He'd glimpsed her through the glass of the observation window a few times, but had been so far away, she'd seemed like a distant image of herself, an unclear photo. Now, she stood just beyond the partition. As if he could reach through the barrier and touch her.

"Hi," she said, and pressed her hand to the glass wall between them.

It was hard for him to put his hand over the same spot, hard as living alone, hard as burning up with feverish need that only she could heal. It was hard, but he put his hand on the glass.

She smiled, and there was uneased sorrow in the softly parted lips . . . in the brown eyes. This wasn't easy for her, either. He knew.

"You look the part," she said, "what they call you now. Lean, ascetic — an eremite, or a monk. Are you a prophet, Brad?"

"They say I am." He wasn't sure he could stay here. It was painful, too much hurt. If she said the wrong thing . . . If she said, *Brad. I love you,* he would go. He would walk into the desert and never come back. For he couldn't live then, not if she said those words.

He couldn't go on living . . . without her.

"Are you well?" Her eyes searched the look of his face, taking in each new line, each strength that the last years had brought to him. She searched, as if nourishing some part of her that was starving.

"I'm healed of the virus, if that's what you mean." He hadn't meant it to sound so abrupt and harsh, as if he blamed her for his life.

She held her thoughts in silence. Words lay unspoken between them, words that could wound and shatter the protective shells each had enclosed around them.

Brad and Jessica.

Jessica and Quinn.

Brad the Prophet.

He wondered, did she know about Cameron? What her son was planning? Was that why she'd sent for him?

"Did you know about my son?" she asked, as if tapping into the thoughts of his mind.

"Your son?"

"Yes, Matthew. My youngest, only six."

100

Prophet felt a tenseness in his muscles relax. "I didn't know you had a boy of six. I knew about Cameron and Trinity, but I'd never heard that you had another child. No one tells me about you."

She looked up sharply at that. The words had hurt her, he guessed. Wounds upon wounds.

"I've had six children, Brad. Seven, counting Trinity."

He was stunned. And then angry.

She had lived a real life, apart from him. She had known love, and happiness, and fulfillment. His world had been ashes, and the stirrings of a single flame. Grief rose up in him like lust. He wanted her to feel the swell of it, to blame her for this unending ache.

"Matthew was my youngest." She looked away from him when she spoke of the boy. "There was an accident in the grain silo . . . almost a month ago. He suffocated."

Prophet's anger dissolved. The consuming fire of love which had shaped his life, returned. "Jessie . . ." Her name was all he could say, all he could offer to loosen the hard knot of pain she carried.

For one instant, she pressed her whole body against the glass — face, shoulders, hands. Her breasts and thighs straining against the clear, unyielding wall. Trying to touch him. Trying to get through.

His body responded, a jolt of feeling that shocked him. If he could have put his fist through the glass to reach her, he would have. He would have walked through fire. Or Hell. Or even death, to reach her. He would have damned them all, broken the wall,

101

and pulled her to him. . . .

But, she turned away.

Her need turned into sobbing tears. She knelt on the ground and her grief for the son she'd lost poured from her. Tears like blood. Tears that carried away the soul of her child. Tears that finally released the boy.

But not her guilt.

"I was thinking of you," she said, staring up at him. "The moment Matthew died . . . I was thinking of you. It was April ninth."

He knew the date. Twenty-five years. He'd wondered if she'd remembered.

"I have a box with a few pictures, and my wedding ring." She was going through torment to tell him. "And I was holding that ring, thinking of you—of us—when Matthew was alone and dying."

Feelings swam at him like sharks, each tearing into his soul. He was moved by the raw hurt of her pain, but his heart had heard words he'd longed to know.

He was part of her life, still. That fact alone, would let him go on living.

"You couldn't have known what was happening to the boy."

"I *should* have known! I'm his mother. I should have felt it. Been with him. Somehow."

More tears, sobs wracking her body. He waited, remaining silent, letting this draining of emotion ease some of the weight of hurt. He wasn't a priest, but she had confessed and he had heard her confession.

Somehow, he knew he must find a way to absolve her of this guilt. It was the one act of love he could do for her. But how?

Her words gave him the way.

"They'll all die," she said suddenly, "the children born in the biosphere. We can't keep them here forever. Something will happen. Another tornado. A flood. Something will end it, and they'll all die." Her face showed a barely controlled panic, as if it might happen in the next moment.

He wondered, did she know about Cameron? About the blood transfusion? Part of him wanted desperately to tell her—tell it now, and feel free again with his conscience. But, he had promised Cameron . . . and knew also that Jessica would never allow such a risk to come to her son. To Quinn's child. The boy would leave the sphere no matter what anyone did to stop him.

By his continued silence, Prophet was giving Cameron Nathan a chance.

"I need your help." Her words startled him back to the reality of this moment.

"I'll do whatever you ask, Jessie—you know that—whatever you need."

"I need a child. Your child." The words were blunt and flat. "If you love me . . . if you have any feeling left for me at all, then find a way to do this, Brad. Please, before it's too late."

All other thoughts vanished from Prophet's mind. He was left breathless by the sudden force and exhilaration of this one primal image.

He and Jessica together, creating a child.

Chapter Thirteen

John Katelo had been up since well before dawn. He stood now with the easy slosh of the lake water at his feet, and the gray-black spires of Montana's jagged mountains at his back. The sun's rays fingered strokes of light across the still-dark sky.

He stood alone in this half-light of early morning, and stared into the direction his sons had gone when they rode off. They had ridden south. It would be warmer for them, the farther south they went. He tried to imagine that they were somewhere warm. That they had food. That they were safe. He tried to imagine these things, but found it hard.

He remembered his own journey too well.

A stirring in the shallow water made him turn. Salena stood beside him. She didn't touch him or ask any questions, but waited for him to speak.

"Thinking of my sons keeps me from sleep," he explained. "In the night, my mind dreams of Seth and Jonathan, of where they are and what has happened to them. I see them clearly in the dream," he said. "They ride their horses toward me, coming home. And then the dream passes, and I am awake. I come here and watch for them."

"Don't look for them so soon," Salena told him.

"Staring at the place where they left won't make the time pass any faster. We let them go," she reminded him. "Now, we must wait."

He smiled, reached for her hand and curled his fingers around her wrist. "All of our children will go, won't they?" He felt the sadness as a heaviness within his heart. "They will go, to find others . . . if there are others."

"And they'll come back." She touched his cheek, her hand warm and gentle against his face. "Each of them. When they've found others, they'll come back to us."

He nodded, saying nothing more to her of his fears for their children. He and Salena had given them life. In the world since the virus, that was a gift beyond any price. He could not live their lives for them, too. Hard as it was, he knew he must let each of them go.

"Why are you standing here? Come out of the water, John."

He couldn't answer her at first. The words wouldn't come. His reason for standing in the shallow water of the lake was more for reasons of the senses than those of the mind. Water was a part of this place, their home. It was the source of life which had allowed them to survive. He felt that the water was part of him, part of each of them. He belonged to it, and to the rich fields of grass and farmland. He belonged to the exposed bones of the earth — the mountains which stood as a shelter to this valley. They were as much a part of him as he was part of them.

"I wanted the water to know how I feel," he said, his words like the spreading image of the rising sun across the sky. He had said what he felt, but would she understand his meaning?

"You see your gods in all things, don't you, John?"

"Is that so bad?"

She bent closer to the water and cupped her hands to it. "I wonder, what would the voice of my religion have made of you?" she asked. "An idol-worshiper, or a saint?" She let the water trickle through her open fingers, then pressed her wet hands to her face. "For me, it's enough that you're here for me to love. You are my blessing, John."

He pulled her up and she came into his arms like a moving warmth. She took his hand, kissed it, and placed it over the damp swell of her breast.

"You are my blessing," he said, and bent his head to the hollow against her heart.

Chapter Fourteen

Willow Gray Wolf's return to her people was more than the regaining of Sagamore's child. She had not come back to the Outsiders as she had left them. She had been changed by the wind. Like the tree of which her name was a remembrance, Willow had known suffering, but had grown stronger for it.

The change in her was so remarkable and so obvious to anyone who looked into her eyes, no one questioned it. She was different from the rest of them. She had been set apart, and was therefore no longer seen as one of the older children. The People considered her a woman now, and no longer simply Sagamore's daughter.

The People said they were happy she was back among them, but they stayed away. No one came close to her. They smiled in passing, but hurried by and did not speak. The children stared in curiosity, but never approached her. Even her own brothers and sisters seemed reluctant to return to the easy sense of family they had once shared.

Her parents did what they could to bring their daughter back into the acceptance of the People, but it soon became clear this would not happen, and they stopped trying. Willow had become something the

Outsiders had no understanding of; she had become a seer.

The first instance of this exceptional ability came only a few hours after Sagamore brought Willow home. Her hand had been badly burned by the campfire, and exhaustion and pain coursed through her in twin rivers of feeling. While her mother tended to cleaning and bandaging the injured hand, Willow began speaking. The voice which came from her was not the mild, sweet one her parents knew. It was feminine, but strong and powerful.

"One returns, and one will go. It is life for life. My gift abides with you."

"What was that she said?" Rosalina Santos asked. She was fifty-four, a round, soft-spoken woman who sometimes talked to herself when washing clothes or cooking. She was a gentle lady, but reacted to Willow's words as if stung, and angry. "What did she mean? Tell me."

"She doesn't know what she's saying." Willow's mother had tried to press Rosalina's questions away. "She's exhausted and in pain. Let her rest. Tomorrow, she'll be better. Go home, leave her to me."

Rosalina did go, then. Nothing more would have been said of the strange words, except that in the morning, Michael, the infant son of Merry Logan lay dead on his cot. It was then that Rosalina Santos remembered the words Willow had said, and the *voice of the Holy Spirit* that she had spoken through.

Other occurrences followed. At first, Sagamore and Elizabeth tried to explain their daughter's unusual behavior by blaming it on her injured hand, saying that she was still sick with fever and infection from the burn, that she couldn't be held accountable for her actions, or her words. They said this the next

108

time their daughter spoke to the People with this voice that was not her own. It was on the day when the male spring lambs were to be slaughtered.

To the Outsiders, the few sheep of this high desert were a primary source of food for the People. When the winter came, only the strongest of the first year lambs had survived the deep snows. The ewes were never touched for food. They were needed for the next year's lambs.

On this day in late spring, a culling was begun among the male lambs. Two or three were spared each year, insuring a continuity of the flock, should anything happen to the breeding ram. On this day, the men and women herded the bleating lambs into the slaughter pens, and prepared to begin their work. The throat of only one lamb had been cut, when Willow Gray Wolf opened the swinging gate of the pens and let the others run free.

"Let the young rams go untouched. Take only seasoned ewes for food." She stood in the corral and turned with arms outspread. Her voice was clear and loud. "Let no one of you touch the young rams. They are holy offerings."

The people grew afraid at Willow's words. For two days, no one dared to touch the lambs. Ram or ewe, no one dared.

On the third morning, the breeding ram convulsed and died. The two remaining adult rams died within hours of the first. Not a single ewe was harmed by this strange malady, nor any of the female lambs. The male lambs dropped as if their spirits were struck from their small bodies in the instant. They fell to the ground dead and remained undefiled by the hand of man.

Two young rams survived. These two gamboled

over the sweet-scented grass, bleating to their mothers for the ewes to let down their milk.

"If we had culled the flock, there would be no rams left," the people whispered. "It was God's truth she spoke. Rosalina was right. Willow spoke with the voice of the Holy Spirit."

For the second time, the People saw this young woman as someone set apart. She was looked upon with honor . . . and with fear.

A third instance of her vision sealed Willow's image with the Outsiders. It was later in the year, on a day of summer warmth, a warning of that season still to come. The children were playing on a sloping hill which reached to the river, across the water from a plateau cultivated with orange and lemon trees. The youngest children were running and rolling down the grassy knoll, sometimes spilling into the cold water at the muddy bank of the river.

There were adults watching. The children had been running and playing on the gentle slope for some time before Willow looked down from the crest of the hill. What she saw was not the idyllic scene of a bright spring game. Instead, she saw a dark basin of rough-thrown earth, a cavernous hole where the side of the hill had been, and collapsed ground damming the river channel.

"Run to the trees!" she screamed to the children. Her voice was sharp and hard, scaring one of the girls into tears. "Get off the hill! Run!" she shouted again, and started down the slope, chasing the youngest ones across the water and into the grove of trees.

"What are you doing?" Natalie Peters, the mother of one young boy, cried out in alarm. "Leave the children alone! Don't touch them with your black arts.

110

Someone stop her! She's gone crazy. She's trying to hurt the children!"

Willow turned back to face the adults. There was anger in their eyes, and fear at what she had done. One of them started rushing down the hill toward her.

"Go back!" she screamed.

The children behind Willow were crying. The adults were shouting to her to let them go. Sagamore, her father, stood at the top of the hill, staring.

And then came the sound . . . a wrenching, tearing break in the earth. The sound was all the warning they had. In that same instant, the ground caved in and sank into itself, carving a deep gouge in the face of the hill, and a landslide of loosened hillside damming the river.

Natalie Peters, the mother who had shouted at Willow to release her son, lay crushed beneath that mound of dirt and rock. The earth rumbled again and a second crack opened along the side of the hill. Once more, the ground gave way and a massive landslide broke and shifted to the river basin.

A thick, brown plume of dust rose from the hillside's collapse, choking the onlookers and clouding the scene of destruction with an eerie moat of swirling particles of loamy earth.

Willow saw her father through this rising curtain of reddish dust. He was still standing on the unsafe ground at the crest of the hill. She wanted to shout to him to move, to call out that where he stood was dangerous, but something stopped her. A look of unconcealed horror was on his face. As the dust cleared, she saw something else. He was not staring at the cave-in like the others . . . but at her.

Father and daughter spoke of his reaction only

once. It was on the same night as the cave-in. In their fear of what had happened, the People shunned her. For a time of awkward silence, Sagamore and Willow chanced to be alone.

"Father?" She could have asked, *Why did you look at me that way?* or, *What have I done, that you fear me?* — but she said only his name and waited.

"I have found my daughter only to lose her again." He didn't look at her when he said this.

"You haven't lost me; I'm here." She was trembling.

"No, Willow is gone," he looked up now, his eyes meeting hers at last, "and you are here."

Her trembling stopped, and she was filled with a hurt so profound, so penetrating, the touch of it seemed to scar her soul.

Later, Prophet came to talk with her.

"Give them time," he said. "They fear you."

"Should I have been silent? Should I have let their children die? Because of me, they lived." Anger boiled inside her in a cold and bitter flame.

"You spoke to protect them. In time, they'll come to see that, too."

His words did nothing to soothe her. "In time . . ."

"It was the same for them at first," he said, "with me."

She stared at him, realizing that all her life she had thought of him as someone different from the rest. With these words of understanding between them, Willow began to listen.

"In the days before the virus came, civilization was a loud voice. It spoke to the People, deafening them to the quiet sounds of the spirit. It distracted them from listening to the words you and I hear. It blocked their ears to that other voice, and blinded their vision to what was before them to see."

"Was the other voice always there?" Willow asked.

"I think it's the voice of the spirit in each of us," said Prophet. "I think it's been with man as long as the spirit has been a part of him. Some hear it clearly, others, not at all."

He touched his hand to her head. "You and I share this burden, and this gift."

"Is it because we were both hurt? Is that why we can hear and see what others can't? Because of the tornado? Because of the virus?"

He shook his head. "Maybe, but I don't think that's why. Earliest man believed that all things were of the spirit. He listened for the voice, and saw its existence in trees and rock and water. He saw his God in what was silent and unseen. Cities and civilization pulled the whole of mankind far away from that direct contact. We lost our need to hear the voice of the spirit.

"Now, the voice is heard again," he went on, "with you and with me. It didn't go away," he told her. "It's always been there, to be heard, to be seen. It has always been."

She considered what he'd said, and knew it to be true. "Will the rest of them become like us? Will they ever hear?"

"Our world is a planet of hungry silence now. What is spoken will one day be heard. This is a time of renewal. We are remade on a new Earth. There will be many seers, many prophets in the days to come. Mankind will hear the voice of the living God, and carry it within him. We are in an age of witness, and are the foundation others will build upon. Hold closely to that voice you hear, to that vision within you.

113

"In time," he said, "the people will know something of that voice. They will hear and believe it, because of you."

In the days and weeks which followed, the child of Josiah Gray Wolf fell away from this new woman. The child of Sagamore died on a desert plain, without the comfort of family or friend. The seer was all that remained.

It was the seer who knew death would come for Rosalina Santos, the seer who spoke the words which filled the People with terror.

"You will die. Prepare your soul."

And the round-faced Mexican woman sickened, daily growing thinner and weaker, until the cancer that ate away at her body claimed her life.

In answer to all those who had turned away from her, Willow turned within. She saw a great fire at the heart of her, a flame that would not be quenched by the fears of anyone. Her spirit nurtured the flame like a quickened child within the womb, and called it holy. She would not turn away from this fire, this knowledge. If all others did, she would not.

Slowly, they came to her. With their questions. With their fears. They came and put themselves before her and said, "Spirit Woman, tell us what will be."

She listened, and told them what she saw.

And thereafter, by this name she was known to them.

As Spirit Woman, she lived among the Outsiders and was given a place of honor among the People. In time, the women would turn to her concerning the best date of conception for each new child. Seeds for new crops would be planted in the upturned earth at the time of her reckoning. And the People would ask her the meaning of the signs they saw in the skies.

She was Spirit Woman, the voice of God in the land of the forsaken.

Chapter Fifteen

Seth's horse caught his hoof on a loose stone of the riverbed, stumbled to the side, and threw his rider into the rushing water. It happened in an instant, and both horse and rider were under the cold flow of the river, struggling for their lives.

The moving force of the water held Seth down. It worked against his efforts to free himself. It was a wall, heavy as rock, pressing its weight on him. Couldn't see. Couldn't breathe. Water punching him like fists, knocking him back, knocking him down. And the horse! Kicking . . . kicking. Black hooves dancing in the water. An avalanche of black-rock hooves.

Seth felt the water smother him. He couldn't rise above the crushing power of it. He felt his body begin to sink into the unyielding net of this river, pulled down, pulled in . . . and he grabbed for Smoke's tail. There was no fight left, only enough strength to hold on. Seth twined his fingers into the long track of the stallion's flowing tail. It moved in the water just ahead of him, a wide fan of shimmering hair.

His eyes were open, but the light was closing like the night. It was darkening in the water, the bright struggle, darkening. Seth felt himself falling into it. Weight like a heavy dream, pressing out all strength. Smothering dark. Black, black, black . . .

Seth was yanked into the light, a catch like a fish clinging to the saving net of the stallion's tail. The horse had broken free of the water and was climbing up the muddy bank. A rush of air swooped into Seth and he felt himself come alive with it. A strength of white light and breath flooded through him. He stared into that light and gasped at the salvation of air surrounding him.

"Seth!" His brother was at his side, supporting him, shaking him loose of the horse's tail. "Are you breathing? Say something!"

He was breathing, though his chest felt caved in, unable to pull enough air into his hurting lungs. He nodded, leaning heavily on Jonathan as they climbed up the slippery bank. "I went under," he tried to explain, the words painful messages forced from his throat and lungs like hard coughs. Tearing. "Went dark . . ."

It was the terror dream come true. The rivers had been his fear on every day of their journey. He'd felt it coming to him, like a knife whistling in the wind of his mind. He'd seen it, known the day would come when the water would engulf him . . . when he would die.

But, he had not died.

"Gotta get you warm," said Jonathan. He began dragging dry brush into a rough pile for a fire.

Seth waited, shaking so hard he couldn't stand. His legs melted under him and he sank rubber-kneed to the ground in an easy drop, feet stretched out before him and sitting. He was left to stare at the churning water that had nearly been his death.

"Don't look at it," said Jonathan. "It's over. You're okay now." His fingers worked the small heat of the fire, feeding it brittle twigs, dry grass, and fanning the tiny flame to a coughing blaze.

Seth heard his brother's words, but kept staring at the water. Jonathan didn't understand. The shaking was from the terrible cold, and from the close touch of his own death. It wasn't from fear—not anymore. The fear was gone. It had been washed away in that surge of white water, in the undercurrent that had pulled him down.

The fear had been his own sure knowledge that this day would happen, that the river would take him. And it had happened . . . and was over. Now, he could go on. It was past him and he'd survived. The terrible dread of it had left him and he felt cleansed of a festering wound that had drained him of spirit and heart.

"Here," he felt Jonathan's strong arms pulling him to his feet, "come over and sit by the fire. You're all right now, Seth. Don't think about it anymore. I won't let anything else happen to you. I promise."

Seth couldn't talk. He was cold and shivering. When he could unclench his jaws enough to speak, his teeth hit together like flaking quartz. He wanted to tell Jonathan not to promise such a thing. No one could keep that kind of promise. No amount of being careful could stop fate from happening. He wanted to explain that to Jonathan. Instead, Seth held the thought inside him. It coursed through his body in easy waves, surging with his blood, surging with the cleansing air in his lungs, becoming as fixed in his mind as his own clear sense of self. He understood now. Life was a risk. Each day, each moment risked everything.

But, that was all right.

Seth stood and walked over to his horse. The black was blowing heavily, visible shudders still rippling over its back and flanks. He ran his hand over the wet neck, feeling the muscles roll beneath the animal's skin.

He lay his head on Smoke's neck, filled his hands with strands of wet, clumpy mane, and held on until the trembling stopped.

The secret meeting between Cameron Nathan and Prophet had been prearranged for 2:00 A.M. at the PAL docking chamber outside the desert biome.

PAL, the acronym for Planetary-All-Land vehicle had originally been designed to conduct exploration studies outside the closed biosphere, just as a vehicle from a space station might one day conduct them on Mars, or another planetary colony. PAL was no longer housed within Biosphere Seven. It had left the sphere over twenty years before, when Josiah Gray Wolf drove it out of the docking chamber and into the desert.

At that time, the people of Biosphere Seven didn't know whether or not human life existed beyond the glass walls of the sphere. They had been cut off from all contact with the outside for weeks, and a desperate sense of isolation had driven them to this dangerous act.

Josiah Gray Wolf had entered the sealed chamber of the PAL vehicle, and using the docking chamber system, had left the sphere. Once Outside, PAL had broken down and Josiah had been forced to leave the support system of the vehicle, thereby exposing himself to the outside air and the virus.

The PAL transport had never been returned to Biosphere Seven. It had been abandoned to the desert at the spot where Josiah was forced to leave it, and where he left his last message for the people of Biosphere Seven before walking out of their lives. "I'll look for survivors," he had said. "If I find them, I'll come back."

All of that had happened before Cameron's birth. He knew of it because he'd heard the talk between his mother and father. Information about the sphere was never kept from him or from any of the Insiders' children. They were a community of technicians, as well as agrarians, botanists, oceanographers, and a hundred other categories of specialists. Each child needed to carry on the knowledge of each adult, in order for the continuance of the biosphere and the people within it.

Because of this, Cameron knew a great deal about his father's work with the computer systems of the sphere. He understood how to safely open the docking chamber — blocking control to the warning alarm programmed into the system. It was a matter of overriding a series of commands in the set-up files of the structural integrity master file. When he had finished, if all went well, he would delete the blocking command and his father would not be aware of any interference with the original program.

He didn't open the outer shield — the docking chamber exit — only the door to the docking chamber itself. There was no danger of contamination to the sphere from this, only danger that he might get caught.

Prophet was waiting on the other side. Cameron could see him through the glass wall. It was dark outside, but the docking chamber had a soft, constant light. They spoke through the intercom.

"When will it happen?" Cameron asked. He was impatient. It had been weeks since Prophet first agreed to find a way to give him a blood transfusion. In all that time, nothing had taken place. "I'm ready to leave with or without the transfusion if we can't find a way to do this. I'm ready to take my chances Outside."

"No. You don't do that, not yet," said Prophet.

"You don't understand. I won't keep waiting. I'm going to be free of here. I won't live as a prisoner. You promised that you'd help me. If there isn't a way—"

"There *is* a way. I've already drawn my blood. I brought it with me tonight."

"What . . . ?" Cameron couldn't think what to say next. He couldn't believe what he'd heard.

"Your mother gave me the means to do it."

"My mother? You told her! You swore to me that you'd keep this a secret!"

"Calm down. Your mother knows nothing about this. I only meant that she gave me the way to do it. She provided me with the sealed plastic bags and medical equipment needed to allow this to happen."

"Plastic bags? Why? If she doesn't know . . . why did she give you those things?"

Prophet didn't answer for a time, then said, "That is a question you can't ask me—or her. It's my only condition of this exchange. What we're doing tonight is an act of faith between us. We're both taking a great risk. You won't violate this trust, Cameron.

121

You won't say one word of this to anyone. Do I have your promise?"

Cameron felt a rush of questions flood his mind, but he held them in silence. What was his mother planning? Why had she sent Prophet sealed plastic bags and medical equipment? And what was this secret? Whatever was happening, he knew Prophet wouldn't tell him.

"I'll never speak of it," he answered. "I swear."

"Do you want to know what convinced me to help you, Cameron?"

It was an unexpected question. He hadn't thought of it. He'd been much more concerned with how they would accomplish the goal. But now that Prophet had mentioned it, he did wonder. "Tell me."

"It was because you said that if things had been different I might have been your father. That was true. I thought about it a long time, and I knew then that I couldn't deny you this chance. If you'd been my son, I would have risked anything for your freedom. That's why I'm helping you."

Cameron was stunned by the bare honesty in this declaration.

Then Prophet added, "If it doesn't go well, I wanted you to know."

Cameron was drawn to this man who had once been his mother's husband. He saw why his mother had loved Brad McGhee, and knew that this man's feelings for his wife hadn't changed in all these years. A grief welled up in him for both of them, for the separation they'd been forced to endure, and the love which had been denied them.

"In a way," Prophet said almost too softly to be heard, "giving you my blood does make you my son.

122

At least, I like to see it that way."

The words had touched Cameron deeply. This man was offering more than his life's blood; he was offering kinship, and a kind of inheritance that would be his if he survived the Outside.

"I see it that way, too," said Cameron. "From this day on, I have two fathers."

They said nothing more of this. There was a danger that he might be seen, and there was no more time to risk being overheard. The rest was up to Cameron. There was work to be done.

Cameron exited the docking area and sealed the desert biome door leading to that chamber. From within the biome, he pressed the outer exit door of the docking chamber, allowing Prophet to enter the docking area and place the sealed plastic bag of blood and sterilized instruments into the chamber. Prophet then exited the chamber, and Cameron resealed the outer door. He then evacuated all the air from the chamber and activated the room's spray nozzles to saturate the entire area—including walls, ceiling, and floor—with a strong sterilizing solution of bleach. Bleach wouldn't destroy the plastic of the bags.

Cameron was completely alone now, and shaking. What he was doing could put everyone within the biosphere at risk. Even with all his precautions, he might be introducing the virus into the sphere. It was a thought which filled him with stark terror. He was alone with his action, his fear, and knew he had committed himself to it. From this moment on, he must follow through with all the steps of his plan.

He allowed the sterilizing solution to sit for an hour, then began reintroducing the air system of the biosphere back into the chamber. It was a slow process, nerve-racking, but it couldn't be rushed. Twenty minutes later, he opened the desert biome door to the docking chamber for the second time that night. Inside, he picked up the two sealed bags — one with Prophet's blood, and the other with sterilized instruments needed to complete the transfusion. Swiftly, he reentered the desert biome, resealed the docking chamber, and fled.

The next step of the plan was to take a bag of saline solution from Diana's lab.

Cameron knew how to draw blood from a vein; he'd done it on the potbelly pigs and the miniature goats when they needed to test the serum white cell count for bacterial infection that had spread through a few of the animals.

If he could find a vein to draw blood, he could find it to receive a transfusion.

There was no time to think about his choices, no time to wait. The blood in the two bags had begun to deteriorate from the first instant of leaving Prophet's body. Cameron needed to act now. He hurried to the place he had prepared, the twin bags — one of warm blood, and one of saline solution — hidden beneath his shirt.

Only when the blood transfusion was completed, and when he was safely back in his room early that morning after deleting the override commands on the computer's system security files, did Cameron's shaking stop.

Chapter Sixteen

May 13, 2018: I know now, it isn't enough to wait for life outside the sphere to be restored to the way it was. The virus has changed our world and excluded us. We are no longer a part of what happens there, unimportant to it. If we can't find a way to heal ourselves, we'll die within this sphere, aliens in this world of our own making, and never become a part of the real Earth again.

Jessica stared at this latest journal entry. She read the words on the screen, feeling again the desperate sense of them. Matthew was dead. And for the other children . . . ? What would happen? Would they die, too, one by one?

Her thinking had changed. The security and structural integrity of the dome wasn't everything. Maybe Diana hadn't been crazy years ago, when she'd tried to escape. Maybe all of them were the crazy ones to have stayed. Wasn't life, the kind of life which meant something, worth even the greatest risk?

She had come to a crossroad in her life, and finally knew there was only one path to take.

* * *

"What are you doing to protect the children born into your biosphere?" It was a question Jessica had asked herself each day; now she asked it of Paul Schefield, leader of Biosphere Two in north Wales.

The communications link had provided both biospheres new information about conditions outside their own areas. Each was an important connection for the other, sharing the experiences of survival in a closed environment.

"We have had setbacks," Paul Schefield informed her. Was his voice sounding more hollow than his usual clipped-syllable dialect? Or, was she imagining that?

"What sort of setbacks?"

"We've lost a few people recently."

Jessica didn't need this drawn-out toying with the facts. Whatever had affected Biosphere Two might just as easily affect Biosphere Seven. Her people and her family were at stake.

"Tell me what happened."

"Three of our young people left the sphere . . . last week, in fact."

"Oh, God."

"They managed to exit the dome before we could stop them."

It was the terror Jessica lived with daily. "Did they violate the integrity of the sphere?"

What she was really asking was—*Have you been exposed to the virus? Are you dying?* But, those were questions she would not ask. She didn't need to. He'd understand.

"We're not sure. There's no way to be absolutely certain, but it's more likely that the air flow was outward moving when they exited. Opening the doors would create a vacuum effect, sucking the atmosphere out."

A week. He'd said it had been a week. By now, they must know what happened to the children who had escaped the boundary of the sphere.

"And the young people who left . . . ?" She kept the question open-ended.

"My daughter, and two boys of eighteen, the oldest children born into our colony," he explained. "All dead."

His words struck Jessica with a force that stopped her breath. For a moment she couldn't speak, or move. Every part of her was as if it were paralyzed, except her mind. She almost wished it could stop thinking, too. It realized what all the rest of her should have felt. And the outrage clanged in her head like a bell, over and over. No. No. No.

"My daughter Katherine . . . she wanted more than we could offer here. She couldn't be happy, I suppose. The two young men, Brian and Kevin, felt the same. You can't stop a thing like that," he said, "a need to be free. I couldn't have kept them here."

"Paul—"

"My daughter died alone. Completely alone. The young men had died a few days before. She crept away so that her mother and I wouldn't see her suffering."

"Paul, please—"

"But, I knew. I knew her every breath. I knew every hurt she felt. Did she think she could hide that from me? Did she think I wouldn't imagine it? I'm her father, and I could do nothing for her, Jessica. I could do nothing for my own child."

"I'm sorry." She said those words over and over,

127

knowing they meant nothing to him, only fillers for an empty space. His daughter was dead. Nothing anyone could say could bring her back—or the two young men who had gone out with her. Nothing anyone did or said could have saved them.

"I'll call you again in a few days," she told him, signing off.

The virus was with them still. There was no question of that. The three teenagers from Biosphere Two had lasted less than a week.

A panic seized Jessica. Time was running out for the children of Biosphere Seven. Her children. They would risk leaving the sphere, just as the three from Biosphere Two had done, or the seal would be broken by an earthquake, tornado, or some other natural disaster. One way or another, time was running out.

She thought of Brad, and knew that she had to go on with her plan. His child would have to be born inside the sphere. He had an immunity to the virus that all of them needed. Maybe, if they were lucky, he could pass that immunity on to the children.

It was a beginning. If one child could be born with this natural immunity, then there was a chance for all of them. That child—once born inside the sphere—might be a source of hope for all the others. If a vaccine could be made using the blood cells from this child . . .

Opening the biosphere for any purpose was a terrible risk. She had weighed the odds and found in favor of this gamble. Without some hope, they were death waiting to happen.

Everything depended on the child being born.

Tomorrow, Brad would bring her the sealed bags containing semen needed for this purpose. So clinical. So antiseptic. Her husband's sperm sealed in bleach-proof plastic. Nothing of flesh would touch them. Nothing of passion, or love.

If she conceived, Jessica would be fifty-two years old at the birth. The understanding of what that meant was seared into her like a branding iron to naked flesh. The child shouldn't be hers. Brad's child.

She could still count herself as a fertile woman. Still knew the cycles of her kind, but they were waning. She was past the normal age of bearing children. And was a realist. The painful truth was, the best chance for the conception of this child wasn't with her. It should be someone younger, someone for whom the chances of success were greater.

If it were only that, her decision would have been simple.

It was much more. There was the danger to the woman. The act of artificial insemination might expose her to the virus which might still be present in Brad's body. That meant she could die of it. And through her the rest of the sphere could become exposed.

It was a danger she wouldn't ask anyone else to take. For that risk, she could only think of one person—herself.

She decided to tell no one. Not even Quinn. He had the right to know, but she wouldn't burden him with this. How he'd feel about it if conception occurred, was something she couldn't guess. He'd know there had been more than an act of leadership to this. He'd know it had been an act of love.

God help me, Jessica thought. I'm risking everything—Quinn's love, my life, the conception of this child, and bringing the virus into the sphere. Everything . . . for a chance.

She thought again of Paul Schefield in Biosphere

Two, and of his daughter Katherine and the two young men who had died in their attempts to escape the enclosed world of the sphere. They had risked everything, too. They'd taken that chance.

Cameron was older than Katherine Schefield had been. Jessica knew his sense of desperation, understood his longing to be free. How much longer before he would take such a risk?

Whatever happened as a result of it, her decision was made. If she died trying to buy their lives back for them, the cost would be one she was willing to pay. If they all died—*God, don't let it be so*—she'd know she had done everything she could.

Life was the right of man.

Freedom was a privilege . . . but one worth dying for.

She would take the responsibility for the dome into her hands, and God willing, into her body. The decision blocked the ringing cry of *No!* . . . the sound that had echoed in her mind since hearing Paul Schefield's news. Louder than that cry was the sound of hope. It filled her mind, heart, and soul . . . and she listened.

The world of the sphere was a living place. For too long they hadn't heard the joy of the human spirit. They had closed themselves to that, but now it flared within her. A tiny flame, it beat its brilliance against her heart, burning with its truth.

Simply to live wasn't enough. Without freedom, the human spirit was contained and couldn't grow. Caged too long, it wouldn't survive. And so, hers was an act of survival.

This child, if she could conceive it, might be the hope of humanity. In her heart she nurtured it, even before its conception.

"Let it be with me," she whispered. "Dear God, let it be with me."

In the many ages of the living Earth, the land was old. It followed a shifting pattern of unfolding development determined at its origin. Oceans became deserts. Alluvial plains became mountains. Chains of islands were born of volcanic eruptions. Enormous land masses folded under continental plates, moving, shifting, molding the land into the ever-changing and new face of Earth.

And the Earth was alive. It produced life. From its fertile ground swelled the seeds of grasses, trees, and flowers. The living fed on the rich minerals of the land. It generated life; it nourished life; it reseeded itself with life. Unassisted by the hand of man, the Earth was its own living force, constantly recreating itself anew.

The land was old, but the living beings on it were new. Man was the keeper of the garden, the hunter, the willful child of the continents who brought their dominion under his care. In the care of man, the living planet began to die.

The waters of Earth, life-giving and unique among all the planets of the solar system, were fouled with the poisons of technology. The pollutants of industry bled rivers of death into the open sea. Into that eternal chalice, the salt-water basin where the origins of all life began, came illegal chemical dumping, raw sewage, acid rain, and oil spills.

The air became thick with the contaminant of man, destroying the protective ozone layer and allowing harmful ultraviolet rays to scorch the vital ground cover into a sterile desert.

The controlling will of man bequeathed a toxic wasteland unto the body of Earth itself, the living ground. Into the valleys rich with minerals and fertile soil, he planted the virulent garbage of mankind. Digging deep beneath the land's surface, he sowed seeds of nuclear waste, time bombs of radioactive refuse, and a chemist's laboratory of unholy weapons.

The living Earth struggled under this stewardship of man. The planet and all its issue began to die. The planet has its own biosphere, that zone extending miles into the sky and miles beneath the Earth's crust, a region where the sphere of life exists. Within the broad limits of this range, the resulting control and authority of humankind was felt.

And then the virus came and cleansed mankind from the world.

The living organism, Earth, reclaimed the garden, reclaimed the great sea chalice, and the air above. Hundreds of thousands of acres of oxygen-producing rain forest went uncut. Manmade fluorocarbons didn't flood the sky. Chemical and oil pollutants didn't clog the waterways. Slowly, Earth began the process of recovery and of regenerating itself. The living planet shifted from the dominion of man, into the dominion of Nature once again. And there, in that unfeeling, unthinking care of Nature, it thrived.

Chapter Seventeen

Seth and Jonathan rode their horses on a bridge over the next big water crossing. Seth could read well enough to spell out the letters on the sign.

"W-i-n-d . . . wind, ri-riv-river . . . Wind River."

Jonathan had never worked at knowing letters. Drawing sounds was as remote as any thought ever got to him, like understanding chicken scratches, and meant about as much. He'd never had the patience to study the marks their mother had cut into the wet sand of the lake shore. But Seth had learned enough to sound out most letters.

"This is the first river I ever saw that had a name," said Seth.

"That don't make it more than water," said Jonathan, unsure of himself on this high platform. "A name don't make it more than it is."

Seth gave him a look of pure dissatisfaction with such a remark. "Why do you suppose they called it the Wind?"

" 'Cause we're hanging in the air to get across it, I guess."

Seth pulled a face at that. "We don't have to swim the river. That's something to be glad about."

Jonathan didn't feel convinced. "I don't much

like looking down on flying birds. I'd as soon swim, as ever do this again."

Seth laughed. "You swim. I'll hold onto Smoke's tail."

They crossed the rest of the way in silence. Jonathan took a deep breath when they reached the end of the bridge, grateful to be off it.

Beyond the river, the ground climbed to a curving road. They followed, letting their horses walk along the softer verge at the side of the paved highway. Grass grew in thick clumps there, and wildflowers were stitched in bright lines along the path like colored seams sewing the land together.

They rode the whole of that day seeing only three bighorn sheep, one moose, and a soaring hawk high overhead. The land was green, and lush, and empty. As day slipped away to a pink sky of late afternoon, the land rose again and they began their climb into the broad-shouldered mountains.

In the four weeks since they'd left home, they had seen just one bear. The grizzly favored the higher ground. Entering the mountains, it was more likely they would come across bear. Neither Seth nor Jonathan had a gun. Their only weapons were a knife and a short, blade-tipped throwing stick. The throwing stick was good for spearing fish and rabbits, and could bring down a small deer if aimed well. It would do little to protect them from a bear.

"Maybe we should stop for the night before heading up into the mountains," said Seth. "Might be better than tracking through an unknown woods after dark."

Jonathan looked at the sky. The shell pink was still a high radiance above them. They could go a long way before dark. "I'd like to get into the trees before we camp. We can make a good fire to keep away anything hungry. You can see the stars better from there," he said as if giving a reason for his choice.

"You can see the stars from here," muttered Seth, but they rode on.

Fir trees poled their long necks into a thick green canopy above them. The sound of the horses startled birds nesting in the hidden, emerald world of the forest. Sharp, scattered cries of the birds and a beating of wings swooping overhead told the riders they didn't belong.

Seth held one arm over his face to protect his eyes from the pointed beaks. "Good thing we're coming into this place quietlike, and nothing knows we're here," he said without smiling. His hand slid to the top of his head. "Ow! They jerked out a chunk of my hair. Scalp's bleeding."

"Bears smell blood," said Jonathan, keeping his face straight and unsmiling. "They've got good noses, bears. They're real hungry in the spring, when they wake up with those cubs to feed." He sniffed the air in Seth's direction. "You smell a little like dinner."

"And you smell a little like—"

Seth's next words were cut off by the sudden rush of something in the trees ahead. It was big enough to shake the thick lower branches of the firs.

Jonathan's hand went to his knife. He held the reins tight on the chestnut mare, but she was starting to shy at the sound. Her hooves picked up and let down in a nervous, jittery rhythm. The black whinnied its alarm, and reared up on its strong

135

back legs. Seth twisted his hands in the flying mane, snugged his body close and hung on.

"Was it . . . ? Did you see anything?" Seth asked when the horse settled down enough to stand on all four legs. "Was it bear?"

"I don't know," said Jonathan. "Something scared 'em. That's sure."

"What do you think? Want to turn back for the night?" Seth laid his hand on the soft warmth of Smoke's neck, calming the stallion.

"I don't know," Jonathan hesitated. "No, we'll keep on a ways. Wouldn't be a good thing to head backwards. I won't do that. Next clearing we come to, we'll stop there."

The horses tossed their heads nervously, but started forward again, into the darkening path between the trees. They moved cautiously, with an unnatural quiet. In a moment, the forest surrounded them and they were hidden from the final light of day. Night was upon the world and they were caught within it.

"The stars . . ." Seth muttered with some disgust.

"What?"

"Nothing."

Night in the forest was darker than night on the open land. Jonathan knew the feeling of being sealed into this black, closed and bound into it. The trees had eyes. The ground was solid black below them, and the sky had disappeared. He felt taken into it, consumed by the weight of surrounding limbs and trunks, and what lay hidden behind the woods. What was it that had moved through the branches? What?

Seth rode beside him, and Jonathan was grateful.

136

Don't let me be alone. The thought came from a place of unknown fear within him. He hadn't recognized it until now, but there it was. The journey would be unbearable without the companionship of his brother. Jonathan was the stronger of the two; he knew that. Being strong didn't mean he didn't need. For the first time he understood how much it meant to him to have his brother with him. How alone the world would be, by himself.

With a new admiration, Jonathan thought of his father, and the terrifying, lonely journey John Katelo had made. He wondered—*Could I have done such a thing? Am I as strong as that?*

Fear was cold and leaden in his heart. It stumbled through him, moving like small jumps into his mind, muscles, and bone. *Could I live completely alone?* Would it happen because he had thought it? Would it unfold into truth? The fear left him chilled, his heart quaking.

And then a worse fear surfaced. It rose from the bubbling cauldron of his mind, hot and steaming as a raw reckoning. It would be terrible if something happened to Seth, and Jonathan were left alone . . . awful even to think about such a possibility . . . but what would happen to Seth if the situation were reversed? What if Jonathan were gone? Would Seth survive? Could he?

Jonathan's mind flashed on an image of Seth, alone and wandering through a forest of dark trees. The deep green of the trees turned black and Seth disappeared into them. Lost.

"Look!" Seth called. "There's a clearing up ahead."

Jonathan's eyes looked into the web of unbroken

branches, at first not seeing anything but the tall spines of trees and the leaves like feathers clinging to their limbs . . . and then lingering on a split in the scene. A lighter dark showed through — a stretch of open land holding the last colors of day, shining like a water jewel against the leafy borders of green and black.

They rode into the clearing, threw back their heads and gulped at the air, as if it were cleaner than that of the bound forest, more breathable. Overhead, a patch of bright stars winked into a sable sky. A three-quarter moon rose above the treetops, spilling a path of white radiance to the clearing below.

Jonathan felt a cool oneness with that moon, and with the stars like scattered fragments of its light. This spot was sacred to him, an oval of open land contained within the dark coil of trees. He slipped down from the mare's back and stood at the center of the space, filling an unspoken need within him. He closed his eyes, giving himself to the healing light.

"Jonathan, look down that path! Do you see? There! Moving in front of the stones."

Jonathan's eyelids snapped open. He couldn't believe what he saw. Not a bear. A faint trace of moonbeam offered a gray silhouette. It was moving before the rocks, stopping and starting like a frightened rabbit. Turning back to stare at them with dark, worried eyes. Not a grizzly. Hiding from them . . . racing to the shelter of the rocks . . . was a man.

"Wait!" shouted Jonathan.

But the figure disappeared. As if it had never

been, the light faded from the distant path. Clouds gathered, blanketing the light of the moon, and the forest closed over the break within this surround of ancient dark.

Seth and Jonathan didn't risk wandering from the clearing that night. They took turns sleeping, kept the fire burning steadily, and waited for dawn.

Chapter Eighteen

A silvered light filtered through the forest with the morning. It passed in uneven spires among the branches of the trees, casting a soft radiance over the land. It was as if the sun had slipped into a sieve and rays flowed out from it onto the dark heart of this green world.

"It was a man we saw, wasn't it?" Seth asked, questioning the night's vision—now, in certain daylight.

"It was a man." Jonathan had seen the figure clearly.

"Was he . . . was he wearing clothes?"

Jonathan's mouth crooked into a tight squirm of a smile. "He was wearing nothin' but naked skin and a beard; that's how I'm sure he was a man."

Seth acted as if he couldn't take it in. His forehead scrunched and his black eyebrows leaned together like knuckles bridging into a frown. "What kind of man would be running around naked in mountains like these? There's branches to stick you when you're walking, rattlers in the brush, scalding sun and freezing nights. What kind of man walks around naked in that?"

"A crazy one," said Jonathan, and the smile disappeared from his lips.

"You think we should go looking for him?" Seth's frown stayed fixed, jagged hawk wings between his eyes.

"We'll look, but we'll be careful."

They ate a quick meal of boiled rabbit from yesterday's kill. The meat wouldn't keep long in the warm weather, so they made certain to finish it that morning, drinking the hot broth of the scraps and bones. They couldn't risk wasting anything, food might become scarce in these mountains.

They saddled their horses and started up the smooth black road. A faint white line ran down the middle of the curving highway, marking the fading memory of a trail. Jonathan wondered about the people for whom that line had meant something. Were they like him? Or, had they been like the man hiding in the forest?

The horses moved at a faster clip as they rounded the curve and headed along a straighter section. Jonathan wrapped his legs tightly to the mare's sides and hung on, wondering what they were getting into, and where this mountain would lead them.

They moved easily up the next grade. The horses were fresh and used to a full day's travel. They were headed up a blind curve, where the road slipped around the side of the mountain. It made Jonathan nervous, not knowing what they'd find around that bend.

Seth's horse was well ahead of Jonathan's, the stallion taking the lead along the narrow highway. Seth twisted back and called out, "Maybe we've come too far. We might have passed him back there."

"Maybe, but I don't think so. The horses would have noticed. Remember how Smoke reared up last night? If the man had been anywhere around here, they'd have smelled him and we'd have known it."

Seth nodded a silent agreement to this.

"Let's keep on a ways," Jonathan said. "We can double back later, if there's a need. I expect we're getting close. He was running in this direction when he took off. We'd best keep still for a time—use our ears as well as our eyes."

Jonathan felt something coming at him. If it had been an arrow, he would have tried to duck . . . but it was something else. His skin sensed it, tingled with a kind of jumpy excitement. They were close. Maybe around the next curve. Maybe in that clump of trees. Somewhere close.

The road slipped around the curve of the mountain like a slithering snake. Seth's horse nosed ahead and vanished around the blind of jagged rock. For that instant, Jonathan lost him. He didn't like it. Didn't feel right. In the next breath, he heard his brother's shout. Just his name—"Jonathan!"—but it was enough. He spurred the mare into a hard run and tore around the mountain curve.

Seth was still astride the stallion, and at first glance nothing seemed wrong. He wasn't bleeding. There wasn't a bear or anything else in plain sight that looked like danger. Then a wider picture came into view—what Seth was looking at—and Jonathan saw a wooden sign with streaks of what had once been blue paint. He couldn't read what the lettering meant. "Look at that," said Seth, pointing.

Higher up the road, above the sign, was a tall fence made of heavy, twisted wire. A bigger sign hung over a gate between two thick posts. Behind the gate was a road leading to a mountain cave.

"What's it say on those boards?" asked Jonathan, for once curious about these strange, written words.

"N-O-R-A-D," Seth sounded out the letters. "NORAD Combat Operations Center."

"What's that? NORAD?"

"It's the name of something, I think," said Seth. He rode closer to the open gate. He read another smaller sign at the left of the entrance. "Cheyenne Mountain Complex. That's this place."

Jonathan rode up to the gate alongside Seth. He stared at the black-surfaced road leading into the wide opening at the base of the mountain. The cave didn't look right. Its face was bare of any kind of rockfall or natural crumbling of stone. The more he stared, the more Jonathan realized that it wasn't a cave at all, but a manmade tunnel. "Stay here," he warned. "Don't follow me."

Jonathan didn't like the sense of being inside a fenced space—even with the gate open. It made him feel caged. He walked the stubby-legged mare through the space between twin doors of wire and wood standing widespread between the gateposts. Seth hung back, watching.

He rode up to the gaping mouth carved in the mountain. One hand reached across and touched the inner wall. Not rock. The feel of it was smooth and cool, hard as stone but not real. It was like the black road leading to it, something man had done.

"What do you see?" shouted Seth.

143

"Some kind of long burrow. Can't see where it goes."

"I'm coming up," Seth called, excitement unmistakable in his voice.

"Come ahead, then. It's all right."

The black trotted up close beside Jonathan's mare. He shied at stepping into the cave, picking up his legs like red ants were at his hooves.

Jonathan said, "We'd better tie the horses if we're going in. We *are* going in?"

For answer, Seth swung his leg over the back of the saddle, pulled his other foot from the stirrup, and dropped to the ground.

"I thought as much." Jonathan scooted off the mare's rump, jumping clear.

They tied the horses' bridles to the fence wire.

"Don't like leaving them tied," said Jonathan. "There could be bear or wildcat around here." He didn't like it, but if they didn't tie them, the horses might not be there when they got back from looking through the cave. Anything might spook Smoke. Without the stallion and mare, he and Seth wouldn't have a chance of getting across this country. They couldn't risk them running away, even if it meant leaving them as staked bait for bear or cat. *Or man,* he thought.

"We won't be gone long." Seth laid his hand on Smoke's muzzle in parting, turned, and they started up the road leading into the dark hollow at the base of the mountain.

Jonathan moved along one side of the dark cavity; Seth moved along the other. The ground be-

144

neath them was flat and smooth, like the black roads they had followed.

"What is this place?" Jonathan's whisper lay between them like a hissing snake.

"That man we saw . . . I think he's here."

"What? Why do you—"

Jonathan's words stopped abruptly, like the dark. A burst of brightness lit the space like a flash of sudden lightning. He raised one arm to cover his eyes.

"Seth! Seth, you all right?"

"I'm here."

"What is it? I can't see you. My eyes . . ."

"I can see you," Seth told him.

The light was so harsh. It hurt unless Jonathan squinted. He could barely make out where Seth was standing. "Stay where you are. I'll come over there."

"What happened?" Seth's fingers were over his face. He was peeking between them, allowing slivers of brightness to pass through the bony cage of his hands. "It's so . . . it's daylight in here. You see it, Jonathan? What made it . . . ?"

"Be quiet. I hear something moving. Up ahead."

Jonathan's eyes had adjusted to the sudden brightness and he could see far beyond where he stood beside his brother. They were in a long hallway made of something like white stone. In the distance was a large, cavelike room. A humming sound came from there, like a wind moving through tall grass. From where he stood the room looked deserted. Wooden crates lined the walls, stacked one on top of the other, four deep.

"Come on," Seth whispered. "Let's look around."

Seth's hands were at his sides now. He squinted in

the harsh brightness, but saw clearly enough to lead the way into the room. "It's like a house under the ground," he said. "Something lives down here."

"Shhh. Listen!"

They waited, silence hovering like angry bees. They heard a shuffling noise, as if something were moving away from them, deeper into the cave.

Jonathan peered inside one of the crates and found boxes and sealed bags. He ripped open one of the bags and a powder spilled out onto the floor. The powder was white, with little flakes of green and red. In the middle of the powder were scattered hard yellow tubes cut into short, brittle pieces. He squeezed one of the pieces between his thumb and finger, and it shattered into tiny shards.

Seth stared at this, a question rimming the corners of his eyes. Jonathan shrugged, brushed the powder off his hands, and they went on.

The room led to another, and another, each stacked with the same wide crates filled with boxes and bags. In the second room there was a long table and twenty chairs. In the third, there were gray metal boxes along one wall. The boxes each had three drawers, which couldn't be opened.

"I don't like it here," said Jonathan. "Maybe we should go back. The horses . . ."

"We came to see if there's any other people," Seth reminded him. "If they're here, we need to find them."

"We don't know that the man came to this place. Who'd want to live in a house under the ground? It's silent as death down here. Remember what Dad told us about the spirits of the dead? They were in the houses like this one."

"That man's not a spirit!" Seth's eyes were bright with a kind of passion. "He's alive, Jonathan. You saw him and so did I. We heard him moving. He's here, and we've gotta find him. We have to know if there are others. I haven't forgotten those stories from back home, and I'm afraid, too," Seth admitted. "If we stay together, we'll be all right."

Jonathan felt a distance come between him and his father's journey, a distance which pushed away the stories that had haunted him throughout his childhood. It wasn't the same for him, that lonely terror. His father had been alone. He wasn't. He had Seth.

Again, Jonathan came to understand how much he needed his brother. Each of them was a core of strength which made the other whole. Seth had changed since the river crossing where he almost drowned. Since then he wasn't afraid anymore, not of risks, and not of death.

Jonathan swallowed his own fear, held it as a living terror within him, and followed Seth.

A long hallway of blank white led to a wall of closed double doors. Each door was nearly twice as tall as either of them. Without hesitating, Seth opened the one nearest, and he and Jonathan stepped inside.

The room was a play of brilliant colors. Blues and greens radiated from glass boxes the size of little windows. A yellow light blinked from one, and a flat orange image shimmered from another. Along every space of the walls were metal boxes, and on top of these the glass cases which trapped and held the burning shades of sky, sun, and grass.

A loud humming shuddered in all directions. It

147

came from the boxes, as if they were breathing out. As if they were alive.

Jonathan would have gone. He would have turned and fled this all-eyed underworld . . . if the sudden scrape against the floor hadn't made him whirl around, tensed and ready to defend his life.

In the corner of the room, flanked by twin rows of glowing lights, stood a heavy-bearded, naked man.

Chapter Nineteen

"Don't be afraid of us," said Seth, stepping slowly toward the man. "You're the one we saw last night, aren't you?"

The man's face was roughly square, a crown of copper-colored hair flecked with white strands, and a thick brush of amber beard, bright as washed pennies in the sun. He was taller than either Seth or Jonathan, broader through the shoulders, with burly arms and legs. And naked. Totally, completely naked.

"You're not Keith," the man accused, his voice sounding dry as deadwood. He looked as solid as a tree trunk, blond body hair covering him from ankle to neck like sun-cracked bark. His skin was rust-gold, and his eyes the bright blue of a jay's wings. He took a tentative step toward Seth. "Where'd my children go? My wife . . . Sara? What have you done to them?"

Jonathan moved up to stand beside Seth. The man had the look in his eyes of one of their bulls back home—ready to rush head down and wanting to gore them. Jonathan didn't like Seth being so close to the man, at least not all by himself.

"Watch him, Seth," he warned.

Seth seemed to be paying no attention. He moved several steps closer, within grabbing range of those powerful arms. "You have children here? And a woman? We haven't seen—"

The man rushed the distance between them, beefy hands swinging like clubs and knocking Seth onto the hard floor, where he began to choke him.

Jonathan picked up the heaviest thing he could find, a metal chair that folded in half when he lifted it, and hit the bull-tempered man across the back of his head. With a sound like a *whoosh* of air, the man crumpled to the floor on top of Seth. Jonathan had to pull the heavy body off him.

He dragged his brother to the far side of the room and stared with a hard press of fear as Seth drew thin streams of air into his lungs. The noise was like something heavy and sharp scraping over metal. Jonathan crouched near him, protectively watching for any sudden movement from the bearded man.

"Jona . . . Jonathan," Seth rasped.

"I'm here. Keep breathing. I ought to hit him again while he's still down." He moved to do just that, but Seth's fingers caught his shirt.

"No. Don't . . . hurt him." The words were hard work, each one causing a pulled line of pain on Seth's mouth, like wounds bursting open. "We scared him."

Jonathan thought it over, then moved to smash the man's skull anyway.

Seth tried to crawl after him. "Don't. . . . Jonathan, please don't."

The metal chair was in Jonathan's hands, his arms ready to smash it down in one final blow that would finish their trouble with this man. And he would have done it . . . but Seth's eyes were silent witnesses, pleading with Jonathan not to kill.

Angrily, he threw the chair against the wall and turned his back on his brother's eyes.

"We came to find people, not murder 'em." Seth's voice sounded less strangled, his breathing easier.

"He almost killed you." Jonathan's muscles began to shudder, his body coming down from that height of terrible anger. Never in his life had he felt so much rage. It left him slowly, bleeding away to leave his body cold and weak. "Like Cody. You looked like Cody lying there. He might have broken your neck."

"I'm all right, and nothing's broke." Seth was on his knees, hands hugging the floor for support and trying to stand.

"But, what if he'd done it?" Jonathan wanted to know. That was the question he couldn't answer. "What if he'd killed you?"

"You'd have gone on without me, I guess," said Seth. "That's what you'd have to do."

Seth sounded sure, as if it were the right thing, the only thing . . . but Jonathan didn't know. Was that really what he'd do? Would he go on without Seth? It didn't seem possible. The terror of that thought clawed at his gut.

Then Seth said something that forced Jonathan to see the truth. "You're Inuit. You'd go on alone, the way Dad did."

The words stung.

"Am I right?" Seth asked.

Jonathan tried to answer, but before he could speak, his attention was drawn back to the man on the floor behind him, who was groaning something that sounded like "Sorrel" . . . and had started to move.

151

* * *

He met her as prearranged at seven o'clock. The soft lights of early evening illuminated the desert.

"Tonight," said Jessica. "It must be tonight."

Her chance of fertility was greatest now. She had counted the days and knew that if she could conceive, tonight would be her best time for doing so. So much was against it. She was too old. Artificial insemination wouldn't be simple. Neither would the added procedure of evacuating the air from the docking chamber and sterilizing the contaminated room with a bleach-solution wash. Still, however slim the possibility, she was determined to try.

"Will you be at the docking chamber door?" she asked. "It will have to be late, close to dawn. We'll pass the sealed bags into the chamber and—"

"There's a problem," Prophet interrupted.

She was nervous, knowing she shouldn't stay long. Someone might pass by, or overhear their conversation. She couldn't risk being discovered even before her plan took place. It would ruin everything. "Problem?"

"I don't know if I can still . . . I mean, I haven't been with a woman for a very long time. Haven't been sexually active at all. I'm not sure I'll be able to . . ."

She hadn't expected that.

"I'm sorry," she tried to ease the awkwardness between them. "It was thoughtless of me not to understand, to anticipate. I didn't know."

"Don't apologize," he said, too roughly.

"I just assumed that there had been other women. In all these years . . ." she couldn't go on. The jealousy she'd felt for the attractive women among the

152

Outsiders, those she'd thought had been with him . . .

"At first I was too ill," he explained. "Later, when it might have happened, there was never anyone I wanted."

She closed her eyes to hide the tears welling there, but they slid down her cheeks.

"Except you," he said, seeing her tears. "You were the only woman I ever wanted, Jessica. Even now, I—"

"Even now?" It was terrible for her to ask, terrible to know the answer.

"I'm not sure I'm capable of ever being more than Prophet, or a friend to any woman now. So much has been lost. My self, really. But if it were possible . . ."—there was a sad and desperate look in his eyes—"it could only be with you."

"What have I done to you, Brad?" She wanted to heal him, to give him back his life and make him whole. She wanted to love him.

"Nothing either of us intended. You're not to blame. Don't carry that guilt. I didn't tell you so that you'd feel responsible."

"Meet me at the docking chamber wall at four o'clock," she insisted. "Promise."

"I don't know what good that will do. I told you."

"Please, Brad. Don't say anything more. It's too dangerous. Meet me tonight." She started to go, then turned back. "Will you?"

His sigh was one of resignation and defeat. Or was it more? "All right. I'll be there."

"I love you." She wasn't sure he'd heard these last words. Her voice had softened to a whisper. She started away, then without turning to face him added, "Bring the things I gave you."

153

"Jessica, I told you, I can't—"

"Bring them," she asked this of him, then hurried away.

They met before the docking chamber's outside wall. Jessica had sealed the stainless steel interior wall between the chamber and the desert biome, to allow them a sense of privacy. It was taking a risk, someone might notice the closure even at four in the morning, but she felt it was worth the chance. They needed a semblance of being alone. She needed it.

Brad was there outside the glass, waiting for her when she arrived.

"You must be cold," she said. "How long have you—"

"Not long. And I'm not cold."

There was a shyness between them, like the painful attempts at intimacy on a first date. She wanted everything to be right for him. This one night was all they had, all she could give him. Most of all, she wanted him to remember it as an act of love.

"I've been thinking about this all day," she began, "longer than that, really. I've thought of you so many times, Brad. Of what it used to be like when we were together."

"I was never with any woman before you, Jessica," he said in a low voice, "and there hasn't been anyone since. Do you imagine I haven't thought about this? Every day of my life? I think of you . . . always. And today—"

"What about today? What did you think? What did you want?" She put her palm on the glass.

His palm touched the glass on the other side, his hand wider than hers, covering it. "I thought about what it was like, loving you. Remember our night

154

in Carmel? The cottage with the fireplace?"

She felt a rush of memory: the yellow light of the fire, Brad's hands stroking a warmth of pink life into her skin, and the full weight of him on her as they made love beside the heat of those moving flames. "I remember. Nothing's ever been more than that night was for me . . . not before, or since."

"Nothing?" His look was so serious. "Jessie, you don't have to lie to me. I know you've been with Quinn all these years, that you have children by him. I understand." Then he laughed, a soft, muffled sound. "I feel like I'm on trial for my life; suddenly, I can't breathe."

"You were everything in the world to me that night," she said, as though he'd said nothing else. "When I think of it, it makes me want you now as much as I wanted you then. There was nothing standing between us—not glass, or years. There was only what we felt inside. Remember, Brad? Remember what you felt for me?"

Her fingers began to slowly unbutton the neck of her nightgown.

"Jessica, I . . ." It was as though he were trying to stop her, but couldn't. The rest of his words went unspoken, and his eyes watched as her fingers slipped from button to tiny button.

"Your hands were warm and the fire was a heat behind us." She pulled twin ribbons at the curve of the gown's bodice, and it slid off her shoulders, slipping to the ground. "You were my love, Brad. I've never forgotten the way it was between us. The way I felt when you touched me . . . here," she said, stroking her hand over her breast. "And here."

"*God* . . ." His voice was a low breath torn from him. "Oh, God."

"Make love to me," she said. "Let me feel you touch me the way you did then. Tonight."

"I want—"

"What do you want?" she asked the question again. Her body began to move with the pulse of her blood. "Tell me that you want me. Tell me."

His eyes caressed her. "I love you, Jessie." She heard the catch of longing in his voice. "I've always loved you."

"These are your hands touching me, Brad." Her fingers stroked the heat of pleasure between them. "You're here. I can feel you with me."

"Lie down," he said.

And she did.

The sound of his voice directed each motion. He spoke to her and she closed her eyes and listened, believing he was next to her, skin touching skin, his body a heat against her.

"I've needed you . . ." His voice sound broken with passion and terrible yearning that had gone unfulfilled too long . . . too long.

She didn't open her eyes, unwilling to stop the waking dream or destroy the illusion. "I'm selfish. I should give you up, but I can't. Never stop loving me, Brad. Never."

"Jessie . . . Jessie." There were tears in the swell of words . . . and release.

For that moment he was with her again. She knew the feel of him against the raw awakening of her skin, inside the heat of her body, and within the fulfillment of her need.

"Open your eyes," he said later. "Dress, and go outside the docking chamber. When you've activated the release on the exterior door, I'll put the sealed bag inside."

She'd almost forgotten that there had been a purpose besides love in this act. And that they were still separated by a world they couldn't change. Everything had happened just as she'd imagined. Now, there would be a possibility of a child. She'd succeeded. But what she hadn't known was how desperately alone she'd feel when Brad would leave her, when each of them went back to the life they lived. Apart.

"I was wrong," she said, her heart breaking within her. "I should never have put either of us through this. It's too hard. Too—"

"It's the only touch of real life I've known for twenty years," he said. "The only love. Don't say anything that'll take it away from me. I won't let you."

"I don't want you to go."

"Jessie . . . we have to be—"

"I'm tired of being strong. I'm tired of hurt and losing people I love," she cried. The tears were locked inside her, dry and painful. "You're part of me. I don't ever want to lose you again."

"You haven't lost me," he said. "Nothing will change that, ever. You're with me until the day I die." The words were a promise she would remember. "Then I'll come to you, Jessie. Wherever you are, I'll come to you. There'll be no walls between us then."

When he left her, there was work to do. She was careful about evacuating the contaminated air from the docking chamber and saturating the surface of its walls and floor with the bleach solution before opening the interior door to the desert biome. The sealed bag Brad had left for her was washed with the bleach solution, too.

She tried to remember his words as dawn lifted the darkness from the world. Alone, Jessica lay in that

157

hallowed light surrounded by the technical equipment of artificial insemination, trying to conceive her husband's child.

Chapter Twenty

"Who are you?" Seth asked.

The man who had been so violent moments before was now hunched forward, arms resting on his knees, in a chair opposite Seth.

Jonathan watched him from the safer distance of a few feet away, his hand still holding the metal chair. He wasn't willing to trust anybody a second time who'd tried to choke the life out of his brother — even once.

"What's your name?" Seth asked, putting the question a different way.

The heavy head lifted until the two men were face to face and the blue eyes met Seth's. "T. J. Parker."

"T. J. . . . ?" Seth repeated the letters. "What's that mean?"

The stranger's eyebrows scrunched together as if pulling the thoughts into place, or remembering. "Tyler James . . . T. J. Parker."

Seth beamed a delighted smile at Jonathan.

Jonathan didn't smile back.

There didn't seem to be any fight left in the man. He slumped like a bag of grain in the chair, looking exhausted. "Who are you?" he asked.

"Seth Katelo. That one who clunked you on the head is my brother Jonathan."

"Are you one of them? From the biosphere?"

Jonathan glanced at Seth. The strange word triggered a memory in him, a memory of his father's stories of the journey from the land of ice, from a place called Biosphere Four.

"What is this bio . . . ?" asked Seth.

"The biosphere? You've never heard of it?" The man was leaning forward in obvious interest. "Where are you from?"

"North of here," said Seth.

"North? Just the two of you?"

"Our family's there."

The man's eyebrows lifted. "Living family?"

Seth nodded.

"How many more?" Parker asked.

Seth turned to Jonathan before answering.

"How many?" the man pressed the question.

"Six," said Jonathan, his voice like the slap of belt leather on bare hide.

Parker twisted around to face him. "You the one that hit me?"

Jonathan nodded, ready to do it again if necessary.

"Well, you did right. I would have killed him, I guess. Out of my head. Didn't know what I was doing."

"You wouldn't have lived long, if you'd done that."

Parker stared at Jonathan, then nodded a grim acceptance of that fact. "I believe you."

"What is this place?" Jonathan asked.

"NORAD," Parker answered. "Built to house the military in the event of a disaster."

"The military?" The word meant nothing to Jonathan.

"The army," Parker explained. Then trying a different response, "You know, soldiers."

Jonathan still didn't know, but let it go. "And

160

those?" Jonathan pointed to the boxes of light and sound.

Parker seemed surprised at the question. "Computers," he said. "Haven't you ever seen one? They hold information like the brain, only they're a machine. They're powered by the same nuclear generator that runs this whole complex. It'll go on forever, I guess, long after I'm dead. Man, too, probably."

"What is Biosphere Seven?" Seth asked again, turning their attention away from this issue. "Is it a place?"

"It's where I started out from," said Parker. "It's a glass city, a long ways south of here. I thought you had to be one of the men from there. You're the first two I've met, other than the Outsiders."

Seth asked, "What's the out—"

Parker started answering before Seth could finish the question. "That's what they called us," said Parker, "the people able to survive outside the biosphere. We called ourselves the People."

Jonathan asked a question of his own. "Where are the wife and children you were asking about?" He was uneasy, not knowing who else might be hiding in the hallways and rooms of this manmade cave.

Parker fell back as if struck. He looked around the room, as if searching for something lost.

"Jonathan," said Seth, "maybe you shouldn't have—"

"He asked us about them, remember? He said 'Keith,' and 'Sara.' "

"Keith?" Parker repeated the name, then stood up. "Where's Keith?"

Jonathan stood, too. He didn't like the odd look in Parker's eyes, or the way he was moving off by himself, as if they weren't in the room with him. "Come over here with me," Jonathan called to his brother. This time, Seth listened.

"You've seen my boys?" Parker asked. His face was a worried mask. "They hide from me sometimes, all of them. I look but I can't find them till they're ready to come out. Keith!" he shouted in a louder, more urgent voice.

"Something's the matter with him," Jonathan said in a whisper.

Seth didn't speak.

"My Sara takes the children away from me sometimes. I think she's still hurt, maybe angry about the way they died." Parker was wandering around the room as if searching the air itself. "Wasn't my fault how that happened . . . except for Jamie." He turned to look beseechingly at Jonathan. "I couldn't let him suffer like the others. He was just a baby. So little. So sweet. I ended it quick for him. That's why my wife hides them from me, I guess."

Jonathan leaned his head closer to Seth. "He's talking about dead people."

"I know."

"What are we gonna do about it?"

"Nothing."

"Can you help me find my boys?" asked Parker. "They were here right before you came. I was talking to them. They told me two men were coming. Can you help me find them?"

"We can't help you," Jonathan answered. "Your family's dead."

Parker stood absolutely still, not even breathing. He stayed that way longer than was comfortable for any of them. When he spoke again, it was in a voice glazed with sorrow.

"My two oldest boys were among the first to die of the virus. Keith, our eldest. Then Michael. Later, it took my wife, Sara. And then I smothered my three-year-old . . . Jamie. A long time ago. Everybody was dying around us. Neighbors. Friends. Everybody."

"How long have you been alone?" asked Seth.

"Long time."

"And the biosphere? Was that where you lived?" Seth pressed him.

"No. The Outsiders found me. We lived in a high desert next to that city of glass. South of here. In a place called Texas."

"Are there other people in that place?" asked Jonathan. "Living people?"

Parker moved back to his chair and sat down. "There were eleven of us at the start. Josiah found the survivors of the virus and led us back to the camp near the biosphere."

"Who's Josiah?" asked Jonathan.

"He was one of them, a man from inside the glass city. He'd come out to find any survivors. Something happened, an accident, and he was never able to go back to Biosphere Seven. He's the leader of the People now, or was when I left them. The children called him Sagamore. It's an Indian name that means the wise one."

"How'd you come to be here all alone?" asked Seth. "What is this place?"

But T. J. Parker had turned back into a brooding silence. He didn't answer any more of their questions. Instead, he sat in the chair and stared at the emptiness of the room, as if expecting to see something, or someone, in the thin plane of air.

Jonathan and Seth left him and went outside to the horses.

"You think there is such a place?" asked Seth, almost before they were clear of the cave. "If it's true—"

"The man's crazy," said Jonathan. "He talks to his dead wife and children, remember? And he tried to kill you."

"I know, but . . . maybe some part of what he says is real. He had to come from somewhere. The wife and children were part of his life once. Maybe this place was, too. It wouldn't hurt to listen," Seth urged, "maybe travel in that direction."

Jonathan felt something stirring inside him, like the growing motion of ashes in a fire. He was being pulled toward this wild man's dream. "Follow what a crazy man tells you? You're serious?"

"I think we should try it."

Jonathan walked to the horses. He didn't believe anything Parker had said for one minute, but it didn't really matter. "Okay. What difference does it make? One direction's as good as another. If it makes you happy, we'll head south."

Jonathan said nothing to his brother about his memory of his father's stories, or the name of that other place — Biosphere Four. If Biosphere Four had been where the virus started, then what would they find in Biosphere Seven, this city of glass?

Jonathan and Seth left the NORAD compound later that same afternoon. They didn't take T. J. Parker with them. The room after room built into the base of the mountain would provide the man with shelter and enough food to sustain him for his lifetime. Seth offered to ride double on Smoke, but Parker refused to go with them.

"I left the Outsiders a long time ago," he said. "No point in going back."

"You gonna be all right here?" Seth's concern showed in his voice and his eyes.

"No," said Parker. "None of us are all right. Are we?"

"Remember something. There are people up north," said Seth. "You ever stop wanting to be alone, you go there."

Parker nodded and turned back into the cave, walking out of their line of sight.

Seth seemed reluctant to leave, but Jonathan gave Smoke's rump a slap and they rode away.

Trinity Adair watched Sidra dive into the ocean to inspect the underwater monitor for saline level, temperature control, and chemical analysis. The central computer gauged these same checklists, but a visual monitor of the sea was also completed as an added assurance of structural and whole-unit integrity.

She stood at the high point of land near the waterfall, afternoon sun reflecting on the bright cascade behind her. As he watched from the secrecy of the rain forest, she stripped off her clothes and dove into the glassy sea.

She was beautiful, her body a curving line of long limbs, full breasts, and rounded hips. Dark brown hair hung to her waist, and rose like a mantle behind her when she dove into the water.

He had waited. Knowing she didn't love him, he had waited. Watching her like this, it was hard to wait any longer. In that moment, he stepped out from the cover of the trees and moved toward the sandy beach.

A loud splash startled him and stopped him from going closer. He turned and saw Cameron's dark head emerging from the water. A solid hurt began to ache in Trinity's chest. Cameron's arms broke the ocean's flat plane of green, stroke after stroke, bringing him closer to where Sidra now floated on her back.

Her arms were stretched out to each side, keeping her level. Her body moved with the gentle undulating motion of the sea. Her long hair floated behind, a trail of fine lines fanning across the smooth expanse of transparent green.

Trinity needed to turn away from this . . . needed to,

but couldn't. Sidra was the woman he wanted. Cameron was his brother. The pain of seeing them together, watching as Cameron swam to her . . . touched her, was a torment to Trinity, one that he couldn't ease. Still, he watched.

Did Sidra know what Cameron was planning? Had he trusted her with his secret — that he was leaving the sphere? And when?

When Cameron's mouth lowered to Sidra's breast, and his hand stroked the length of her slender body, the strangle of a cry broke from Trinity's throat. Sidra's arms went around Cameron's neck. In an agony of both lust and anguish which could not be appeased, Trinity tore himself free of this intimate scene and rushed away.

A bitter fury rose in Trinity against his brother. It raged for an instant into a quick-kindled flame, burning over Cameron's deceit with Sidra, burning over his plans to abandon them all, burning . . . and then was gone. He couldn't hate Cameron, not even for Sidra. They were brothers. More than that, they were friends.

He couldn't blame Sidra or Cameron. If they were genuinely in love — and he believed they were — that had to come before any feelings of his.

Trinity made up his mind to help Cameron in whatever way he could. No matter what happened, he'd always defend Jessica's son. He would be forever grateful for the kind of life Jessica had given him, caring for him during all these years since his mother died. And he knew that Cameron meant more to her than anyone else in the world.

A loneliness descended upon Trinity. In a surrounding full of people, he was alone. He thought of his real mother, Maggie, and felt lonelier still. Both his mother and father were dead. He was the only orphan in the biosphere.

It should have been Sidra, he thought, stumbling through the trees, running from the pain. *She should have been mine.*

A brace of trees was just ahead. He slumped against the trunk of one, digging his fingernails into the bark. "Mother!" he cried out, pressing his cheek against the rough face of the wood. It wasn't Jessica he called for, but his own mother, the blood parent he couldn't remember. "Mother, help me. I'm so alone. Please . . . please, help me."

The tree supported him as he slid to the ground, cradled him and gave him solace. The soft earth cushioned his fall. He sank into the bed of leaves, crushing them beneath his hands and knees. The scent of life rose up from these crushed leaves, pungent and green-smelling.

At that moment it seemed as if the Earth itself was his mother, comforting him with the strength of her trees, the softness of the ground, and the perfume of life rising from the crushed leaves like a gentle caress. This was the mother he had been given — not a woman of his own flesh and blood, but the biosphere — a living world which sustained and nourished him.

He was the first child born of the sphere. He thought of Maggie Adair's Bible and the stories he had read from the book of Genesis. The likeness was unmistakable. He was Cain. Like Cain, would hurt and jealousy make him take his brother's life?

"I'll never hurt him," he vowed. "I'll never do anything to hurt either of them. It won't happen that way, not through me. I won't let it." The Earth was his witness. He was a child of this land, this place. He swore by the unbroken bond between himself and the living sphere.

He lay on the bed of soft leaves until evening, feeling a comfort he had never known. This day, he'd called upon the unseen God of this place . . . and had felt an answer.

For the first time, he knew he wasn't alone.

Chapter Twenty-one

Cameron and Sidra had made love for the first time in the secluded cove on the wet shore of the sea. He hadn't told her he loved her, not used those words, but he *had* loved her. His body had spoken for him. Now, they were quiet in each other's arms, the passion stilled. Her dark hair lay against his neck.

"Am I going to be with you, Cameron?"

"What?"

"Am I going to be a part of your life? I need to know." She hadn't moved from the embrace of his arms.

"You *are* a part of my life," he said.

"Am I?"

He sat up. "What do you want me to say?"

"I want you to tell me if you're leaving."

Could she know that he'd already given himself the transfusion? "Why do you want to talk about such things, especially now." He tried to kiss her, but she twisted away.

"You haven't given me an answer."

What could he answer? One part of him believed she deserved to hear the truth. The other part silenced him. It was too dangerous for anyone else to know. If

169

he told her, she might find a way to stop him. He couldn't let that happen.

"You know I want to leave," he admitted. "I've always been honest with you about that. But the way things are, how can I?"

Her green eyes were solemn witnesses. "If there were a way, would you go without me?"

"Sidra . . ." he tried to reach for her.

She pulled back. "Would you?"

"Yes." The word slipped from him — the truth, and a burden of guilt.

She didn't speak. Her green eyes looked away. For a time the space between Cameron and Sidra widened, though neither had moved.

"I'm not sorry about today." She said it as if she knew it would never happen again. "Whatever else happens, I'll never be sorry for this. And I'll always love you, Cameron." She stood up and started to go.

"I didn't say that I was going to leave."

Her eyes said, *Don't lie*. Her lips said, "Don't."

The pain of that single word brought him to his knees. He watched in numb silence as she walked away.

"What is it, Sidra? What's troubling you?" Cathe Innis stroked her daughter's long, glossy hair.

"I'm all right."

"No, you're not. I know you, remember? What's making you so unhappy. Tell me."

For several days now it had seemed to Cathe that Sidra had been pulled inward by some great sadness she wouldn't share. It hurt the mother to feel this distance come between them. She loved her daughter, perhaps this one more than any of the others, and yet never felt that the girl was like her in any way. Sidra had always been her father's child. Her ways were Indian, like him.

Even in her features and coloring, Sidra resembled Josiah, as though Cathe had been no part of her.

Josiah had given Cathe this child on the night before he left the biosphere. They had made love in his room, and his hair had been a black weight in her hand, like his daughter's was now. His back had been as straight as Sidra's, and his eyes were her eyes, too.

I've been with her all her life, thought Cathe, and he hasn't been around her for one single day — yet, she's a thousand times more like him than she'll ever be like me. Dominant genes will out, the botanist in her thought, and knew a sense of loss at this acceptance.

"I'm going to bed," Sidra said. The sound of the door closing announced that her daughter was gone.

She is gone, Cathe thought. *I can't keep her. As much as I want to hold her forever as a child, to protect her from all hurt, she won't be kept by me or anyone. She's free, like Josiah. That sense was born in her and nothing I do will ever change it.*

Cathe turned instead to the balance of her life, to Daniel Urquidez and the seven other children she shared with him.

A sense of desperation brought Sidra into the night. It was late, nearly four in the morning. She hadn't slept, couldn't remain in her mother's quarters either, a room which made her feel as though something alive and struggling within her were suffocating. Quietly, she left the housing biome and walked.

The recycled air of the sphere was too close. She couldn't draw a deep enough breath. It was this night, this terrible night. She felt as if she were drowning, and no one could save her.

It wasn't going to happen, not the dream she'd believed in for so long. She and Cameron would never be

171

together. Her world felt broken and nothing made sense anymore. There wasn't enough air. There wasn't enough life. She couldn't live like this. The shuddering beat of her pulse rocked her body, and she began to run.

He doesn't love me; he doesn't love me; he doesn't love me enough.

That was the truth which tore at her. That was the ache she couldn't ease. He could never be completely happy with her, not here. It wasn't really her, she knew, but this place. It was the biosphere itself which was driving Cameron away. The Outside was her only rival for his love. The Outside would take him from her. His mind was captured by it, and his heart.

She dropped to the ground from exhaustion in the desert biome. Sand cushioned her fall. As the sound of her thudding heart and pulse lowered, she could hear the magic of the desert rise up and surround her.

A Texas tortoise moved across the warm sand, and a leaf-toed gecko scrambled over the soft ground before her fingers. She heard the puffing sound of the knight anole, inflating its rose-colored dewlap, and the scurrying rustle of the spiny lizard and blue-tongued skink. It was a living world, this biome, with spadefoot toads, tree lizards of the thornscrub, and the flapping wings of pygmy kingfishers. There were bats overhead, and the unsettling shuffling of snake, or desert rat.

And something else.

There was a sound coming from behind the connecting wall between the docking chamber and the desert biome. Sidra was close enough to hear movement coming from within it. Someone was in there.

Then, all at once she knew. Jolted by this understanding, she rose to her feet and raced to the steel door.

172

"Cameron!"

He was leaving; she knew it.

"Cameron!" she cried his name again. Screamed it. He would go without her. In an instant it would be too late. All of the air was gone from her lungs, and she couldn't breathe. Couldn't move . . . except to hit the button which opened the docking chamber door.

Amazingly, no alarm sounded when the steel wall slid open. Nothing changed. And he was there, as she'd known he would be.

"Go back," he said.

"You're leaving."

He didn't deny it.

"You'll die out there." She was looking at him for the last time. When the outside door opened, there would be no coming back. He would be contaminated with the virus. Sick or not, he would never be allowed to return to the sphere.

"People have lived. Josiah did. I've taken a chance. I've done something," he said.

"Something?"

He seemed to hesitate before speaking again, then told her. "Brad McGhee gave me a blood transfusion. If it worked, I'll have his immunities. He survived the virus, and so will I."

"Prophet?" She couldn't believe it. How had they done this? "I don't know what you did," she said, "but it's too dangerous to leave. You don't know that you're protected. I don't want to lose you," she said at last, and then stopped. There was nothing else to say.

"Sidra . . . I can't stay. I won't spend my life in a cage. That's what this is, a wonderful, beautiful cage. I'm going out. Live or die, I'm going."

She knew that nothing else she could say would change him. "I'll help you," she said at last. "I'll press the buttons for the doors."

"That would make it safer for the others," he admitted. "I'd have left the outside door open, and then warned them from another area of the sphere. I didn't want to ask for anyone's help, to get anyone else in trouble, in case it goes wrong."

"I'll do it," she offered, and moved back into the desert biome.

"Sidra," he called to her, "will you kiss me goodbye?" He stood in the docking chamber, looking lost and alone.

"No." She pressed the activate-docking-system button to trigger both doors in a timed sequence.

The outside glass door wouldn't open until the inside biome door was sealed. The stainless steel panel was already closing. In one moment, he'd be lost from her vision and from her life. In three minutes the docking door would open and he would step Outside. She followed the heavy door as it closed, moved with it, her eyes holding him to her still . . . still.

"I love you," he said when the door was almost closed. "Remember that."

It was the only truth she had ever wanted to hear.

Without hesitation, Sidra stepped inside the docking chamber. The steel door sealed with a loud mechanical click. And she was there beside him.

"No! What have you done?" He looked stricken. The Outside door was activated on automatic release. It would open in a matter of three minutes, and there was nothing he could do to prevent it. "Why Sidra? Why?"

"Any world would be a beautiful cage if it kept me from you."

He turned away, furious at first . . . then twisted back and pulled her into his arms. His kisses were on her cheeks, her eyes, and her mouth.

"I don't care anymore. Whatever happens," she

174

said, "we're together."

He nodded, as if unable to speak.

They watched the glass door of the biosphere lift and open. The first true breeze of their lives, cool and scented, moved like a caressing hand, touching them.

Together, they walked free and stepped Outside into a world of night, beneath the press of a billion brilliant stars.

Chapter Twenty-two

The campfire warmed the man and boy. They sat around the circle of flames as other hunters had done thousands of years before. The man would teach the boy his skills, and one day the boy would pass on the knowledge to another. It was the way of a tribal people, the wisdom of an elder of the clan given to the young.

Shepherd Hallinger fed broken pieces of mesquite into the lowering fire. He poked at the charred remains of the thicker wedges of burning wood, breaking them open and scattering the embers around the new dry kindling. The snapping brands blazed into a pool of uneven, sharp-sided light. When the fire was a constant mass of steady flames, the boy sat back and listened once again as the man spoke.

"The land is a witness to all we do."

"A witness?" Shepherd asked, not understanding what Sagamore meant.

"It carries our mistakes within it," he said. "We don't hurt ourselves alone by our actions, but the ground below our feet, the water which feeds the green life on our world, and the air we breathe. We're all part of the same home, children of one mother, and we need to learn to live together."

"Is it true?" Shepherd asked. "Were there really cities that pushed at the sky? Were there people as thick as grass?"

"Not as thick as grass," Sagamore told him, smiling at the words, "but we were many, and the buildings of the cities were far taller than trees."

"How did the hunters find game in places like that?"

"Our game was of a different kind. We filled our stomachs with the rich broth of want instead of need. And we forced our will upon the land."

"Where did the animals go? When the cities covered the ground, where did the deer and cattle go?"

"They found few places," said Sagamore. "We took their portion of living ground and buried it beneath concrete and steel. We smothered nature, and many of Earth's animals died."

Shepherd felt a sense of awe in the knowledge that a world of people had lived on a different Earth before he was born. It was frightening to think of them. They were stories of an earlier age of man, not quite real, like distant gods whose voices could still be heard. "Man died, too," he said, thinking of them.

"Man died by the work of his own hand," said Sagamore.

The day's hunt had gone well. Shepherd had taken his first pronghorn. The meat from this kill would feed not only those of his mother's house, but put food on the table of Crystal Rivers, an unpaired woman of the camp.

Shepherd had no feelings of sadness at the loss of so much of mankind. He had never known a world different from the one he knew now. Still, he understood that it must be harder for Sagamore. He had been one of them, the old ones of that earlier age. To Shepherd, Sagamore was like one of those distant gods, speaking of things the boy had no understanding of, and re-

177

membering a time when man was thick as grass upon the Earth. Sagamore was wise, Shepherd knew. He had lived beyond the end time of the old ones. He had survived when the others had not.

"You are the eldest son of your mother," Sagamore said to him, surprising Shepherd. It was the first time tonight that Sagamore had spoken directly to him, and not only answering a question. "You are the first of the young men of our camp."

"I'm not the oldest," Shepherd told him, thrilled to have heard himself called a man.

"There are others who are older," Sagamore agreed, "but you are the first."

"The first?" Shepherd wanted to understand. He wanted the words to mean what he hoped they meant: that Sagamore thought him special, that this wise one noticed him as being apart from the rest of the boys of the camp, that he saw him as a man, like himself.

"You are the novice now, listening and learning," Sagamore told him, "but one day the novice will be called upon to lead the People."

This was much more than any dream Shepherd had ever imagined. He had only hoped to learn the ways of a hunter, the ways of a man. What Sagamore had said frightened him. He didn't know what a novice was but he knew what it meant to be a leader of the People, to be one like Sagamore, and had never wanted such a thing.

"I'm just a little boy," Shepherd told him, denying the longed-for standing of a man. "I couldn't lead the—"

"Shh," Sagamore stopped him.

It was clear to Shepherd that Sagamore was listening to something; his face turned to catch the sound. Shepherd could hear nothing but the soft wind, and the crackling hunger of the fire. He turned to look, but couldn't see into the dark beyond the fire's ring of light.

Sagamore rose from the circle of stones, his hand grasping the throwing spear from its place on the ground at his side. His back was to the flames, his eyes watching the living night in the distance beyond them.

"What do you hear?" Shepherd whispered. Even the wind had stopped, as if listening, too. The silence was a heavy burden for a child; he couldn't hold it within him. "What is it?"

"Be silent, and don't move from the safety of the fire," Sagamore warned him.

And then he walked from the circle of light into the swollen dark, leaving Shepherd afraid and alone.

Later—the boy had no way of knowing the space of time—a sound scraped in claws of terror over the shuddering still. It pulled Shepherd to his knees, heart racing, and gasping in the cold truth of the hunter and the hunt.

The long night pooled in black rivers across the sky. The stars moved along the course of the rivers, shimmering from their washed beds, glittering a hope of dawn. Clouds scoured the skies like polishing sand, clearing away dreams and fears. Slowly, slowly, the pale light of morning shone through the covering dark.

They watched the morning lift into the broad canopy of sky, seeing it clearly for the first time, and not segmented between triangle panes of glass.

"It's an ocean," said Sidra of the sky. "It's upside down hanging in the air above us." She curled in closer to his side, pressing her back against the glass wall of the biosphere.

"It's time to tell them," Cameron said.

"No, not yet. We've had this such a short time. It's

179

like all of this is ours, as if there isn't anyone else in the world. I don't want to give up that feeling so soon. Please, just a little longer."

He leaned closer and kissed her. "I wish I had all the world to give you," he said, "and mornings like this one for the rest of our lives."

She twined her arms around his neck and pressed her face against his. "Don't let me be afraid, Cameron. Hold me," she said. "Hold me."

He could feel her heart beating against him, and her breath was his breath. The morning air was cold and silent. There were no sounds of machines, only the slow breathing of the woman beside him, only the quickening of his heart at her touch.

"I never wanted to hurt you," he tried to tell her. "Never."

"Shh," she whispered, and kissed the words from his lips.

His hand moved from the silky skin of her neck to the warm weight of her breast. In this first dawn of their new world, on a pillow of white sand, beneath the pale blue of an overturned sea of sky . . . they were all that mattered.

He had made the fire last all night. With the morning, he let it fall into itself and die. There was light enough to see his way. Putting his feet in the marks Sagamore had left upon the earth, Shepherd followed the footsteps.

He was alone now, in a wilderness which stretched far beyond even the boundaries of this unknown desert. A certainty came to him that Sagamore wouldn't be there to lead him home, that he would need to depend on his own skills to find his way. That sure sense prepared him for the rest.

He found Sagamore in the cool pink and gray luster of dawn. Sagamore's face hadn't been harmed, untouched by claws or teeth, but his chest was laid open, the dark stain of blood soaked into the ground. Beside him was the body of the bear, Sagamore's hunting knife still piercing its neck.

Shepherd dropped to his knees beside him, then realized that the bubbling sound he heard was the drawing in of breath. He watched, disbelieving his ears at first, then saw the rise and fall of Sagamore's chest.

"You're alive," he said, touching his hand to the man's arm.

Sagamore's eyes opened. "Who's there? Brad? Quinn?" He looked at Shepherd, but didn't seem to see.

"I'm here, Sagamore. I found you."

"Shepherd? The bear . . ." He struggled as if trying to rise.

"You've killed it," Shepherd said. "It's there beside you. See?" Shepherd lifted Sagamore's head so he could see the bear, and the knife still embedded in the animal's thick neck. The bubbling sound grew louder with this movement. Sagamore coughed, and a froth of red spilled from his mouth and trickled down his chin.

"Tell me what I should do," he said, frightened by the sound.

"Go home."

"Go home?" Shepherd hadn't expected that. How could he go home? "You're hurt. I'll stay with you."

"You can't heal my hurt. Go back, Shepherd. Go home to your mother."

"I . . . don't know how," the boy admitted. "I'll get lost. Don't send me back alone, Sagamore. I'm afraid. You'll get better," he bargained. "We'll go home together. Let me stay with you."

It cost Sagamore to speak; Shepherd could see that on his face. Each word was an effort, each breath painful. "I can't walk. You can't carry me. I need you to go . . . to bring help."

Shepherd wanted to cry, wanted to press himself close to Sagamore's bloody arm and never move. It was too hard. Could he find the way back by himself? The desert was fear, bleached white ground, rattlers coiled beneath the only shade, and hunters like bear and puma stalking his trail. With Sagamore he had felt safe. Now, he would be alone. On the desert, he might die.

If he didn't go for help, Sagamore would die.

He took off his shirt, wadded it into a thick pad and pressed it over the open wound in Sagamore's chest. He slipped his arms into the sleeves of his thin jacket. It would protect his skin from the blistering sun and keep him warm at night.

"Follow the marks we left," Sagamore said. "Remember what you were taught."

"Don't die."

Shepherd stood and turned to go.

"Wait," Sagamore called to him. "To protect you . . ." In his open palm was a bear claw. It was stained with blood. "His." Sagamore leaned his head in the direction of the slain bear. "I'm alive; he's not. It's a totem," he said. "Take it."

Shepherd stretched out his hand and took the dark claw. His fingers closed, squeezing into a fist, and the sharp point dug into his flesh.

"Now, you're safe," said Sagamore. "Go."

Shepherd moved away quickly, before his fear could stop him. The claw was a reminder of Sagamore's strength and Sagamore's words. He kept the point of it against his skin, giving him courage.

He had wanted to become a hunter . . . to become a

182

man. Now would be the greatest hunt of his life, following the faint track of his own trail across the seamless desert.

Chapter Twenty-three

Jessica heard the sound through a thin veil of sleep. She had been dreaming of swimming across a blue-green lake, the water warm as sun against her skin. Her arms moved in perfect symmetry, reaching high into the space of cooler air above the smooth surface, cleanly cutting her way through this unseen track. She could see the wedge of land far ahead of her and struggled for it, knowing that if she could reach that shore she would find a hope of peace.

The repeated knocking intruded on the illusion. Like a stone thrown into the still water, it distorted the comforting images of the lake and the land. Relentless and insistent, it forced her into wakefulness and shattered the dream.

She sat up, all her senses tensed, alert.

"What the hell . . . ?" said Quinn, rolling over and pushing his full weight onto his back. His eyes were blue cups, deeply shadowed and staring blankly in the slow change from sleep blindness to waking sight.

The steady pounding came again.

"I'll go," Jessica said, not waiting for him. She was moving toward it, a warning sense hurrying her step. She pulled the knitted shawl around her and ran.

Others were up too. They'd heard it. She saw them crushing against each other in the corridor between the habitat sector and the ag wing. They were pressed against the glass: Cathe and Daniel, Diana and her three daughters, and Trinity. Cathe was screaming.

Jessica felt it coming . . . a wave that would hit and knock her down. It roared in her head, diluting the sound of Cathe's screams, of Quinn's calling to her from somewhere in her past. It was gathering like the head winds of a storm and coming. No way to stop it. To force the images back.

And then she saw him standing with his hands still balled into fists on the glass. Outside.

And he was Brad. For that instant he was Brad. She remembered it all, saw it again . . . the yellow pustules on his face, the eyes that spoke of seeing death, the hopelessness and fear.

But it wasn't Brad; it was Cameron.

"Mom."

He was calling to her. She couldn't move, but she heard his voice.

"Mom, I'm sorry. Please understand. I couldn't live that way, not anymore. God, please don't look like that. Say you understand. Mom . . ." He was crying, fingers splayed and open on the glass as if reaching for her.

She saw Sidra standing beside him, knew why Cathe was calling her daughter's name over and over. They had gone together. The lovers. Left the dome and taken their chances as a pair. Sidra, Josiah's child . . . inheritor of the stars.

The images rushed at Jessica, leaving her breathless as they crashed and exploded into colored fragments, sending a surge of blue-green waves from the placid lake of her mind. Someone was calling. She heard Quinn shout, *Jessica!* but she slipped beneath the water, falling, falling, into the warm embrace of unseeing dark.

"When you are the hunter, notice the land you're passing through. Which way are the mountains? Find a point you will remember, a tree, hill, or river—something you can see from a long distance away. At night, use the stars to guide you. You will never be lost if you mark the places of your journey in your mind. Your eyes and your mind are the first weapons of the hunter."

Shepherd remembered the strength of Sagamore's words. On that morning two days ago, the warning had seemed of small importance. Now it was everything. Only the memory of all he had been taught, and his own courage, could bring him home.

He felt small. The size of the land seemed larger than it had been before, the empty spaces wider. It would be so easy to become lost. A trembling panic rose up in his heart at that thought, sending a quaking into his legs, into his strength. He held the bear claw tightly, squeezing the hard blackness of it until the sharp point pierced the skin of his palm.

It was easier to fear. Controlling that fear and thinking in the way of a hunter was hard. It didn't mean he couldn't cry. Tears washed his cheeks many times. They comforted him. It did mean he couldn't stop. To stop was to let Sagamore die alone on the desert. To stop was to wait for his own death, too.

A bright heat swam on the air surrounding him. The hard baked ground shimmered and glinted white-gold in the full sun. Shepherd's eyes felt burned by the light but he shaded them with his hand and went on. He remembered the morning he and Sagamore had started out from home. The sun had been at his back then. For hours he had felt it against the nape of his neck and scorching through the cloth of his shirt.

If it's in my eyes now, he thought, *I'm going the right way.*

Long ago, Sagamore had been alone on the desert, too. Shepherd tried to remember all that he'd been told about the man the Insiders called Josiah: how he had been trapped outside the biosphere unable to return, how he had wandered alone over the land of death looking for survivors, and how he had brought them back to tell the people of the biosphere that there was life outside the dome.

Josiah Gray Wolf had become Sagamore the leader.

"One day, the novice will be called upon to lead the People," Sagamore had told him. The words had frightened Shepherd. What did he know of leading anyone? Why had Sagamore said that of him? Had he seen something Shepherd couldn't see? Had he known this would come?

If he knew that, Shepherd thought, *then he knew I won't die in this desert. He knew I'd live . . . to lead the People.*

The idea gave him a moment of comfort, a small promise of hope, and then a bright thread of fear. If what Sagamore had said was true, if Shepherd was meant to grow up to be the new leader, did that mean Sagamore was going to die? With this fear pulling him onward, Shepherd hurried his steps across the desert's unyielding ground.

Spring softened the stone-white earth with brilliant splashes of bold color. A solid stand of white prickly poppy flooded one rough-cut mesa. The flowers reminded Shepherd of large, broken eggshells with flakes of gold inside. A bee could drink from such a

187

cup, or a bird. He broke the stem of one that had three flowers branching from it. A thick white sap oozed from the broken end, wetting his palm. In the desert, everything must have moisture, or die.

Shepherd stopped in the field of poppies and took a long drink from the goatskin water bag. If he pushed himself too hard, he would drop from too much heat or too little water. He didn't let himself sit down but stood quietly in the soft morning breeze, waiting while the thudding of his heart slowed to a normal beat. He drank once again, and moved on.

The day had a stillness, traveling alone. Shepherd had never known such silence. The large family of camp was a noisy, busy place, loud with children's voices and the calling of one woman to another, or a man's shout ringing from the fields. Even tracking with Sagamore, there had been the sound of another's steps, his presence heard in the soft rub of clothing brushing together, the crush of gravel beneath his feet, and the pull of breath beside him. Even without words, Sagamore had filled the empty space with sound.

Now, Shepherd was alone and heard the silence. His ears, as well as his eyes, were trackers, and he listened for the sounds he had missed before. What was common was his own heartbeat, the hard cuff of his breath, and the soft crush of his moccasins on the dry ground. What was uncommon was the high squeal of a coyote pup, or the slap of wings from the brown hawk overhead, or the scraping noise behind him.

He twisted back. Nothing.

But the sound hadn't come from nothing. It was real and had followed him, a constant scraping on the hard-packed ground.

What scrapes the ground when it walks? Claws.

There were rock outcroppings behind him, stacked stones covered with thick brush. He walked faster— his eyes, ears, and the nerves of his skin seeing, hearing, and feeling every change.

If it's a bear, Shepherd thought, what will I do? He felt a heat of fear surround him. In that heat he walked, and knew he wasn't alone. The wilderness was threatening . . . at every step, behind every shrub, in every choice he made. He didn't let himself panic, but made his choices wisely, as he thought Sagamore might have done.

After a time, the scraping stopped.

He kept going.

Sidra and Cameron ran from the terrible sounds of Biosphere Seven, their parents' cries ringing in their ears.

Cathe Innis would not be comforted. "Sidra!" She screamed her daughter's name over and over, until the others were begging her to stop. "Sidra," she wailed, the sound of the one name drawn from her as if in torment.

Quinn shouted at Cameron, his voice rough and cracked with emotion. "Do you know what you've done? You've killed yourself and your mother. Look at her! She won't live through this. What were you thinking, boy? Oh, God. What were you thinking?"

They stood outside the glass, listening until they couldn't listen any longer. The guilt was too strong, the pain too great. Sidra put both hands over her ears, holding her head tightly as if to block the sound of her mother's cries. She broke and ran first; Cameron followed.

Sidra ran in the direction she had seen the Outsiders go home when they had visited the sphere. She didn't know how far away their camp was, or if she could see it from the bluff, but she needed a distance between her and the shattering screams of her mother.

The bluff was the sharp drop from the upper plateau, an edge where the land sloped down a crumbling hill to the lower mesa, along the river's bank. Sidra stood at the brink of this drop, her legs trembling, staring at a space of unending land spreading outward as far as she could see. There were no boundaries here. No walls. No biomes. This was the Earth as it was meant to be. She breathed in the reach of it, the infinite span of sky, land, river, and mountain. It calmed her terror.

"Look at it," said Cameron, coming up beside her. His breathing was ragged and strained, like hers. "It goes on forever."

They stood at the edge of the bluff, feeding their souls on the sight of this unending land. In the distance, they could see the Outsiders' camp. Near the adobe huts were cultivated fields of growing crops.

"My father said I killed my mother."

Sidra had no words to comfort him. Her own wounds were too deep. That they had done this to their families was a grief they couldn't lessen for each other. It was a mark branded deep into each of them, and would never leave. She imagined it imprinted into her bones, into her blood. Words wouldn't wash it away.

"Did you see her? My mother . . . ?" asked Cameron. "She fainted."

"I saw everything."

"I never wanted to hurt anyone." He turned back to stare at the sphere. "Why does it have to be like this? It's our lives; why couldn't they just let us go?"

Sidra could feel his pain, the same misery tore at

190

her, but she didn't look back. The decision had been made, and their only choice was to go forward. Without a final glance at all that had been her life before, the biosphere and the family she left behind, she started down the hilly slope toward the Outsiders.

Cameron caught up with her, and they moved out into the open world together.

Chapter Twenty-four

The camp of the Outsiders was awake and busy when Cameron and Sidra came down the hill and walked into view. The children saw them first, and like a warning of yapping dogs, ran toward the two strangers, shouting and alerting the attention of every man and woman within the loose framework of the camp.

Willow was alone before her adobe house, kneeling on a reed mat and grinding corn into soft yellow-white meal. She looked up as the strangers approached. She knew Sidra at once. The girl had the unmistakable straight frame, dark hair, and expressive eyes of her father, Josiah Gray Wolf. The cornmeal fell from Willow's bowl onto the braided mat, and she stood.

From all around the camp, the people were crowding around the two strangers. Willow could hear the sharp intake of breath among the older women, and the quick hard words of the men. The children ran in noisy circles around the tall, dark-haired man and the beautiful young woman.

It was as though she were seeing another image of herself. The high cheekbones and the sharper angles of their faces were the same. They were of an equal age, though Willow knew Sidra was one year older. Their height was the same, about five and a half feet, as though molded from one shell. *My sister,* thought Willow, and moved forward in the crowd.

"Cameron!" Prophet shouted, and the People pulled back, making an open space for him to approach the newcomers. Even the children stopped their frantic racing around the young couple, retreating instead to their parents. Prophet was a man many of the children feared, for his stern eyes and distant manner. Willow saw this and knew that they feared her, too. She and Prophet were different, and would never be wholly accepted by the People as one of them again.

Willow watched, and as Prophet moved toward the man called Cameron, she moved closer to the dark-haired woman, Sidra. At last their eyes met, and Willow knew a calm and instant familiarity with another person, something she had never felt before. The feeling was certain and unexplainable. They were more than sisters of the same father, she knew in that instant; they were sisters of the same spirit.

"I am Willow, eldest daughter of the People," she spoke loudly enough for all to hear, and touched Sidra's arm. "For my father, I welcome you, my sister." She leaned forward and kissed Sidra's cheek. They were of one height, one coloring, one blend of their father's nature. Standing together, they were clearly two halves of one whole, and all who saw them noticed.

"For your greeting and welcome, I will remember you with love all my life," said Sidra. She returned Willow's gentle kiss with one of her own. "Please," she asked, "where is my father?"

"Come into the compound," said Prophet, not answering her question. He led them toward a large, bare circle in the center of camp. "The People will want to know why you left the biosphere, and as much as you can tell them about life beneath the glass dome."

Willow followed, dropping back until she was one of the last to crowd into the gathering. She remained on the higher slope at the back of the compound. From here, she could see well into the distance, along the desert's crest, and watch for her father's return. She had felt a certainty of fear about him all night. She knew, just as she had known of the landslide, and the death of Rosalina Santos, something had happened to Sagamore, her father.

She had not spoken of this seeing with her mind to anyone. The People wouldn't thank her for telling them both Sagamore and Shepherd were in danger. Many already thought her a force against nature, something unclean and evil. She wouldn't willingly add to their distrust of her. She might have said something to Prophet, but now he was kept busy with the two from the biosphere. To calm her fears, she listened to the voices of her sister and the man called Cameron, and waited.

Shepherd walked in aware and observant silence. He didn't try to keep himself company by humming, or singing. Instead, he listened to every sound of the high desert, cautious for his safety as a hunted animal. He was the long-eared jackrabbit, the pronghorn antelope, and the small, feral cat.

The desert was a land of hard beauty. It threatened him with its wide, unending space. He kept his mind clearly on the mountain range ahead. That was his point of focus. To that, he added the rock formation in the distance—the one he and Sagamore had

194

passed—and the angle of the sun overhead. There were many other markers, some looked for, and some remembered as he saw them. They were his map, leading him home.

The wild beasts of the desert didn't run from him. He was a small boy and of little danger to them. The stand of five Texas longhorns watched unmoving when he passed close to them. With Sagamore at his side, they had broken and run. The bull had shaken his shaggy head at them and pawed the ground with sharp, black hooves. Now they remained, watching him with calm, brown eyes. Even as he passed, they lowered their heads back to the rich spring grass.

Shepherd tried not to think of Sagamore as he was now, injured and dying. Instead, Shepherd remembered Sagamore as he had been just one day ago, teacher and tracker, guiding a young hunter through the desert. The distance seemed great, and barely possible. Had they come so far?

The day stretched into long shadows. He heard life move more freely on the sun-baked earth. Cooling night approached. Shepherd hurried his steps. In the dark, tracking his way would be much harder. And, too, hunters prowled the night. To be safe he needed to gather dried grass, mesquite branches, and build a fire to last him through the night. To be safe he should stop now and wait to try going on until morning.

But Sagamore was dying. He was this man's only hope.

Shepherd drew a line with the bright North Star he saw overhead, straight to the range of blue mountains in the distance. He would lose sight of the mountains soon, but the star would be his guide through the dark.

It can't be much more.

If he kept walking . . . if he didn't let his fear of the night allow him to stop . . . if he didn't fail Sagamore, he would be home before morning. Holding to his courage and all that he had learned, Shepherd forced himself to go on, moving in steady passage across the unmarked face of the desert.

Soon, night spread its blanket of black across the sky. The last pale mark of day narrowed to one bright line of red and gold, then disappeared. A wide, chalky moon rose in full splendor over the tracker and the land.

The memory of Sagamore's words led Shepherd like a blaze through the closed cave of dark. "You are the first of the young men of our camp. One day, the novice will be called upon to lead the people." He remembered this and the totem, the bear claw. "Take it," Sagamore had said. "Now you are safe."

With the point of the claw sharp against the palm of his hand, Shepherd carried the weight of those words into each step of the future. If he was to lead the People, first he must find his way home.

Willow brought Cameron and Sidra into her own house. She had lived alone since the time of the tornado. The People came to her in this small adobe shelter, with their questions, with their fears. She was the Woman of the Spirits, and although they feared her, still they came.

She poured a mug of herbal tea for each of them. "Drink this," she said. "It will calm you."

Cameron hesitated, staring suspiciously at the contents of the brew. He took a tiny sip, tasting. Sidra picked up the mug and drank.

She trusts me, thought Willow.

"What will happen when my father returns?" Sidra

196

asked. Her eyes were deep recesses in her face, hollowed by exhaustion.

Cameron slipped a comforting arm around Sidra's shoulders, and she laid her head against him. "Prophet says we're welcome. Why do you want to question that? If he says it's all right, then it is. Isn't that right?" He turned to Willow.

"Our father is leader here." Willow's words made a point of including Sidra in this, their shared birthright. "When he returns, Sagamore will decide what must be done."

"Done?" Cameron pushed the mug of hot tea away, as if it scalded and threatened him.

Willow tried to see and understand what it was about this man that made her sister love him. He was a shining light, like the flash of silver on a fish's scales, but that shining was thin as the brightness on the water. Only a reflection of the real light from the sun. She wondered—*What was Cameron's sun? Who, or what, had been the source of light that he was a faint reflection of?*

"It must be for Sagamore to answer," she told Cameron.

Willow left the shelter. Going out into the night, she again felt the strong sense of fear for her father. She could hear two children of the camp laughing, running through the winding paths between the houses. Women called to them, and the night raced on with its stir of expected sounds.

The silence was within her. Terrible, and nearing. What did it mean? She wandered a distance from the camp. Her need was to be apart from the others, alone. A full moon shone down across the desert, making the hard ground shimmer in its polished light. *Where are you, Father? Where are you?*

"Don't worry about Josiah. He was the one who

197

found all the survivors. Remember? He's the best tracker there is."

She turned. Prophet stood a few feet behind her, the moon casting an unnatural pallor to his face. Willow had seen death before, in the infants who had not survived their first year. Death was a gray-blue corpse. And Prophet, with the moon's pale light upon his face . . .

"You feel it, too?" she asked. "This danger?"

Prophet walked closer. He shook his head. "Only that you're worried. Anyone can see how you watch for him."

She turned back to the shimmering desert. It would be the path to bring him home. If she stood and waited . . . If she drew away from them all and listened for his step.

"Why did you help them, my sister and the other one?"

"Cameron is Jessica's son. The girl came with him."

It was enough of an answer. She understood. For him, the young man was the one of importance. For her, it was the woman.

A scrape muffled on the hard-packed sand. Too far away. She couldn't see past the flat, smooth dark.

"Father?" She ran ahead into the sea of dark, wanting, needing it to be him.

"Wait!" Prophet called to her.

She couldn't.

"Father!"

A wind rose in leathered fury behind her eyes, in the vast reaches of her mind, roaring. She heard the shrieking keen of it, rising . . . rising against the solid crown of her skull. It was the pounding of her blood, this wind, a force she could not silence, or deny.

"I'm here." The thin voice sliced through the air.

Some part of her heard. The words were whispering wings beating against her ears. The voice hidden as a thread in a field of grass. But, she heard.

"This way!" she shouted. "Where are you?"

"What is it?" Prophet asked, beside her now. "I heard nothing."

"Where are you?" she cried again.

And then, the pinpoint of that voice pierced the night again. "I can't see you. Where . . . where?"

Willow didn't wait to ask if Prophet had heard it, too. She ran. He followed her, deeper into the dark coil of the desert, toward the brimming cry of that sound.

"Shepherd!" she called out, for she knew now who it was—and who it wasn't.

"Don't leave me! I can't find you," he cried.

And then she saw him. He was the shape that moved against the dark. He was the stillness in the wind. She ran to him, knowing long before reaching the boy that he would be alone, and that the fears she'd held for her father had come true.

Chapter Twenty-five

Jessica had learned that she was pregnant on the day before Cameron and Sidra left the biosphere. The urine test had been conclusive. Blue meant positive. Quick-read pregnancy kits had been stocked in the lab's communal pharmacy since the day Biosphere Seven began its human occupancy. The designers of the project had assumed it might be a concern, with five women and five men sharing living space in an enclosed environment.

She had known one day's joy of her pregnancy, and now . . .

It was as though God, if there were a God, had given one child and taken away another. Why had it happened? Was it because daring this pregnancy was wrong? Risked too much? Had she been playing God, herself? Was that why Cameron would . . . her mind fought against the word *die*.

She knew a fear, too, for this unborn child within her. What legacy had she given any of her children? Matthew? Cameron? And now this infant? She wondered — Was it so wrong to reach for life? She was the new Eve of the Garden, not reaching for the fruit from the tree of knowledge, but from the tree of life.

Quinn had treated her gently, protecting her from everyone in the sphere, keeping them at a distance for a few days. They all had their questions, she knew. Had the sphere been contaminated by Outside air? Had the seal been breached? And how had the computer's warning system been altered?

She knew Quinn was protecting her, and was suffering, too. Cameron was his son. How much longer would Quinn go on loving her, she wondered, when he learned the truth about the child she was carrying? Would any of them understand?

Why tell them now? What would it change?

The more she thought of it, the more certain she became that she must keep the truth of this child's conception to herself. It would be easy enough to let Quinn assume the child was his. For the sake of all of them, it was the best decision.

Lastly, Jessica thought of Brad. Memories of the night when their child had been conceived replayed in her mind. She saw again the look of awakened longing in his eyes, heard his words. "You're with me until the day I die. And then I'll come to you, Jessie. Wherever you are, I'll come to you. There'll be no walls between us then."

All the while, it had been Brad helping Cameron to leave. Brad had given the blood for transfusion. Brad had known and kept the truth from her. Even then.

The place under her heart where the baby grew felt unnaturally still and cold. She pressed her hand over the spot. An act of love had begun this child. A betrayal of that love had killed the heart in her, for it.

Cameron! She pulled back from the terror of

her son's death. Couldn't think of that. Couldn't wonder . . . Would it be slow? Would he die calling out for her? Cameron.

Her hand fell away from its place over the knotted cold below her heart. Resting both hands in her lap, she stared into soothing nothingness. One full day and night had passed since Cameron had gone. Looking out through the skylight of her room, she saw the dawn.

It was the morning of the second day. She went to the computer terminal and entered the journal file.

May 25, 2018: We have lost them. With the loss of the children, the hope of our world has gone. Cameron and Sidra have chosen probable death among the Outsiders, over a controlled life within the sphere.

What hope can I have for this new child I carry? My firstborn is beyond my help. When will the end come for this child, too? For all the children of the sphere? God help them. Cameron and Sidra have found their freedom, at last.

Shepherd Hallinger was unhurt by his ordeal in the desert. He had followed a trail through the night, set by the stars and his memory of the landmarks he and Sagamore had passed. Beneath the light of the full moon, he had found his way.

In the adobe shelter Willow questioned him. While he waited for her to speak, Shepherd noticed the two strangers, a man and a woman he had never seen before. The man was a blank space, someone Shepherd didn't know or care about. The woman was another face of Willow.

"When you left Sagamore," Willow asked, never saying the words, *my father,* "did you leave him water?"

"I gave him his water bag. He had forgotten it at our campsite."

Willow accepted this without comment. She knew her father had *forgotten* nothing. Her next question was more difficult for the boy to answer. "What did Sagamore say to you? What were his words?"

Shepherd remembered each word clearly; he had repeated them out loud each time he began to grow afraid on the journey home. They had guided him, as much as the stars or the moon, or any landmark of the desert. But were these words for Willow to hear? Were they meant only for him?

As if understanding his concern, Willow said, "Sagamore is the leader of our camp. His words are for the People. You carried them home to us. I must know the last things he said to you."

Then Shepherd told her all that Sagamore had said. That he was the first of the young men of the camp. That one day the novice would be called upon to lead the People. Shepherd repeated it without embarrassment or pride. They were Sagamore's words.

"He gave me this," Shepherd added, pulling the bear claw from his pocket. "He put it in my hand and said, 'Now you are safe.'"

Willow lifted the bear claw from Shepherd's two outstretched fingers. He watched her as she stared at the dried blood, turning and turning the point of the claw. In one sudden movement, she forced the dark point of it deep into the center of her palm, then pulled it free. A gush of blood pumped and spread into a thick lake of red held in the cupped well of her hand.

The two strangers pulled back, shock showing on their faces. Watching Willow, Shepherd didn't think she was aware of them, or him. She was seeing other worlds, other faces. Her action had surprised him, too, but tracking across the desert alone had given him a calmness he couldn't easily explain, or understand.

"Come close to me," Willow said to Shepherd. "Let my hands touch you."

He didn't fear her. His mother, and some of the other people of the camp were afraid of "the Indian witch." He knew. Shepherd was young enough to remember Willow as she had been with the children, as one of them. He came forward without any dread of her, and remained very still while she laid her cool hands on his forehead, face, and arms. Her blood touched him in red smears, but he made no move to wipe it off.

He watched her now, her eyes closed, a small movement just beneath the skin of her brow. She was Spirit Woman, he saw that clearly, and was struggling now to help Sagamore. The unknown woman beside her watched with silent eyes.

A shudder trembled through Willow's hands. She gasped, pulled away from Shepherd, and seemed to come back to them at last.

"Sagamore lives. We must hurry."

As if forgetting all of them, Willow rose and started for the door. Something stopped her. She turned back, her dark eyes fixing on first Shepherd, and then the woman sitting across from him.

At first, Willow didn't speak, as if not believing her own thoughts.

Then, she said to Shepherd, "I know you are tired. Today has been another time of birth for you. But you must come with us now to guide our way. We will find him only through you."

His legs ached with exhaustion, but he stood up to go with her.

To the woman with silent eyes, Willow said, "Our father will need both of his daughters. If you would have him live so that you may know this man, you must come, too."

The woman who looked so much like Willow stood and moved toward them.

"Sidra, don't!" the stranger shouted.

"She can't go with you," he said to Willow. "What if she gets the virus? She'll be out there in the middle of the desert."

It was the only time the man had spoken. Shepherd stared at him, wondering at this response. Why did he believe the woman would get the virus?

"If the virus has touched her, she will die no matter where she is," said Willow, as if explaining the obvious to a small child.

"I want to go," said the one called Sidra.

"Don't force her to do this!" The man sounded afraid. "She can't leave this camp until we know if . . ." He let the final words fall unspoken.

Willow touched the woman's face. "No one will force you. My sister, will you come with us?"

"Sidra, please listen!" the man cried out.

If she had heard these words, Shepherd could not see that they had made her hesitate. "Yes," said this one who might have been Willow's own reflection in the water. "I'll go with you."

In the end, it was a band of six people — Willow, Sidra Innis, Shepherd, his father Skeet Hallinger, Stephen Wyse, and Prophet — who crossed the land of the high desert to find Sagamore.

Cameron Nathan was not asked, and did not join them.

Josiah Gray Wolf — Sagamore — had been alone on the desert before. He thought of that other time, as he lay wounded beneath the furnace-bright Texas sky, caught in one solid core of pain. So much had changed of his world. So much ended. So much begun.

The thought of dying didn't frighten him. He had seen an entire world of mankind die. Should his own death be the cause of so much greater fear? No. He knew that this, too, would come to him, to all of them.

The thought which troubled him was not that he should die, but if he had done enough. Could they go on, these people he'd gathered? Would they remain united as a clan? As a tribe? Or, would they splinter into fragments at his death?

He had claimed them as a band of survivors, a gleaning of the final harvest, not the scattered, single remnants of humanity. But, would they remain one people after he was gone? Had he given them enough reason to become one nation? That was the pain which tormented him as he waited beneath the Texas sun. Whatever the cause that had brought these few together, it must be a concept of faith and belonging which would keep them bound to one another now, and into the future.

Josiah reached for the water bag near his hand. He lifted, tilted, and poured the last of the liquid from the goatskin pouch, fighting against choking on the warm trickle as it touched the back of his throat. The splash of lukewarm droplets against his skin made him shake with chills, telling him how hot he was with fever, and how much in the grip of steadily spiking infection from the bear's claws. His shoulder was laid open to the bone, and there was one flayed tear of flesh across his chest, the wound covered and stopped like a plug with Shepherd's wadded shirt.

A puddle of new bright blood led away from the bunched-up shirt, and pooled at Josiah's side. The smell of it would bring animals soon. Smaller predators wouldn't be lured in too close, not even by the strong smell of fresh blood. This was man, the hunter. They would wait until the end, until he either fainted, or died, before they would risk approaching. Knowing this, Josiah worked constantly at staying alert and awake.

He knew also that if another bear found him, and if it was aggressive enough, there would be no fight. Death would follow in a few agonized moments. The knowledge had brought little comfort as the time had stretched from day to night, once more to day, and now, was dropping toward night again.

Without water, he was certain, this would be his last day.

The fever worked at his mind, skewing his thinking into slants of strange and unknown realities. He tried to remain calm, to listen for the voice of

207

his own spirit, to stay on his own path, but other voices called to him. Other fingers closed over his flesh and pulled him toward places he didn't know or understand.

His mouth was dry, fever burning through him. The sky boiled, bubbles of white froth closing in to touch him . . . to drop its heat in pearled nets, lowering softly with the clouds of night.

His eyes closed for a moment. He saw his mother as a young woman bathing in the river. The water was patterns of dark and light, marked by the twisting leaves on the trees near their home. He sat on the bank of the river watching her, unashamed. If she saw him, she gave no notice of it. He watched, captured by the cool breeze along the river, by the vision of his mother, and by the changing colors on the water. One part of him felt drawn to this place. He moved closer to it, wanting to join his mother in the cooling river. His mind moved toward it, knowing that once in the water, he would never return to the world of man.

With a sudden stop to the images, the vision blurred and faded. Josiah's eyes opened. Something he had felt, rather than heard, pulled him from the peaceful beauty of the dream. Something was moving in the tall grass, not far away. Now, he could smell it. Wolf.

The wolf had caught his scent, too. That much was clear.

Josiah tried to sit up, but the cage of his chest was broken, the bones crushed by the bear's paw. One shoulder was mangled to the white bone; the other, could not lift his weight. He looked around for a weapon. Nothing was near him except the water bag. His hunting knife was still embedded in the neck of the bear.

He heard the wolf's snuffling, following the scent of blood. Whether it was the bear's blood, or his own, Josiah didn't know. It didn't matter. The scent would draw the wolf in close enough to see him. A healthy wolf wouldn't normally come anywhere near man. Either the strong odor of bear had masked Josiah's human smell, or the wolf was starving.

With his left hand, Josiah clawed at the ground, digging a trough of finger grips, and dragging his body with the strength of that one good arm, closer to the bear's carcass . . . closer to the knife.

And then he saw it. The lone wolf stood with its forelegs braced and ready for attack. The ruff of hair around the back of its neck rose in stiff hackles from the gray-black coat, and its ears lay flat against its skull. A low, warning growl shuddered from the broad chest and throat, and the black skin of its muzzle was cinched back tight, revealing an open-mouth snarl.

Josiah scraped a fistful of dirt and rock into his hand, and with a loud cry, threw it at the wolf.

The animal bolted for the brush.

Using his legs to push him, Josiah dragged and scooted across the ground, close enough to touch the bear. The stench of the animal was strong. It had been two days since the bear had been killed. No wonder the wolf had been drawn in by the fetid smell of putrid flesh.

He heard the animal tracking back and forth behind the brush. It had seen the bear carcass, and was hungry enough to stick around. He'd scared it off for a little while, but it would be back. He had to get the hunting knife before that happened. Without a weapon, Josiah knew he was helpless.

Pushing his back against the bear, he scooted up the mound of flesh, stretching out his good left arm to try to wrest the knife free from the animal's neck. The rank smell of the bear enveloped him, choking the muscles of his throat and closing the passage of air into his lungs by its heavy reek of corruption. He felt a surge of vomit rise within the spasmodic muscles of stomach and throat, but forced it down.

The wolf's low growl came again. Closer now. The sound of it stretched across Josiah's senses—hearing, sight, taste, and touch—a live current, shocking him into desperate action. Pushing from his legs, he shoved himself higher and reached for the embedded knife. Pain tore through his chest, ripped flesh pulling against this strain.

His hand caught the wooden handle of the knife.

Why was the wolf alone?

The question tugged at Josiah's mind, pulling, even as he pulled at the knife. A wolf hunted in a pack, unless the wolf had been injured, or chased off by a dominant male. An injured wolf was far more dangerous, for like Josiah himself, it had become desperate.

The knife caught at the bear's flesh as Josiah tried to jerk it free. A fresh sheen of blood pumped from Josiah's chest wound as he struggled to pull the lacerating blade out of the animal's thick neck. The thought was clear to him. He would die, or he would live, from the agony of this one act.

From the corner of his eye Josiah saw a streak

of gray-black. It blurred and lifted into the air . . . and the sudden weight of the slavering wolf hit the bear's head. Triangulated jaws snapped closed on the meaty sag of the bear's thickly furred neck, a thin space from the hunting knife, and Josiah's fingers.

The wolf's back arched, ears flattened against its skull, dark mouth drawn up in savage threat. Eyes like angry yellow jackets watched Josiah's every move, even as the wolf's teeth ripped chunks of fatty flesh from the bear's carcass. The deep growl said, *stay away.*

But Josiah needed the knife. Without it, he was defenseless. His hand tugged harder at the wooden handle, feeling it begin to give and move under his grip. He knew that if he stayed where he was and kept struggling for the knife, the wolf would attack him. He was too close to the animal, and it was afraid. The smell of blood was strong.

Forcing himself tighter against the bear, and closer to the wolf's jaws, he worked to wrench the knife free. He could feel it, a tautness between him and the wolf, like a breath of fists. It shoved at him, saying, *go away.* But he couldn't . . . not without the knife. The wolf would come for him, sooner or later. He knew that. Josiah's one good arm kept jerking at the knife. He didn't have a choice.

They came into the air together, the hunting knife and the wolf. Each, blooded and deadly.

Josiah's arm hit the side of the animal, knocking it back. The wolf's stance was low, legs braced, head and neck drawn forward into one sharp line. Its lips tightened into thick black rope over the pointed teeth. A long, deep growl forced itself through the wall of the hard-muscled chest, rigid throat, and clenched jaws.

Josiah struggled to sit, to brace himself for the moment when the wolf would hit him with its full weight. It would come in low, rushing for the open wound of his chest, drawn to the blood. If that happened, Josiah knew he would die. He was too weak to fight for his life.

He struck at the wolf's head with the knife handle, driving it back. "Go on!" he shouted. "Get out of here!"

He heard a quick yelp of pain, and then the growling began again. Deeper.

The sky had darkened into seamless gray. *Night of the hunter,* Josiah thought. Before dawn, one of them would die.

He didn't dare to throw the knife. If he missed, there wouldn't be a second chance. The wolf's crushing jaws would be on him in that same instant. His only hope was to keep the wolf back with loud threats and hard jabs from the blade.

A rolling howl caught at the center of the lowering night, pulling a dread of dark from the sky, and into Josiah's heart. It came again, the first, answered by another, higher call. And more. And more.

The wolf didn't move. Its ears lifted into straight peaks, listening. The tunneled cries came again, hollowing a core through the rooted night . . . finding them.

And then the wolf lifted its head, and answered.

Josiah knew that death would come now, in this circle of yellow eyes. He felt its nearness in the rasping scuff of claws moving over hard-packed earth. He had waited for the boy to find his way, for the others to come for him, but now . . . he could wait no longer.

He was alone. Alone, he had been born. Alone, he had gone out of the biosphere and into the world of the Outsiders. Alone, he would face death. Josiah held the knife tightly, braced between his one good arm and his chest, and waited for the circle of wolves to close . . . to rush for the kill.

Chapter Twenty-six

Cameron Nathan had not joined the others in the search for Josiah Gray Wolf, or Sagamore, as many of the Outsiders called this patriarch of the People. Instead, while they walked the face of the desert looking for Gray Wolf, Cameron walked the boundaries of the camp, finding a balance of peace in the quiet of the orange and lemon groves. He stood at the hill and watched the swift-moving current of the river. Spring rains and snowmelt from the nearby mountains had turned the flat ribbon of gray-green water into a surging flow, cascading over the sides of its earthen banks.

The world beyond the biosphere was an accessible land, unrestrictive, yet captivating. In the short time he had been a part of it, Cameron felt that he had become like a sponge, one which could never absorb enough of this place. The mountains were the only barriers to the vast distances in any direction, and it was possible to go beyond them. Gray Wolf had done it, when finding the first group of survivors.

The land went on, stretching past these mountains, into green valleys and forests, flat grasslands

214

and verdant hills. He knew the reality of such places through the words of his mother.

"There are two great oceans on either side of this wide plate of land," she had told him, "the Atlantic and the Pacific. Their waves lift and touch the sky, then crash down against the drum of deep-sea basins. The sound of those waves, surging out and pulling back in a slow constancy of liquid motion, is the pulse beat of the Earth."

He knew of the legends of the land, by the stories of his father.

"The land's alive, Cam. Never forget that. Hidden beneath the hills and mountains, beneath the oceans and forest floor, there's a cauldron of life, and unending source of abundance. From it comes spring wildflowers and trees, plants of every description, animals of the rich grasslands, all predators and prey . . . and people. Man has lost the power to destroy it now. Oh, we've tried," his father had laughed softly, "but it was put there in the making of this world, and will be there as long as the Earth abides."

To his mother, the pulse of the planet's life was in the deep oceans; to his father, it was the cauldron of the living earth. To Cameron, his world was a blending of both ideas. To him, the land would always be the living force, but he would hear its heartbeat in the message of the sea.

Cameron Nathan knew no god. Nor, did he honor any system of ethics, or religion. He was unsullied by faith. His eyes were innocent of vision, or belief. He came to this new world as an empty vessel, waiting to be filled.

And he didn't think of dying. His mind wasn't

caught in that web of dread and fear. Instead, he saw the green of orchards, leaning their heavy boughs into a leafy cascade over a running river. He saw the earth's abundance, bursting with the force of life . . . in trees, in plants. The desert floor was carpeted with tiny flowers, yellow, purple and red. He moved his feet carefully, not wanting to crush them.

He hadn't gone with Sidra and the others. Hadn't become a part of that. His world was open for the first time, a bountiful paradise. With every step, its treasures were given to him. With every glance of his eyes there was more, and more.

He was reborn into this place, a grown man—like Adam, set into the Garden. And like that first man, he spoke the name of all that he saw. For that day of beginning, he had no bond with any people, but walked the plains of Earth, a part of the living land.

The day held them in its heat, a hot wind blowing over the desert. The searchers found little comfort in the late afternoon's humid breeze at their necks, the warning of a storm building from the south. Sultry clouds gathered beneath a force of leaden sky.

The wind dropped with the weight of moisture-laden cumulus, pressing against the solid boundary of earth. In between, the searchers felt the wet, sweltering touch of rain that would not fall. The sweat of that immured cloudburst beaded and glistened on their necks and foreheads like a sheen of oil on cold water. They felt the throb of this imprisoned thundershower in the rocking pulse of their blood. Like the lowering clouds, their skins were walls swollen tight with water cells, and aching with the tension of the coming storm.

The boy led them, through the flat sheet of baked earth, across the unmarked wilderness, into the reach of swollen foothills pressed like rounded toes curving out from the mountain's base. When Shepherd's legs stumbled, the men carried him on the wet shoulders of their backs.

For one hour they would have rested—the three men, two women, and one boy—but Willow pressed them onward, saying there was no time. "If we wait," she told them, "Sagamore will die."

It was hardest for the boy, no more than a child in years. He led them through the desert, following the faint track of his own footsteps until night. When it was too dark to see the prints on the ground, he recalled the line of the stars against the mountain, the landmarks of the twisted mesquite, and the break in the hill at two-stone canyon.

Through the tracking skills of the boy, the searchers found the high valley in the crease of land below the timberline. From there, the voices of the wolves led them.

Now, lightning seared the edges of the hidden sky, and thunder broke the shattered vault above. Hard rain fell and hit like pellets, making their skin burn with the impact. Clouds covered the moon, and the guiding stars were lost behind the constant downpour.

Only one thing could be heard above the thunder and the rain. Only the growling of the wolves. They ran toward the sound, each of them shouting and calling.

"Josiah!"

"Father!"

"Sagamore!"

They ran, dark shapes racing across the muted edges of night. Into the circle of wolves, they ran. Thunder pealed and rippled in one long resounding drum across the heavens. In the next flash of light, Shepherd saw him.

"Sagamore!"

The figure was still as rock, the hunting knife held straight up, wedged between chest and arm.

Shepherd's legs trembled in exhaustion and fear, but he stumbled forward. "I came back. I found you," he cried. "Sagamore . . ." The word was a whisper, too softly spoken to have been heard by the other searchers. "You can't be dead."

Shepherd knelt in mud beside the body, his foot touching Sagamore's leg. "I came back," he said again. "I found my way, just as you told me, Sagamore. I brought them to you."

There was no light. Rain and clouds had blacked the stars and moon. Shepherd leaned closer—his tears slipping down wet cheeks, mingling with the falling rain—and touched this second father's face.

Beneath the child's fingertips, the man's lips moved.

"Sagamore?"

In that moment, the torrent stopped. The clouds shifted, and a curving line of silvered moon shone down upon them. Sagamore's eyes were open, looking at Shepherd.

"The bear claw . . ." The words were hushed breaths.

Shepherd's hand dug into his pants pocket, fished

218

out the sharp curl and placed the claw in the center of Sagamore's palm.

The long fingers closed around it. A deep sigh was breathed into the well of night. "Now," said the bear killer, the hunter of men, "now, I am safe. Today, I will die."

And then Willow was there. She knelt beside them, lifting her father's head into her lap. Only— Shepherd could see—she wasn't Willow now. The look on her face wasn't that of the girl he'd known all his life—the one who'd chased the children, laughing and playing as a child. She was Spirit Woman.

"You will not die, Sagamore."

Shepherd heard the words she chose and understood. She had said Sagamore, and not Father. She was not acting as any man's daughter now. "I have brought a power to heal you, stronger than this wound."

Sidra stepped into the shaft of moonlight.

"Child . . ." The word itself was the sound of life renewed. It was spoken with a strength that was beyond death. Josiah lifted his head, fighting against the pain, struggling to look at Sidra. "Is it possible?" he asked. "You're here? Outside?" The effort was too great. "But, how did you . . . ?" he tried to go on, then fell back, exhausted.

"Your firstborn has come out of the biosphere. Look at the face of your daughter," said Spirit Woman, pushing Sidra closer to the injured man. "Know that you must hold onto life, Josiah Gray Wolf, to guide her. You are Sagamore, the gatherer of man." Spirit Woman joined Sidra's hand to that of her father's. "This day, your daughter has come

219

searching for you. For her sake, you must live."

The rain lifted from the desert, and a warm wind blew the clouds north. The searchers lifted Sagamore onto a litter and carried him back to the camp of the Outsiders. His wounds were deep. For many days, he lingered between the spirit lands of life and death. It was said among the elders, that it was Sagamore's two daughters, Sidra and Willow, who brought him through the injury and long weeks of illness which followed. Through their healing and their care, Sagamore — Wise Leader — was given back to the People.

In the memory and mythologies of the many distinct and varied clans of New Earth, those who in years to come would spring up like tough Texas grass across the open prairies, Shepherd Hallinger's trek across the desert to save the patriarch Sagamore, would become the telling of an epic journey of faith and destiny — the story of a strength given to those chosen to lead the People.

Direct descendants of the man, Shepherd, would define their own call of faith by this earlier claim. "We are the inheritors of Shepherd the Tracker. We of the Tracker's bloodline are called upon by Sagamore the Hunter to be leaders of the People."

The many descendants of Sagamore were to become known as the Wise Ones, Spirit People, those men and women set apart by nature — not of the People, but living for them. Only descendants with a direct bloodline to Sagamore were counted among these holy ones. And of these, the most sanctified were individuals whose family links could be traced in an unbroken line from Sagamore's two eldest daughters, Willow Gray Wolf and Sidra Innis.

An odyssey of belief was begun and charted on that long trek back into the desert. The journey, led by a nine-year-old boy, would one day lead an entire people onto the pathway to the beginnings of their faith. The name of Shepherd, like that of Sagamore, Prophet, Spirit Woman, and Sidra, would be returned to the breath of Father Sky—the air above them—by the whispered prayers of the many clans and nations sprung from the legacy of these, the first People of New Earth.

Chapter Twenty-seven

He was born in the first hour of morning. The bruised purple sky above the Sahara was the only roof over his head. His mother, a Berber of the Gued'oula tribe in North Africa, named him Zechariah, son of the shooting star. The streak of light was an omen at his birth, and his mother said of it, "This child of my body will be like the spear of heaven, a star to shine across the earth."

He did not have his mother's dark hair and Mediterranean coloring, but bore his father's stamp, the look of the tribe from the Dadès River valley: pale skin, blond hair, and blue eyes, like many of the Berber people since ancient times.

His mother pierced her infant's left earlobe with a thin ring at his birth, a recognition of his having been born on a Wednesday, a day all Berbers considered to be a sign of good fortune.

Zechar, as the boy had come to be known, grew up on the southern slopes of Morocco's High Atlas Mountains, along the strip of fertile land just north of the Sahara. The Upper Dadès River cut through the High Atlas, creating a valley that was a green corridor of life fifteen miles long and three miles wide. To the north were these tiered black mountains of Morocco. To the south was the Sahara. Zechar was born into the fortresslike village of Ait Attig.

His mother, Itto, braided her son's hair in the likeness of the village saint. As he grew older, she wove a wool burnoose for the boy, and kept him warm at night in the pressed-mud house with the coarse grass she gathered for fuel. Each morning, Itto walked a half-day's trek into the mountains, and cut the thick grass with her sickle knife. Before the sickness came to the village, she had done this chore with the other women of the *igh*—the extended family of one common male ancestor. Now, there were no others. She went into the mountains alone. Bundling a hundred-pound load of heavy grass upon her back, Itto would walk bent over by her burden, and return to the village in time to prepare the family's midday meal.

Before his death, Zechar's father, Nuri ibn Ziyad, had kept a donkey to ride into the fields to work, but women could not be seen in the shameful act of riding a donkey, or mule. It was the way it had always been. *"Aya d'asrif,"* Zechar's mother would say. *It is the custom.*

Little change had come to the families of this valley for thousands of years, isolated from all invaders as they were by the bleak mountains and the unconquerable desert. Even Islam was new. Its teachings had come to them only a thousand years before from the Arabs. In all other ways, they were unchanged from their long-distant forefathers.

The Berbers were, as their ancestors had been, a people closely related to Egyptian, Basque, Iberian, Pict, Celt, and the race of men from Gaul. The same megalithic dolmens and monuments found in pre-Christian Europe, England, and Ireland, could be found in this northern region of Africa. It was said among their *amhars*—or chieftains, that the Berbers were descendants of the noble Avrigha, or Afrigha, a tribe of ancient days.

They spoke a Hamitic tongue, not the Semitic of the Arab nomads. Some said they were the descendants of Ham, second son of Noah. The Egyptians had called these distinct people Lebu. Romans called them Numidae, a name borrowed from the Greek *nomad*. To the Greeks and Romans, they were also called Berber, or Barbari—the barbarians. Always, it had been so. Nothing had changed.

Their ancient god was nature. Much of that earlier faith remained with them still, sharing religious beliefs with the teachings of Islam. Like their relatives the Celts and Picts, they were a warlike people of sturdy independence, never completely subjugated by any outside force. Self-reliant, they drew their strength from the sea of desert, and the sheltering black mountains surrounding them.

Itto M'Hand, Zechar's mother, spoke to her son of the time before the sickness had come and plucked the souls of men from the earth. She told young Zechar of Haroun M'Hand, her father, an *amrhar* of the Gued'oula tribe in Morocco's Rif valley.

The beauty of his mother's dark eyes were outlined by thick, black shadow made from antimony and grease. A narrow band of black and red tattoo marked a line from below her bottom lip, down the center of her chin. Her colorful scarf, weighted with beaded wooden slats to cover her long braids, moved in a graceful, feminine rhythm as she bent her head to work, squeezing the bag of goat's milk curds as she spoke.

"My father was long-boned, dark, and narrow as a cage. The Tuareg men of my valley were like him, tall and lean. He had a sharp narrow nose," she described this maternal grandfather to Zechar, "and thin, hard lips. He was a fearless horseman, like all the Tuareg men, and a raider," she said with pride. "My father carried a rifle, a curved dagger, and a long straight sword."

Her hands took up the cooking knife, and she cut food for her son to eat. "I remember the Awashe. It was a time of feasting and of song. My mother served the men of our village wild boar's meat, and fig brandy. Our men claimed Islam as their faith, but they did not always remember the laws of their religion. Some still heard the voices of our ancient gods. Our women would dance, their voices rising to a piercing cry, their many-colored robes whirling to the sound of the drums and singing." Itto moved in quick steps, as though the music were still there.

"Through the day and into the night, my father and the other men would shoot their long guns into the sky, and ride their swift horses across the valley, showing the fine harnesses and shining collars of their stallions." She clapped her hands to her face, remembering. "My father's was the finest of them all."

"What of Haroun M'Hand's gun, dagger, and sword?" the boy asked. "Did my grandfather use these, too?"

"I cannot tell you if my father killed any man," Itto said in a still, calm voice, "but it may be so. He was of the old way, not tamed by any government or power. He was Imazighan," she said the Berber word for freeman, the only name the Berber people called themselves.

"You are like him, little bird," she said to the six-year-old Zechar. "You were born in the year after the death time of man, when all the world lay dying. You were the only infant of our village to live that year, to survive the sickness. Your father, Nuri, died when you had survived two winters. He was stronger than the others, and lived long enough to give you life."

"But, my father died, too," said Zechar.

"Yes." Itto stared into the eyes of her son. "I saw him begin to grieve for the people who were no more, and I knew his spirit would soon leave his body."

Itto put the food she had prepared before her son: goat's meat with its savory fat sizzling in a seared crust, a platter of thinly sliced cucumber, watermelon, onion, and a bowl of rich yoghurt. To this, she added three round wheels of flatbread, and a large cup of hot, treacly mint tea.

The young Zechar waited while his mother took up her place at the weaving loom. Wool from the mountain sheep was twisted into thin strands and tied to nails at the top and bottom crossbars, forming the warp. His mother's quick-moving fingers pushed her wooden shuttle through and between these strands, slowly building the fabric of a finished cloth. His mother's weaving was the work she did at night, when she and Zechar waited for the morning in the pressed-earth house, with only the sound of the fire to fill the silences between them.

"I am of my father's tribe," Itto told her son. She didn't look up from the work of her hands, but spoke clearly. "I will not grieve for the ones who are lost to me; may they be in Paradise," she said gently. "You need not fear losing your mother, too, my son. I will not let my spirit lift from me until the time you are old enough to carry your father's rifle, dagger, and sword. On that day, you will be a man."

For the next twelve years, Zechar lived with his mother in the hill camp beside the Dadès River. The water was the color of green ice, clear to the gravel bed beneath, but flowing with the verdant blush of life, the green of grass and forest. Zechar and Itto worked the ground with hoe and spade, using the strength of their arms and backs, disdaining in the Berber way, the lesser labor of a donkey and plow. They planted in the first thaw of spring, and opened the long rows of *targas,* or irrigation channels, to water the fields of wheat and barley.

Together, they drove the sheep and goats to each

of the rich meadows which formed the valley. They remained as shepherds with their flock, guarding the young lambs and kids from the mountain cat, and packs of wild dog. Their life was simple. They lived beneath the open sky, and each night Itto named the stars of heaven for her son, calling on the ancient memory of her people. She pointed to the ones they called the Female Camel, and the Great Bear. These led the way to the Pole Star. Every moment they were together, she taught him something, as if she knew there would not be enough time.

"The sky is the foundation, the ground of the next world," she explained to her son.

He lay on his back, staring at the heavens. "The sky is beautiful," he argued.

Itto nodded. "If it is so beautiful, and only the ground of the next world, what must the heaven of that place be?"

Because of his mother's teachings, Zechar learned to see things clearly, without a blind of forced beliefs or customs to conceal his understanding of the truth. Itto did not teach her son the ways of her husband's faith, Islam. Instead, she sent Zechar on small journeys into the desert, there to find the new religion she was sure awaited him.

The isolation of their home didn't seem so strange to him. It was all he had ever known. He was a part of nature and the animals with which he lived, just as the Berber people had always been. Isolated from the earliest times, by mountain and by desert, the Arab name for the Berber

228

homeland had always been, Jazirat al Maghrib, the island of the west. The green valleys rising from the desert were islands in the great sea of the Sahara.

For all the years of his childhood, Zechar and Itto found a way of life in this small home. In all that time, no traveler found his way through the cut in the High Atlas Mountains. They remained alone, the boy and his mother.

"I have heard of men called *soufis*," Itto told Zechar on one morning in his sixteenth year. She said it as though they had been talking of such a thing many times before. "These men are the mystics of the desert," she answered Zechar's curious stare. "Once, they lived in isolated monasteries, wore long woolen robes called *soufs,* and had *baraka,* the God-given power to perform miracles. If any of these holy ones have lived," she said, "it may be that you will find them."

Without further explanation, she shaved her son's head, gave him his father's rifle, dagger, and sword, and sent him into the emptiness of the Sahara where religious thought was purified, to become such a visionary.

Chapter Twenty-eight

In Arabic the name for desert is Sahra. It is the only name for this land. The rolling dunes are called an *erg,* or sea of sand. Like the sea, a man could drown in them.

It is an Arab saying which declares that Allah has made the Sahara stark and harsh, so that He might find one place on Earth to walk alone in peace. Berbers know this is not true. The broken land was made for them. They are the people of the desert sea.

Zechar had girded his face and head from the harsh glare of the afternoon sun. He peered through an eyeslit in the indigo head veil, a cloth of five yards long, wound around his head to protect him from the blowing sand, and from spirits which might enter a man's soul through the unprotected openings of his mouth and nose.

He stopped beside the clean pool of a *guelta,* knelt and brushed aside the green surface scum. Tiny red larvae danced like specks of brilliant fire in the water. He pulled the veil below his mouth, cupped his hands and drank.

In the distance, a stretch of gravel plain, or *reg,* fanned out below the mountain range. Once, a river had run its course across this ground. Now, this broad band of wide, flat earth was all that remained of that channel of rushing water and grinding rock. A lone sandstone pinnacle stood like an accusing finger pointing to the sky. The great *reg* was vast and unshadowed, burnished to a patina of white-gold beneath the endless furnace of the desert sun.

Zechar lowered the goatskin water bag from his shoulder and dipped it into the cool water of the pool. The bag swelled, filling into a tight, rounded pouch. This, Zechar slung back over his shoulder, feeling the wet touch of the bag dripping against his arm and side.

He had counted one complete turning of the moon since the day he left his childhood and his mother's house. In all that time, he had seen no one. The wind was his companion. The shifting dunes were the villages of this land, and empty space was the silence of the desert.

Beneath a slate-colored sky of late afternoon, he walked the hard beauty of the *reg*. The ground was hot under his sandaled feet. It fought against him with each step, yielding nothing. The first stars of evening pierced the brooding sky, and the thin curve of a crescent moon hung on the heaven's last ephemeral light.

Across a small dry wadi, he saw the red leather tent.

Zechar's feet raced the dark. With only a thin, curved line of moon to guide him on this path, he would soon lose sight of the tent until dawn. This was the first tent he had seen, the first people.

231

His sandals broke the brittle ground into cracks, and his breath was a sounding force, like the hollow wind. He ran hard, coming to a sudden stop before the tent dyed with the clay of red earth.

The man sat on a wool rug before the wide, square tent. A long goat's hair robe swathed his crossed legs and draped in folds onto the blues and yellows of the worked rectangular throw. His hair and face were shrouded in the winding cloth of a white muslin head veil. The sweet scent of hashish rose in a puff of smoke from the kif pipe, whose stem disappeared into the loose bands of the face cloth.

"Salaam aleykum," Zechar offered.

"Aleykum salaam."

The man motioned Zechar to sit beside him on the rug. "You are welcome, stranger. Rest before my tent. You walk the desert alone?"

Zechar noticed the hazel eyes of the Tuareg, cautious and searching. He looked only at them as he answered. "I am of the Gued'oula tribe, from the hill camp by the Dadès River valley. I came to the desert to find my understanding."

The Tuareg nodded. "May Allah who sees all, enlighten you. Are there no others of your people to walk this journey with you?"

"I am alone."

The Tuareg stood, and it was then that Zechar noticed that the man was over six feet tall. A long sword encased in a red leather scabbard hung from his waist. His hand was on the hilt of that sword, and had been, Zechar realized, from the moment a stranger had approached his tent.

Instinctively, Zechar's hand reached for the hilt of his own sword. He had rushed to this place, he realized too late, with the wisdom of a fool. The two men watched each other's eyes, wary and distrustful.

"You will be hungry and thirsty after so long a journey." The Tuareg let his hand drop from the sword hilt, lifted the grass-matting wind flap, and disappeared into the tent.

Zechar waited, watching the Sahara night close in around him, and feeling a sense of peace descend with the cooling dark. The soles of his feet began to ache, complaining of every step they had traveled. His body seemed to sag in upon itself, and a tiredness wrapped around him like a winding cloth of the dead. Letting the slow weights of exhaustion take him, his eyes began to close.

The soft whoosh of the grass matting pulled him from the opiate of sleep. He turned his head toward the sound and saw a young woman. Her face was unveiled, in the open manner of Berber women. In her hands was a wooden bowl of goat's milk. Without speaking, she knelt and put the bowl before him.

Her eyes were dark mirrors outlined in black, shining medallions against the paler planes of her face. These eyes looked at him directly, and spoke in that instant of an untamed spirit caught beneath the passive rivers of her soul. She wore a headdress of braided wool, its bright colors spilling down her cheeks and onto her shoulders. Her thick, dark hair was twisted into loose coils beneath the beaded covering, clasped and held as if

233

by twined fingers . . . and beautiful. *She* was beautiful.

"I am Moussa ag Hamadi," said the nomad, reappearing from his tent. "This woman is my daughter, Rhissa."

"I am Zechar al Maghrib." He had spoken before thinking, casting aside his father's name and calling himself after the island of the west. This act of new allegiance surprised Zechar, but he made no effort to correct it.

The woman's eyes didn't meet Zechar's again. Before her father's stern gaze, she became as smooth of all interest in him as the goat's milk.

Hamadi spoke a few quick words to her and she left them. "Remain with us tonight," he said to Zechar. "My daughter prepares a meal."

Rhissa ag Hamadi built a cooking fire. The two men sat in amiable silence before the small light of that blaze. Zechar watched the woman slip chunks of goat meat and onion onto long, thin skewers and set them between two rocks, over the open flames. The smell of the roasting meat, its rich fat spattering and sizzling on the fire, made him know how hungry he was.

They ate millet porridge, goat meat, and crisped onions. The men sipped hot tea from tiny glasses. In the distance, a fennec fox yipped, and beside the fire a camel-spider raced across the sand, waving its menacing palps. The woman left them, going back into the tent.

Zechar had not known the need for any woman, had not known this one existed, but now his desire for her was as powerful as the night, as powerful

234

as the purpose of his journey across the desert. His eyes stared at the grass matting of the tent flap.

When the fire died low, Hamadi spoke in the quiet of that sound. "Allah who knows the innocence or guilt of a man's heart has sent you to me. He has brought you out of the mountain valley to this lonely place—to us. I put my trust in the One Who Gives Breath To The Desert Wind. Stay with us for a time, Zechar al Maghrib. You are welcome here."

Two full moons passed in the time Zechar spent in the camp of Hamadi and his daughter. With them, he lived the life of the desert nomad. During the days, he rode out with Hamadi on the backs of groaning camels and found new places of greenery to pasture the herds of goats and sheep. In the late afternoons, he helped Rhissa gather firewood from the brush and thorn trees growing near the small oasis of the well. He lent the strength of his back to tilling the small garden of watermelon and onions, and to building a brush fence around the vegetation to keep out the goats.

Each morning and each night, he and Hamadi took the four camels out to feed upon the leaves of the acacia trees and drink their fill of water. Zechar sat on the narrow saddle, and with a cry and a slap of the reins, urged the obstinate animal to its feet. The hind legs rose, throwing Zechar forward against the pommel, then the forelegs stood and he was pitched in a nauseating up-and-down motion across the dunes of undulating sand to the well.

While Hamadi sat in the shade of the wadi, Zechar drew the leather bucket from the well and poured water into an enamel bowl. The camels drank as fast as he could pour. When at last the small herd had drunk its fill, they wandered away to taste the green buds of the acacia trees. Then, Zechar began hauling the water for the sheep, and the goats. Twice a day, his back ached with the exhausting labor of this act.

Twice during the many days he was with them, Zechar and Hamadi hunted gazelle, chasing the fast-moving creatures from the backs of their camels until the gazelle tired and were easily speared. Hamadi's eyes were beryl jewels, green and bright with the excitement of the chase.

"Allah has given me a son," he said, reaching across the space between them and touching Zechar's shoulder with a broad, firm hand. "You are Imazighan," he said the Berber word for freeman, "like me."

On these nights, when the rich meat filled their hunger, Rhissa's eyes would linger on him, and she laughed in unguarded happiness at his stories and his smiles. She never spoke of the day when he would leave them, but he thought of it often.

In the long evenings, Hamadi questioned him about the world beyond the desert. "Have you seen people in the cities? What do you know about the sickness? Is it finished, at last?"

To all these questions, Zechar could only answer, "Coming here, I passed no one between this

236

tent and the mountains of my home. The cities are empty vaults. If the sickness still lives, I have seen nothing of it."

On one such night, he could see the pupils of Hamadi's eyes staring at him like darker islands within a dark sea. "My wife is no more. My children, but for Rhissa, are no more," said the Tuareg. "Our people were once as many as the wild Barbary sheep. Like those untamed sheep, we drew our strength and our lives from this desert. Now," he said, turning away from Zechar and looking into the endless black, "the cry of a night bird has filled this place."

Zechar knew from his mother's stories that the cry of a night bird meant an evil spirit. But, the Sahara didn't feel that way to him. It felt like newly fired land, swept clean of evil. He felt as if each step he traveled was a claim to this inheritance, this birthright. The Sahara was his home, and his destiny.

"You will leave us soon, is it not so?"

Zechar could find no way of denying the truth. "There is something more which awaits me."

The nomad made a small noise deep in his throat, a resignation to the unalterable hand of fate. "You did not find this tent by chance," Hamadi turned back to face Zechar. "You were led to us."

Zechar could not argue this. It seemed the same to him.

"What will become of my daughter when you have gone? What awaits her in this place?"

The thought had come to Zechar, too. He knew

that Rhissa had come to like him. Her easy smiles and laughter told him that much. And something else . . . there was a kindling of need between them. It burned steadily and grew brighter with each passing day, each night. Thoughts of her had dimmed that other fire, the vision which had led him to the desert.

"You have become one who is as a son to me," said Hamadi, "and brought joy into the stillness of my life, a peace I had thought never to find again. My daughter would keep you with her. I would have you live among us. You must choose, Zechar. Stay here and claim my daughter Rhissa as your wife, and the pastures of my land as your home. Or, go into the desert alone."

He thought of his mother in the pressed-earth house at the base of the mountain. Was she wondering what had happened to him? Had it been her dream, or his?—this journey of understanding. For Zechar, to find a life in this place, with these two people, was enough. The *soufi* mystics of the desert—if there were such men—could be found in years to come.

"Here, I will remain," Zechar answered. "I will be your son, husband of your daughter, from this day forward."

"Through you will be the beginning of a great family. I had believed my line would die with me," said Hamadi, "that all who had gone before would end on this desert. Yet, even here you have come to us. Truly, Allah has granted me peace."

Hamadi stood and called Rhissa to come to him. "Will you have this man?" he asked. "I

238

would not give you to any husband, against your will. Do you like him well enough? Will you agree?"

Zechar watched her face. She wouldn't look at him, or her father, but stared into the flames. "I like him well," she said softly, "and will agree." Her answer given, she stepped back into the tent.

The two men sat again for a time, each silent in their thoughts. At last, the Tuareg rose to his feet and said in too loud a voice, "I will not return this night." Hamadi then strode out into the endless black beyond the light of the fire, and was gone.

Zechar waited in the shell of night which remained. A sense of loneliness hollowed the air around him, as if he, and only he, were there in the desert. Hamadi's words had brushed against the deaths of mankind. Zechar had been born during that time, and had been spared. But, he was alone.

He thought of Hamadi, and also of his mother, Itto. They were the last of those from another age. They remembered. Zechar couldn't remember what he had never known. The past was locked away from him, a time when the world was far different from the one he knew today. The memories of that time . . . in his mother's words . . . in Hamadi's eyes . . . they were stories to Zechar. Not real. Not of the world he knew.

He sat before the blind of dark until the fire had burned low, then rose and went into the tent.

Zechar held the tent flap open, the amber light from the dying fire cast a near-liquid glow on the woman's skin. She was bare to the waist, and as he stood looking at her, she dropped the white muslin skirt to her ankles, and held out her arms . . . to him.

Chapter Twenty-nine

June 21, 2018: We are eighteen, living within the protective walls of Biosphere Seven. I carry a new child into the hope of existence, but have lost two children this year — Matthew, and Cameron. Cathe has lost her daughter, Sidra. We are eighteen.

Cameron still lives among the Outsiders. The children within the sphere talk of nothing else. Each day, the first question they ask is, "How is Cameron?" Their hopes have been quickened by his act, and they wonder when they might try this same method of gaining immunity.

I wait. How long before we know for sure? How long until I can look at my son and not ask myself — Is this the last time I will see him alive?

Sidra's survival is another case. We believe it is because her father is Josiah Gray Wolf that she hasn't become ill with the virus. If Josiah has a genetic protection from the sickness, it may be that he has passed this gene on to his daughter. None of us can be sure.

I tell myself it is possible that the virus has mutated to a slower contagion period, or has somehow ended. I want to believe this, especially now, but I am afraid to hope. Until I am sure, I can't risk more of our children to this still unproved speculation. We will wait, Biosphere Seven and I, until enough time has passed that we can be certain it is safe to go out.

I think of it, too. Returning to the Earth outside the sphere is a hope none of us have been able to completely bury. It is a part of us, that bonding with the land, our home. I wonder if the child I bring to life will ever walk beyond these walls of glass. Will it, like Cameron, be a citizen of Earth—or of Biosphere Seven?

Jessica saved the file and exited the journal. She knew she had not recovered from Cameron leaving the sphere. Would never recover. The thought dwelled with her, like the growing child within her body. It was a constant awareness, as though she had three hearts: one beating below her breast, and one beating in her son, and one in the child she carried. She knew the cadence of them all.

In his way, it was Trinity who had been her salvation. It was he who sat beside her in those first days after Cameron and Sidra left the sphere. It was Trinity who took on the function of leading the people in her stead. Not Quinn. Like her, Quinn had foundered. Cameron was his only son, now lost to him forever.

She and Quinn each hurt too much, and hadn't

found a way to comfort one another. She had told him of her pregnancy, but not whose child it was she carried. He hadn't asked. His silence was as telling as his accusation would have been; it said he didn't care.

Jessica pushed her chair back from the console, concentrating on the effort it would take to rise from this comfortable place. She felt as if there were no energy left in her . . . that even the small exertion of lifting her body from the chair was too great. What did it matter? What did *she* matter?

A knock sounded at the door of her room and Trinity came in without waiting for her answer. He looked so young and strong, light shining in his redblond hair. *Like his mother,* Jessica thought. The quick image of Maggie Adair flooded the space between them like a rush of color and sense. He had always been Maggie's son—not Jessica's. But she loved him. And he was her strength now. He cared for Jessica, as she had once cared for him. That was the link between them, not one of mother and son, but one of caretaker.

"I think you'd better come with me. Somebody's got to talk some sense into Diana."

Jessica didn't move. She smiled at the incongruity of the thought. "Diana doesn't listen to me. Never has. What's she plotting now? A coup?"

"You're not far wrong," said Trinity. "She's got some wild notion about Cameron's transfusion . . ." he hesitated before going on, "and about something else. She says there's some lab supplies missing, sterile bags, tubing, and other provisions that might have been used for the purposes of artificial insemination."

Jessica felt the muscles of her chest wall constrict, squeezing like a closing fist. It was hard to breathe. *How could Diana know?* It had to be more than the missing supplies. *How had she found out?*

"I'll talk to her." She stood up, ready to go with him.

"Mother . . ." Trinity took her arm, turning her to face him. His eyes were the same deep blue as that of the planet when seen from space. They looked at her now, as if searching for a truth he couldn't see.

"We live in this separate place, Trinity, but we're not all the same, even those born into the world of Biosphere Seven." She tried to put so many thoughts into what she was explaining to him. He needed to understand. He was the future. If she could give him her own knowledge . . . now, before the worse times came, it might help.

"It's wrong to think of ourselves as a separate people. Some of us want to believe that being a part of this place makes us more important than those beyond these walls. Some of us fear the Outsiders. We're all simply human," she told him. "Remember that."

What else was there? That she was sorry? She wasn't. That she'd been wrong to risk it? Yes, perhaps. But a child grew in her, a child who might bring them out of their confined existence in this Eden. A child who by its blood might set them free.

"Come with me," she held out her hand to Trinity. "You might as well hear about this now."

Together, they left the peaceful setting of the habitat wing and walked in fertile silence toward

244

Diana's lab.

It had been four full days since they'd crossed the Colorado River into Texas. Seth read out the words etched into a road marker of rough granite, "State of Texas. We're still here," he told his brother, "wherever here is."

"Big place," Jonathan observed.

"Nice country," said Seth. "Good grassland, water, cattle. A man could live here."

Jonathan twisted back in the saddle. "You got a home, Seth. Up north. Remember?"

"I know. I just meant it's peaceful here, that's all. We don't have cattle like that up north." He leaned back and hooked his leg around the saddle horn, staring at a bull in the pasture. "Look at the size of the horns on him . . . a man could stretch out full length, tip to tip. He's something, that one."

"And mean," Jonathan reminded him. "Remember how a bull like that one came rushing at us when we crossed the river? Wanted to knock you onto the ground and gore you with those horns you admire so much. Would have done it, too, if the black hadn't been watching him and struck out in the other direction. Not too smart, your bull."

"He's smart as he needs to be. He's wild, Jonathan, like all cattle used to be. They never tamed up, his kind. How smart is that? All this time," Seth kept admiring the bull, "people putting fences around cattle, making them soft, gentle. Not him. He never broke."

"Don't taste half good," said Jonathan, "that's why." They had slaughtered a young bull three days

245

back, and the meat had been as stringy and dry as brown rope.

"The cattle at home have more fat on them," said Seth. "They're lazy, never have to go far to find a valley of sweet grass or clean water. They'd die in this dry place. But look at that one. He makes this land feed him. He's tough."

"To eat." This was far as Jonathan would budge. "You through staring at him? Maybe we could ride on now?"

They rode on until the sky began to bleed red-orange, then drew up beside a creek and set about making camp for the night. Deadwood was plentiful. A recent storm had cracked branches from the scattering of trees and cast them neatly in clumps that were easy to gather. Jonathan had a fire laid high and sparking licks of yellow flames before twilight.

A good aim with a river rock had earned them a supper of game hen. Stretching the bird between two forked branches over the fire, they settled back to watch the stars come up and wait for their first taste of chicken in a long while.

Jonathan kicked at a branch, sending a shower of hissing copper embers into the dark pearl of night. "You think that naked man knew what he was talking about? I mean, about this glass city we're searching for?"

Seth eyed him soberly over the roasting meat. "We found Texas, didn't we? He set us tracking this way, and we're here. If he said there's a glass city, I expect to see one. And he has a name—T. J. Parker. I don't think he'd thank you for calling him 'that naked man,' like he wasn't human or something."

Jonathan turned the chicken over, laying it quickly back on the forked branches and sucking his fingers to ease the burn. "Humans might come into this world naked, but if they've got any sense they don't stay that way."

"What made you think of him, anyhow?"

It was hard putting his thoughts together into words. He'd been feeling it coming on, like a wind rushing at him. Getting stronger with each day. "If he's right, we'll find people there. The way he was talking, there might be a lot of them."

"That's what we came to find," said Seth.

"I know that. It's just . . ."

"Just what?"

He didn't want his brother to laugh, not at this. He pulled the roasted chicken off the forked sticks and laid it on a rock to cool. "Seems like we're headed for something, Seth. You know how it gets before a storm?"

Seth dipped his head a time or two in a nod.

"That's how it feels to me . . . like that shimmer in the air before lightning strikes. It's been staying on me like a mist that won't slick dry. And I keep wondering, what is it we're heading for?"

Seth shifted and reached for the chicken. He cut himself a hunk of white meat and dropped a piece of it into his mouth, chewing fast to keep it from burning his tongue. "I've never been able to tell what day the snows are going to melt, or when the sun will start breaking up the ice on the river. It happens when it's ready. I guess we'll know what we're heading to," Seth told him, tearing off another bite, "soon as we get there."

Jonathan twisted off a rounded leg and sucked

the tender meat off the bone. He could see it Seth's way, if he tried. But no matter what words Seth put to it, the feeling was still the same. They were coming to something . . . good or bad, he didn't know. The sense of it was shuddering through him, and he felt it getting stronger every day.

"We came here looking for this, didn't we Jonathan? To find people, that's what brought us across those mountains and rivers, to this land. People. I couldn't turn back now. Could you?"

It wasn't an easy thing to answer. *Could he?* He could, and maybe even wanted to. *But, should they?* That was a winter river locked with ice. The answer was froze up, like that river, but would be there when the time came.

"We'll keep going," he said. "We've come this far; we'll see it through."

Seth stretched out beside the fire. "We've seen a lot coming here—a river I nearly drowned in, T. J. Parker, that Texas bull today. I don't believe it's all for nothing, Jonathan. I think we're heading where we're meant to go."

Jonathan eased onto his back and stared up at the stars. The sky was a river and they were rocks rolling downstream. He couldn't see the end or the beginning, but he guessed he'd know it when they got there.

Listening to a rustling of soft wind blowing through the leaves on the trees, he closed his eyes and gave himself over to exhausted sleep.

Chapter Thirty

Diana Hunt glared at Jessica from across the lab tables. She had once been a beautiful woman, thought Jessica, but now there was a hardness to her eyes and mouth, and a thin, brittle look to her body. She had become much too thin.

When did this happen? Jessica tried not to stare, but the woman's gauntness was disturbing. The thought wouldn't go away. *Something's gravely wrong with her.*

"Did you think you could get away with this new scheme without anyone noticing?" Diana rested her hands palms down on the table. She leaned forward, supporting her weight against it. Her face was paler than normal and there were deep circles under her eyes.

God help her, thought Jessica, suddenly sure. She's in the final stage of cancer or something else equally terminal. An alarm was ringing in Jessica's head. Did Diana know? Jessica couldn't concentrate on what the woman was saying, or on the venom Diana was trying so hard to inflict. Her mind was fixed on the fact that without any doubt, Diana Hunt was dying.

Trinity seemed unmoved by Diana's appearance.

"Why don't you tell us what you're imagining, Diana."

Can't he see how sick she is? thought Jessica. *Or, am I the last one to have noticed?* A sting of guilt came with that realization. She was the leader of the team, but she had put aside her responsibilities to them and concentrated only on her own needs. She hadn't really *seen* Diana. What else had gone unnoticed?

"Whose child are you carrying, Jessica? Is it Brad's?"

"You're crazy!" shouted Trinity, his face turning red with anger. "Is that what you're accusing her of? You sit here in this witch's lab, dreaming up things to hurt people . . . My mother's too old to be pregnant."

"She's not your mother, and she's not too old." Diana's dark eyes were busy spiders dancing over a thickening web. "Tell him how you risked the life of everyone in the sphere to have Brad's child. It's true, isn't it? Tell him!"

"I've heard enough of this," said Trinity, turning to go.

"Wait," Jessica stopped him. "You need to know the truth. I am pregnant, and it is Brad's child."

"What . . . ?" He stared at her in disbelief. "Brad's child? Have you both gone crazy?" he asked, staring in turn at first one, and then the other woman. "He's an Outsider. And you," he said to Jessica, "you must be in your fifties. It isn't possible."

Diana's hard laugh mocked him. "Obviously, it is."

Jessica touched his arm. He pulled back as if

250

she were a fire—and could burn him. "Why? What have you done?"

"Trinity, I—"

"You and Cameron, both of you were willing to risk all of us for yourselves. For what you wanted! You could have brought in the virus. You could have killed us all. Why? For another child?"

"For Brad's child," Diana corrected him. "She did this secretly, putting her desire to bear her husband a child above everything. She shouldn't be leader—a person like that—she shouldn't be leader anymore."

Trinity was glaring at Jessica, a look of shame and outrage in his eyes.

"It wasn't the way Diana said. I did it for all of you," Jessica tried to explain. "Not for myself. I did it to save the children of our world. We can't go on losing them. They'll leave us. Cameron and Sidra proved that. I had to do something, and the danger was too great to allow the other women to take the risk. I did it for everyone in the bio-sphere."

"Liar!" cried Diana. A paroxysm of unremitting coughing seized her. Her neck and face darkened, purpled with lack of air. Still the strangled coughing tore at her thin frame. A froth of blood spattered over her lips and chin. She dropped to her knees and folded onto the floor.

Jessica hurried past the lab tables to the stricken woman. "Diana . . . Come on, Diana. Breathe." She struck her sharply between the shoulder blades. "Breathe!" Diana's eyes were open, but she wasn't making any sound. Jessica saw all struggle and awareness go out of the dark, spider eyes. The wasted body caved in upon itself, and in that instant, Diana Hunt was gone from them.

Jessica glanced at Trinity; he was fixed in place, staring in shock. "Help me," she called to him.

Diana had stopped struggling. There was neither breath, nor pulse. Jessica started breathing into Diana's mouth, beginning CPR.

"Okay, I'm here," said Trinity, suddenly beside Jessica, and took over the chest compression.

Together, they worked on trying to save Diana's life until Jessica couldn't breathe for her any longer. She collapsed onto the floor next to Diana, crying tears of exhaustion and defeat.

"It's not your fault," Trinity tried to comfort her. "You did all you could. We both did."

But Jessica wouldn't be comforted. "Look at her. Her body's ravaged with disease. How long has she been sick, Trinity?"

He didn't answer.

"How long?"

"The last four or five months, I guess. That's what Alix and Lara told me. Her daughters had been taking care of her. She had them. It wasn't as if she was alone."

"I never noticed," Jessica reproached herself. "I'm supposed to be a leader to these people—all of them, not just those I like—and I wasn't there for her. She was right about that. I haven't been there for anyone—not for a long time."

Trinity helped Jessica to her feet. "I said a lot of things tonight. It was a shock, finding out about the baby. About Brad. I still can't believe it."

"Trinity—"

252

"Wait. Please . . . let me finish." He started to speak, stopped, then started again. "What Diana said, that's between us. It won't leave this room."

"You believe me?" Jessica needed to hear his answer.

"I believe *in* you. The rest doesn't matter."

It wasn't what she wanted to hear, but she had to accept it.

"Does Dad know about the baby?"

"Yes."

"Does he know it's Brad's?"

"No."

Trinity looked wounded, as if trusting anyone had become too painful.

"I didn't lie to him, Trin. He didn't ask. I think because of Cameron. He's hurting too much to ask the right questions."

Trinity let go of her arm and stepped away. "I won't be the one to tell him."

They left the lab together. The others had to be told about Diana's death. Her daughters had to be comforted. Jessica did that.

She held each of Diana's three daughters in her arms and said, "I'm sorry. I'm so very sorry."

That night, when she lay beside Quinn in the stillness that pretended to be sleep, she felt the first movement of the baby in her womb.

It was into the first hours of morning when Trinity heard the soft scratching on his door. He hadn't been asleep. The night was too warm, and his thoughts too clouded to allow the peace of sleep to claim him.

"Who's there?" he called from the bed.

The silence held no answer. The scratching came again, and for one irrational moment he was afraid it was Diana, come back from the dead to rake her nails across his face. His hand hesitated on the lock, then turned the knob and pulled the door open.

"Cassi. What are you doing here?"

She didn't speak. Cassi never spoke. Sometimes Trinity wished that he could be like that—hold all his thoughts inside, never share them with anyone.

"You'd better come in." He stepped back to make an open space of the doorway. "I'll fix us a cup of tea. Would you like that?"

She nodded.

He closed the door and let her wander around his quarters while he boiled water for the tea. She picked up things, put them down, and picked them up again. He watched her move from object to object, touching the surface of everything, lingering at chairs, table, and bed.

He poured the hot water over fresh tea leaves in the diffuser. He liked the old brown earthenware teapot. It was one of the things that had belonged to his mother. Somehow, using it made him feel closer to her. He set it on a wooden tray with two mugs and a jug of goat's milk.

When he came back from the apartment's small utility kitchen, Cassi was sitting in the middle of his bed.

He rested the wooden tray between them and sat down beside her. "Do you like milk in your tea?" He picked up the jug of milk, but she lifted her mug, holding it away from him. "Okay, okay." He

254

laughed. "No milk. I don't like the stuff, either." He touched her hand and she lowered the mug, allowing him to pour out the hot brew.

She was fragile-looking, with an innocent's face, wistful blue eyes, and a sleek mass of shoulder length, dark hair. Her cupped hands held the mug to her lips, sipping and blowing on the steaming drink.

"I'm sorry about your mother."

Trinity didn't know what else to say to her. Of course, he imagined that she must be upset by the day's events, but she didn't seem to be. Her behavior seemed casual to the point of peculiar. But then, like everyone else within the sphere, Trinity knew Cassi wasn't exactly normal. She didn't speak, and that was enough of a problem to deal with, but she didn't seem to understand things, either. He couldn't help but wonder about her. *Does she even understand that Diana's dead?*

She looked so alone. The orphan in him was moved to pity for her. He didn't try to talk anymore. Instead, he sat on the bed and waited while she drank the mug of tea. When she was finished, he loaded the teapot, creamer, and mugs back on the tray and carried them into the kitchen.

In the moment that he was gone, she changed. Her eyes had rounded with tears, and the silence of the sobs which shook her shoulders broke his heart.

"Oh, Cassi." The hurt he felt for her was too strong to be put aside. He sat down again beside her on the bed, his back leaning flat against the wall, and held open his arms. "Come here, Cassi. It's all right. Come here."

255

Like a child, she curled into the space his arms made, and let herself be comforted. In time, her breathing slowed to a gentle rise and fall against his chest. She slept. He watched over her through the night, holding back all danger of any hurt until dawn.

Chapter Thirty-one

They followed the Colorado River deeper into the summer heat of Texas. The grassland was a gold-green, fast turning brown. The horses' necks hung low, and the sound of their hooves *plop-plopped* in the cooling water. Nothing moved on the air. The day was brass-bright and parched as baked clay. The water deepened, and they moved up on the bank.

"Watch yourself!" called Jonathan. "There's a hole up ahead. I'd swing around it if I were you."

Seth hadn't noticed the bowl-sized sink until then. He reined the black to the left, higher up the riverbank, and looked down on the basin as he passed it.

"You've got a good sense for trouble," said Seth. "There's a copperhead in that hole with a body thick around as my fist."

Jonathan didn't look at it as he passed. "You need to give a better glance at where you're going—not let that horse do all the looking for you. He's a skittish animal, anyhow. Probably would've stomped it. Snake might've bit him, and you. Can't trust the judgement of a skittish horse."

Seth thought that through and said in his horse's

defense, "He got me this far. I guess he'll do."

They had been climbing all day, the ground rising at an angle and facing them into the sun. The glare on the water hurt Seth's eyes. It was crack-glazed, like the sky. *Too bright,* he thought. *Too hot. Too far.*

When the river forked, they took the smaller branch, just as T. J. Parker had told them to do. He'd called this branch of the river the Ware, and said it would lead them to the Outsiders. They followed it all that day.

There was plentiful game on the land. The Texas cattle dominated whatever grassland they entered, but Seth also saw pronghorn antelope, a few elk, hare, wild turkey, and barnyard fowl that had been turned loose and managed to survive. There were fish in the river, and quail perched in the trees overhead.

"A man could live in country like this," Seth said as much to himself as to Jonathan.

"A life like that naked man up north?" Jonathan didn't look at Seth when he spoke, but kept his eyes on the rise ahead of them. "You'd be alone, don't forget."

Seth wouldn't let his enthusiasm for the place be put down. "If there are people in the biosphere, I wouldn't. Parker said people lived there."

Jonathan did turn and look at Seth now. "Parker talked to his dead wife and children, too. I wouldn't put much trust in what a naked man living in a cave tells you."

But Seth *did* put his trust in Parker's story. He had thought of little else since that day. A city made of glass, and a camp of Outsiders living by the Ware River. It was coming true, all of it. He couldn't understand why Jonathan wouldn't see it. It was as if he'd closed his mind to what was happening. They'd made it to Texas, they were on the Ware River, and they *would* find the place called Biosphere Seven.

"I've been thinking about home," said Jonathan. He rode abreast with Seth, his body sitting easy in the saddle and his eyes searching the trail ahead. "I've been thinking maybe we ought to go back."

"Go back . . . ?" He couldn't believe Jonathan had said it. "After we've come this far? You want to turn around right before we get to where we've been heading to for so long, and go back?" It made no sense. Why was Jonathan fighting him? Why now? "What's the matter with you? You're acting more skittish than my horse ever did. Are you scared of meeting people, Jonathan? Is that it?"

His brother's arm swung out and connected with Seth's head, knocking him off his horse. Seth hung for a sickening moment at a sideways tilt, then felt himself catching air until the ground hit him. His shoulder landed first, then the wind got knocked out of him. For a terrible moment he couldn't breathe. He was staring up at the sky, gasping like a bird dropped from its nest.

Overhead, he could see Jonathan still sitting the chestnut mare. He didn't get down from the horse or try to help. He just sat there watching. "I'm not scared . . . not of people, and not of you. Remember that."

A whistle of air came piping in, and for a time, all Seth could do was lie there and let breath come back to his body. *Funny,* he thought, *how pretty the sky looks when you're down here just try-*

ing to breathe. And the underside of the leaves on the trees. And the birds . . . He heard birds singing. No, that was his chest trilling like a warbler.

When the air quit making that sound, he still stayed put. It was nice where he was, and he had no need to get back onto that horse. Jonathan had made himself scarce, riding up ahead a ways. Seth didn't care. He just lay flat on his back and let the sky and trees surround him. He might never move again.

He had no way of reckoning real time, but it seemed like a long while since Jonathan had left him. He heard the mare's hooves thumping along the soft riverbank, and then Jonathan was down from the horse and standing over him.

"Have I killed you, or what? You ever gonna move from that spot?"

"I like it here fine." Seth tried shifting his legs. They seemed as if they might be able to lift him, but he made no effort to try standing. His back still felt like he'd been hit with a small tree, and his head was aching from its contact with Jonathan's arm.

"It's okay with me. Stay sprawled out like a pole-axed heifer. If you're not interested in seeing the camp I found of those people . . . I'm willing to sit here. It'll keep."

"You found the camp?" Seth jackknifed into sitting up. Then slowly, slowly, he lay back down. His head was leaning heavily toward falling off to meet his toes. If he stayed flat on his back, it might keep hooked onto his neck a little longer. He wasn't going anywhere.

"This looks like as good a place as any," said Jonathan, observing that Seth was still flat out.

"We'll make camp here tonight."

Seth didn't argue.

By morning, Seth could stand. His shoulder was swollen into a tight drumhead where it had met the ground edge on, but his braincase felt as if it might remain fixed to his neck. At least he could walk without falling down. That was an improvement.

"Think we ought to just ride in?" asked Seth.

"You know any other way to do it?" Jonathan brought the horses up from the riverbank, where he had taken them to water.

Seth didn't. It was ride in, or stay put. He saddled the black, stomped out the night's fire and tied his blanket to the back of the saddle. Ready to ride.

Jonathan hadn't made a move. He was leaning, his back against a tree, looking like he might have been planted among the woodland. His arms were crossed over his chest, and he was staring at the ground near his boot toes, paying no mind to Seth.

"You coming?" Seth had to ask him.

"Not sure, yet."

"Not sure? We've been riding our butts off on these horses, risking our lives every day, and you're *not sure*. What's the matter with you, Jonathan?" He could feel a fury building up behind his eyes stinging like hornets. "I don't care what you're thinking. Understand? We came here together, and we're going in that camp together. Hear that?"

"I didn't mean to knock you off your horse." Jonathan's boot toe was digging a trench in the soft, woodsy ground.

Seth had wondered what was coming next. An "I'm sorry" had always been a hard thing to wrench from his brother. As long as Jonathan felt like apologizing, Seth didn't need to hear the words. But he knew Jonathan needed to say them. He kept still and let him get on with it.

"There might have been some truth in what you said . . . 'bout how I feel meeting those people. Women, maybe. You got more gall than I do. It's sitting in me right now, like fat worms crawling in my belly." He gave a soft, embarrassed laugh. "I don't know if I can do it."

Seth stayed where he was, knowing he couldn't get closer than this. His brother was looking like a trapped animal, ready to strike out at anything. "About you hitting me," he started, "I've got a hard head. It'll heal. But don't do it again."

Jonathan smiled at that.

"About the rest," he let all his brother's doubts about himself and women go unsaid, "I'm a year older than you. That might account for something. The way I see it, you got no cause to worry. You've always been the stronger one of the two of us. Nothing's changed."

Jonathan didn't look convinced. "I don't know what to say to women. I saw them. There's more than one young woman in that camp. I watched them for a while. They were drawing water from the river."

Seth could feel his heart shaking at the thought.

"I might have rode up to them right then, but I couldn't. It was like I stood there and froze solid. Couldn't take one step forward."

This was going to take another kind of approach. He had to get around his brother's fear, without calling it that. Seth hadn't expected this—to be so close, and have Jonathan turn nervous on him.

262

"You'd go in with me if we had to fight something, wouldn't you?"

Jonathan raised his head. "You know I would."

"You've got to see this like another kind of fight. Like it was with T. J. Parker. You really mean to send me off into their camp alone? Anything could happen. I don't know those people any better than you do. They might kill me—like Parker tried to do—if I ride in by myself. We're brothers, Jonathan. We watch each other's backs."

He almost had him. He could see a motion in the eyes, a willingness, picking up speed. Jonathan's feet were moving back and forth, ready to jump. "What happens if you find a woman and I don't? Then, do we split up?"

"No. We don't ever split up. We stay together no matter what. That's the way it is now, and that's the way it's going to be." He hadn't thought it through before this moment, but knew that was the right answer.

"Dammit then," said Jonathan, "let's ride. I can't take thinking about this no more." He saddled the mare and swung up into the saddle.

Seth hitched his foot into the stirrup, too.

Together, they rode the last distance of their journey—Jonathan out front breaking the trail, and Seth following his lead.

Cameron stirred from sleep and listened to the sound of birds trilling and chirping from the green-leafed branches of the orange and lemon trees. The thick adobe walls protected them from the already hot Texas morning. Summer was here, in days of shimmering heat and polished-silver skies.

He lingered in this drowsy awakening, and laid

263

his hand on the woman beside him. Sidra murmured from beneath the sweep of shining hair that had fallen over her face. She was still holding to that dark light of sleep. Her body was curled into it.

His hand slid along her bare skin. She lay on her side, facing away from him. He followed the rise up the hill of her hip. The curving line of her body was a foreign and exotic land, and he was the new arrival, anxious to touch upon its boundaries.

He moved closer, the length of his body touching hers. One arm closed around her, and he held the fullness of her breast against his hand. All of her yielded to him, the softness of her body, the scent of her hair, the taste of her skin on his tongue. She was the other half of his nature, the other half of his humanness.

They came together like the air above and the water below, each moving in a smoothing glide over and through the other. She was the rushing river, and he was the shuddering wind. Desire climbed with their bodies and he lifted her, a gale force against the white-water rapids of rolling swells and enclosing surge.

The water crested and met the rising storm, higher . . . higher . . . until the fierceness of the gale broke, its strength abated, its power subsiding into the lessening hold of the river.

He lay back breathless, drawing away from her.

And heard the shrill cry of children calling out that two strangers were coming into camp.

Chapter Thirty-two

Sagamore was too weak from his injuries to go outside his adobe house and meet the two young men on horseback. In his place, his daughter, Willow, stood at the center of the camp and waited for the strangers to approach her.

The children raced alongside the stallion and the chestnut mare, reaching out curious hands to touch the flanks of the animals. Neither they nor Willow had ever seen a man sitting astride the back of a horse.

The men were young, nearly her own age. The one riding the stallion was tall and narrow-limbed as a sapling. The one on the mare seemed to be a darker version of the other, with a broader body and a wider head. She was wary of them, but didn't move away, even when the horses moved nearer.

"You are welcome among us," she said in greeting. "I am Willow, Spirit Woman to the People."

Seth swung his leg over the saddle horn and came down, grimacing when his foot touched the ground. He held the horse's reins loosely in his hand and walked to where Willow stood. She noticed that he winced when he moved, as if injured.

"I'm Seth Katelo. This is my brother, Jonathan."

"Why have you come to us, Seth Katelo?"

He didn't glance around at the camp, like the one still on the horse did. When he spoke, his eyes watched only her. "We left our home in the north when the first days of spring broke the river ice. Our journey's been long, four times the full moon has covered us with its light."

"Why have you come so far?" she asked.

"To find other people."

It was a simple answer, and one she could accept.

"Are there no other people in the north country?"

He nodded, slightly. "Our father and mother, one brother and three sisters."

"No one else?"

"No one, except the wild man who calls himself T. J. Parker, living in a cave between there and here."

The name rushed at her in a flood of memory. *T. J. Parker.* She saw herself again as a child, watching the broad back of this man as he walked away from their camp, and out of her life. Parker, the grieving husband and father, the man who could not live among the People. All this time she had believed him dead. Parker, a wild man living in a cave. The image was painful; she forced it from her thoughts.

Her gaze lifted to the stranger still sitting astride the mare. "You have come so far to be among us, Jonathan Katelo. Now that you are here, will you not come down from your horse?"

He didn't swing his leg down from the horse as

his brother had, but held to the saddle horn and lifted his weight from the animal's back, lowering himself to the ground. He stood the earth a harder force than his brother's lighter stance.

A quick vision came to Willow when she met the eyes of this man—it was of earth, breaking from the core. He was the power beneath the mantle of rock. In his silence, she knew him. He was the strength of the land, and the spirit bound in it.

"Your horses will be thirsty," she told them. "My brothers will take them to the river to drink." She reached forward and took the reins of each horse and led the animals to where her two younger brothers, Yuma and Jared, stood before their father's house.

The two strangers followed Willow through the camp, meeting and learning the names of the men, women, and children of the People, and finally coming to the distant adobe shelter that was the home of Spirit Woman. She drew back the woven blanket which served for a door and entered the narrow house, motioning with one arm for them to follow.

The harsh light of the outside day dropped to a cooler shade inside the thick walls of the earthen room. The brothers sat on two twisted-strand rugs, each one thick with the blended textures of sheep's wool and goat hair. Willow sat on a mesquite-wood stool her father had made and given to her.

"T. J. Parker told us of your camp," began Seth, "and of another place . . . a city of glass."

"The biosphere," said Willow.

"Then it is real," said Jonathan. His forehead

creased into a frown, as if he were troubled by the thought.

"It's real, and not far from here," she told him. "The leader of our camp, Sagamore, once lived within the sphere. He came out to find the People. If he were stronger, he would tell you of how he went alone into the empty cities and found ten survivors. He brought them to this place."

Seth's eyes were shining and eager as a child's for her story. "Parker, the man we found, said he was one of those first ten. He spoke of a man called Josiah Gray Wolf."

Willow nodded. "Some are known by more than one name. I am called Willow, but also Spirit Woman. My father is both Josiah Gray Wolf and Sagamore. Another among us was once Brad McGhee, but is now called Prophet. We three have changed . . . becoming other than we once were."

"Why do they call you Spirit Woman?" The look in Jonathan's eyes was gentler now, not shining mirrors of his soul, like Seth's, but calm brown earths staring back at her.

Where she might have answered this question from anyone else, she wouldn't answer it for him. Instead, she pretended not to have heard, and busied her hands with preparing food for them. He didn't ask the question again, but she knew it was between them — a silence that would somehow find its answer in time.

Throughout that day, the elders among the People came to the small earthen house. One by one, those of the ten Sagamore who had gathered so long ago, sat on the twisted-strand rugs and spoke of the homes they had left behind when they came to this place with that first band of survivors. It was as though the two strangers drew the stories from them. In fact, neither Seth nor Jonathan even asked.

Willow watched the expressions on the two young men's faces as they listened to the heartbreaking memories of each of the survivors. Willow's own mother came, and told these strangers about her first husband and the three children she had buried.

"It was a time of dark fears," Elizabeth Cunningham said, "an ending of the old world. I never thought to live beyond it. Josiah changed that; he found us and brought us here. Josiah is a man who by the strength of his actions has altered the course of our world, and reversed the final days of mankind. This camp is our second chance. The People are our hope."

To the house of Spirit Woman came all of those who were left from the original ten survivors: Emily Pinola, Stephen Wyse, Merry Logan, Skeet Hallinger, and Crystal Rivers. All but Sagamore himself, and Prophet. With Willow sitting in silence beside them, they told the stories of the ending of their lives, and of their rebirth.

Prophet didn't come to Seth and Jonathan that day, or even during the long night which followed their arrival at the camp. Instead, he stayed beside Sagamore, nursing his friend through the dark lines of suffering and fear that lay between the space of life and death.

Sagamore's recovery had been slow and painful.

Infection still seethed in the wounds and recurrent fevers sapped the needed strength from him to heal. At times, it seemed as if the worst was over, that Sagamore would come back to the People whole and strong. He would know a few brief days of improvement, and then the fever would come to him again.

This had been one of the worst days. Almost from the moment the young men had come into camp, Sagamore's fever had begun to climb. Prophet had been with him and recognized the signs of trouble. Without telling Elizabeth of this, he had urged her to leave her husband with him and to go speak to the two strangers.

"She's seen enough of sickness and death, my wife," said Sagamore when Elizabeth had gone. "My life lingers like a spirit lost. Can't decide between living and death."

"I've decided for it," Prophet told him. "You're living. I carried you back from the wilderness on my shoulders. I'm not about to let you go now."

"Fine words from a man who claims to be a channel to God. Don't you think you ought to let the Creator decide?"

"Are you arguing with me for trying to save your life? You're too mulish to die. Now lie still and stop complaining. Act like a sick man and rest."

"I heard the children shouting. Someone came into camp today," said Josiah. "Who?"

"Must you know everything? Stop wasting strength talking. Your lungs have a hard enough time drawing a clear breath. Here," he offered, holding a cup of water to Sagamore's lips, "get a little fluid into you before the fever spikes."

Sagamore drank a few sips. "It reminds me of the days when I was gathering the survivors," he said, his voice losing force, becoming faint and breathy. "How many more of them are out there? How many—"

"That's enough questions," said Prophet. "Now it's time to fight the fever."

Sagamore said nothing more. The familiar heat of the fever took him, and in the delirium which followed, he saw himself standing at the center of a circle of unfolding cloth. The cloth was colorless, a transparency which showed the greens, browns, and blues of the living earth beneath it. Spread out upon the cloth were people: those survivors Josiah Gray Wolf had claimed, and others . . . so many others. The circle of mankind floated over the face of the land, unfolding in an ever-widening cascade from the center, that place where Josiah stood.

"Wake up, Josiah," Prophet's voice came to him as if spoken from a long distance away. "Open your eyes and have something to drink. Wake up," he insisted. "Here, try a little juice."

Josiah opened his eyes to a brightness that was morning. The dark had passed by. Not this time. Death would not have him yet. The fever had broken. His body was weakened, but still fighting to live.

He tried to speak. The lining of his throat was dry and sore. The words cracked and were lost to hard-drawn breaths.

"What is it?" asked Prophet, leaning closer.

271

"What can I get for you?"

"The strangers . . ." said Sagamore the leader of the People, "bring them here."

Chapter Thirty-three

Cameron saw the two brothers on the day they came into camp.

"It means there are others out there," he said to Sidra. "We could search for them, you and I. We could leave here and find our own place."

Sidra pulled the fat ears of corn off the stalks. The basket she pulled behind her was full, and needed to be carried back to camp. She should have turned away then, but wanted to hear what Cameron had to say.

The thought of leaving had come to her, too. In the three months since she'd left the biosphere and followed Cameron to this lonely place, the camp still didn't feel like home to her. The People, as they called themselves, were a nation, a colony; she and Cameron were the Outsiders here.

"Where could we go?" she asked, willing to consider his idea.

"North. We could find good farmland, where the heat doesn't kill the crops and the mosquitoes don't eat you alive. There's a whole country of rich land to be had." He stood up, stretching his back and looking out over the rows of corn stalks. "I feel bound here," he said. "I don't belong."

Sidra felt this same alienation. Even though the man called Sagamore was her father—and Willow and the other six of Elizabeth Cunningham's children were her half-brothers and sisters—she felt apart from them. The truth was, she didn't want to stay here, either.

She didn't ask, could we survive on our own? Or, could we find our way across the desert? She was willing to take those risks. Leaving the sphere had been the greatest act of courage in her life; anything beyond that was a lesser bridge of faith. What she did ask was, "What about Biosphere Seven? They're waiting to see if the blood transfusion has worked for you, if the virus—"

"It's been three months! I'm not going to live my life like one of Diana's lab animals. The transfusion worked. They know that. Maggie and Mike died within three days. I found the way out of the sphere, the way around the virus," he said. "If the others want to try it, that's up to them."

His face was flushed from the heat of the day, and with the intensity of his feelings. Even his eyes had a bright, uncommon light to them, as if the need for this thing burned within him.

She leaned close and kissed him. He was everything to her, all the world that mattered. "I'm always running away with you," she said, smiling. "When do we leave?"

He pulled her close. The breath left her lungs as his arms hugged her closer still. He was strong and his skin smelled of corn, and dry earth, and—

The small blister was beneath the collar of his shirt.

She didn't gasp; his arms held her too tightly.

When that first instant of shock and recognition was over, she slipped the fingers of her hand to the back of his neck, slid them under the loose cloth . . . and felt two more blisters along his shoulder. Her hand drew back in sealed-white fear.

Everything disappeared: the cornfields, the mountains beyond them, the sound of the river in the distance. Cameron disappeared, too. She felt him pull back. She was left staring into a kaleidoscope of harsh, blinding light, turning . . . turning . . . until she felt the ground beneath her fall away.

"Sidra?" she heard his voice call.

She tried to answer. Tried to come back to that place she had been, to a world grown green and earthy, and full of hope.

"Sidra?" The sound of his voice was lessening, with the light.

The brilliance shattered . . . and she was lost.

Jonathan woke in the house of Willow Gray Wolf. It was a dawn unlike any other he had ever known. All night, he had slept on the familiar ground of a woman who was not his mother or his sister. He had been beside her, close enough to touch her skin if he had reached out — all that day. He had seen the whole of his life in the silent judgment of her eyes.

And the world was changed.

"Sleep here tonight," she had offered her house to the brothers.

"But, where will you sleep?" Jonathan had asked, not wanting to put her out of her home.

"My family will still have me." She had smiled at

the words, as if they held a secret. "For tonight, let this be your home, and the People your family."

Seth's slow, shallow breathing told Jonathan his brother was still asleep. And so, until Seth woke, the house was Jonathan's alone. His thoughts about the woman, Willow, were his own, too. He held them against his naked soul like a softness he could touch.

Before yesterday, there were horses and river traces, and winding trails to follow into the wilderness. There were deer and rabbits to hunt. There were mornings of sameness, each day like another. Now, the morning came as a new being to him. It was a hushed filtering of light he had never seen. It covered him with promise, and with the first real understanding of his lifetime, of what he was living for.

A crush of footsteps on the hard ground outside the doorway brought Seth awake. He twisted up from sleep, sitting bolt upright, his eyes staring and empty, like the twin barrels of a rifle.

"Easy," said Jonathan. He stood and pulled on his pants, moving barefoot across the room, then drew back the woven-blanket door and stepped out into the light.

Willow stood a few feet from the doorway. She didn't notice him at first. Her head was lowered, staring at something on the ground. He moved a step closer, and she glanced up.

Her eyes were lost rivers, hidden crossings to her soul. He looked, but couldn't see into them. The boundaries were too deep and dark.

"My father has sent for you. You and your brother must come with me."

"Is there something wrong?" He felt it, knew a change had come to her, saw it in her eyes.

"My father almost died in the night. When the fever was at its worst, I fought for him," she said simply. "I went into that place where the heat struggled for his life . . . and brought him back."

Jonathan did reach out to her now, for she seemed to still be in that place of heat and suffering. He touched her face lightly with his hand and said, "Come back into this world, Willow. There are those who need you here."

He hadn't questioned her strange words. He knew that what she'd said was truth, at least to her. The People called her Spirit Woman, and that was not without cause. For him, it was a simple trust in this one woman. Without doubt, he believed her.

It didn't happen immediately, but something did change in the way she looked at him, some flickering of remembered light within that well of lonely dark. He saw the slow return, as if she had been pulled away from herself and was drawing back.

How much had she given of herself, Jonathan wondered, that her father might live?

"My father is the strength of the People," Willow said, as if she had understood his unasked question and was trying to explain. "His life is of great worth."

"What worth is Spirit Woman to the People? Isn't her life worth something, too?"

A faint smile traveled over her lips. "Less," she said. For an instant, she was there with him. Then, she turned away and walked quickly back to her father's house.

When Jonathan pushed the blanket aside and

went back into Willow's house, his brother was dressed and leaning against the far wall. There was no smile on his lips.

"Why does he want to see us?" Seth asked.

"Who?" Jonathan's mind was so full of crowded thoughts, he really didn't know who Seth meant.

"Sagamore . . . her father." Lines of worry stretched in unseeded rows along Seth's forehead. "If he's so sick, almost dying, what does he want with us? I don't like it. Maybe we should ride out of here."

Jonathan couldn't believe what he was hearing. "Only yesterday, I was the one who didn't want to come to this place. You were the one who insisted that we'd come so far . . . that you wanted to find other people, remember?"

Seth's brooding scowl remained fixed. "They're not like us. Did you hear what she was talking about? Spirits and bringing people back from death. I don't believe in all that—and neither do you."

Jonathan was stunned by his brother's reaction. "Dad talked about the spirits of the dead on his journey across the snow and ice. He told us both about them."

"I don't remember any of that," said Seth stubbornly.

"Don't remember? He told us when we were little. You were older than I was. What's the matter with you? What's happened since last night?"

Seth moved away from the wall, walking closer to where Jonathan stood. "He told you things he never told me," said Seth. "You always were more like him. Inuit." He said the name like a challenge.

"What's this really about?" They'd never argued about their father's feelings for each of them before, and although what Seth had said about Jonathan's being more Inuit was true, it had never mattered to either of them, until now.

"That woman," said Seth, "she's all you're thinking about."

Jonathan didn't know what to say. Things had gone just the opposite of what he'd expected—maybe the opposite of what Seth had expected, too. Jealousy was a big part of all this sudden anger. It had risen up like a diamondback between them, shaking the rattles of its tail.

"I *am* thinking about her," he said calmly, "and if that's wrong, then I don't know what we're doing here."

"We came here together," said Seth. "Just don't forget that."

"I don't get it." Jonathan had slipped one arm into his shirtsleeve, but now tore the shirt off and threw it from him. "You wanted us to come here and find other people. This wasn't my idea in the first place. You wanted us to find women. Remember all that talk? Now we're here and there's one I take an interest in . . . and you start yelling like I'm dragging you over rocks. What's goin' on in your head, Seth? You'd better tell me the way this game works. What's eating at you?" He reached out and grabbed his brother by the arm.

Seth twisted away. "I don't want to talk about it."

"Don't want to talk—" Jonathan started, but Seth was moving out the door.

"Hurry up!" called Seth. "She said her father wanted to see us. Let's go." He stood outside, a few

279

feet away from the house, kicking ruts in the ground with his heel. A minute later, he started off alone.

Quickly, Jonathan snatched up his shirt and boots, ran ten spread fingers through his hair, and still shod in only one booted foot, hopped outside to join him.

The house of Sagamore was no larger than any of the other adobe shelters. The harsh light and heat of the desert summer disappeared within the three-foot-thick earthen walls. Seth and Jonathan entered the house after Willow, and followed her to the room at the back where her father rested.

To Seth, who on their journey had grown used to days of open air and sunlight, the dim rooms were cheerless caverns. He felt as if he were entering the den of a wounded bear, and was wary of each step he made into this brooding place.

A woman with light hair and eyes met them at the entrance to the sleeping room. She blocked their passage with her hands pressed to either side of the doorway.

Willow made no move to urge the woman aside, but waited patiently next to the doorway, her head slightly lowered in deference to her mother.

"My husband can't see how ill he is," said the woman. "All night his life has swung on a thread between living and death. You won't say anything to upset him." She looked at each of them, and especially at her daughter, Willow.

"Beth, bring them to me," called an exhausted-sounding voice beyond her.

With a final warning glance, Elizabeth Cunningham stepped aside and let the three pass into the darkness of the room.

A single high window opening gave a slant of light to the muted space. Its shaft of brightness seemed directed onto the man propped against a hill of pillows where the wall met the bed. He was almost sitting, his body inclined in an awkward pose, looking caught and held—like a drab-colored blanket sliding off the wall and into the layered folds of bedding.

"Stand closer," said Sagamore.

Seth and Jonathan moved to the side of the bed and stood where the sick man could see them better in the shaft of light. Willow stood at the other side of the bed, waiting in the dark.

"Your names?" asked Sagamore.

Seth spoke for them both. "Seth and Jonathan Katelo. Our father was from the Siberian biosphere."

"Katelo?" Sagamore's brow pinched into a frown. His eyes stared at them, as if searching their faces for some hidden truth. "You're from the Siberian biosphere?" he asked.

"They're from the north country, Father," said Willow.

"Wait . . . let them tell it." Sagamore's face was a scowl of pain, or anger.

And then, Seth made the connection. "Our father, John Katelo, was the Inuit interpreter. He escaped the biosphere."

"Inuit interpreter? John Katelo . . . Yes, they would need an interpreter. I understand." The scowl lifted. His body sank back into the softness of the bedding.

"He thought we were lying," said Jonathan.

Willow glared at them. Her eyes were harder than her father's had been.

"It was a question my mind asked," said Sagamore.

So, he had heard.

"We knew of no one who survived Biosphere Four. Your father brought life out of that place." It was a long speech for the sick man, his breath coming in hard-earned gasps for moments after.

Seth gave Jonathan a let's-get-out-of-here hit on the leg. They turned and started to go.

"You are welcome among the People."

Seth looked back. Sagamore had lifted up on one elbow, the muscles of his face drawn and weak, but his eyes still burning fire. "You may live here among us, sons of John Katelo."

Seth simply nodded, but Jonathan answered, "Thank you. We will. My father brought life out of Biosphere Four, and the Siberian winter. We bring it here, to the People."

Seth couldn't believe Jonathan had said such a thing. His brother's words shamed him. He looked back at the injured man in the bed, believing he would see the same look on Sagamore's face. But the old Indian was laughing.

Jonathan's laugh followed. Then Willow's.

Seth didn't get it.

Seth was grateful when Sagamore's wife, hearing the loud sounds, rushed back to her husband's side, and giving black looks to each, hurried them all from the room.

When Sidra had fainted, Cameron had carried

her from the cornfield to the shelter and stayed with her until she felt stronger. By evening of that same day, it was Sidra who was caring for him.

By nightfall, the yellow pustules were everywhere on his body. His handsome face was swollen, and made grotesque by them. The fever raced through him, and quickly, he became too sick to stand. He collapsed to the floor of the earthen house, and had to be dragged by the two women, Sidra and Willow, to a loose mat of gathered blankets.

The shelter, a storage shed, stood empty and awaiting the time of fall harvest. Willow had acted in her father's place and given Cameron and Sidra permission to live in it while they decided where their house should be built. Now, it seemed this shed might be the last place Cameron Nathan would ever live.

"How can it be the virus?" Sidra questioned Willow. "It's been three months. It's past the time. No one else lived this long before. . . . It can't be the virus."

Willow laid a comforting arm around her sister's shoulders.

"It is the virus. You know it, and I do."

Sidra stood trembling, no longer denying the words.

Willow drew her a few steps away. "The People are afraid that both of you have brought sickness into camp. You must stay here with Cameron. Don't go outside the shelter. Not now. It isn't safe."

"But, I'm not sick. There's nothing wrong with me."

"Nothing was wrong with Cameron," Willow reminded her, "before this morning."

The words filled Sidra with a new terror. She had fainted today. Did that mean she would get the virus, too? Would her face be covered with painful, hideous blisters? And would fever claim her life, as it now fought to claim Cameron's?

"I'm not sick," she said again, this time more forcefully. "I'm Sagamore's daughter. He was never sick with the virus. I won't be, either."

Willow poured cool water into a shallow basin and dipped a cloth to lay across Cameron's brow.

"Let me do that," said Sidra, taking Willow's place. "I care about him. You don't."

"I'll be back later," Willow said, turning back at the door to the storage shelter. "Remember, for your own safety, don't go outside this room."

She closed the wide doors, and left them alone.

We're trapped inside walls again, Sidra thought.

Cameron seemed only dimly aware of what was happening. Bathing him with cool water wasn't keeping the fever down. He groaned and stirred, restless within his cage of pain and unending heat.

"How can this be happening? Cameron, you're not meant to die," she cried, sinking to her knees beside him. "You brought us out of the biosphere. I never would have dared that without you. You'll get well, Cam. You have to. You'll be better soon, and we'll go away. I promise. Only, don't leave me. I love you. Please, Cameron." She pressed her face against his. "Please, don't die."

If he heard her words, she couldn't tell. His skin was hot, and his breathing labored. As the night slipped into the still-dark hours of early morning, it became the only sound she heard, the hard pull of his breath.

284

Once, in that half-light before dawn, his eyes opened and he stared at her. She was sure that he recognized her, that he knew she was beside him, fighting the heat of his fever with cooling cloths.

"Cam? Listen to me. Think of Prophet. He lived through this. You will, too. Can you hear me?" Her eyes blurred with pity for him. And love. "Cameron . . . It's going to be all right. Everything's going to be—"

She heard a long sigh of surrendered breath, and then no other sound followed it. The morning waited, holding back its light for that one moment. Nothing changed.

But, everything had changed.

She didn't cry out his name. She didn't scream. The sound of her pain was within. It wailed like the voices of the damned, like the voices of the Earth, dying. *Her pain was within.* It was his name she heard . . . in every sense of her body, every thought in her mind. It was his name surrounding her.

She lay down beside him, cradling his lifeless body in her arms.

A new dawn lifted into the skies. And the sun rose to meet the heavens on the morning of that day.

Chapter Thirty-four

The child, Zecharia ibn Ziyad, had been born in the green valley below the High Atlas mountains. But the man, Zechar al Maghrib, had been born again on the dry, windswept *erg* of the Sahara. The rising desert dunes were the breasts of his mother—this land. The deep wells hidden within the dry wadis were the veins which crossed beneath the desert and gave it life. The emptiness of the Sahara was a lonely quiet, but became to Zechar the wellspring of a faith which was born beneath a crowded sky.

Day after day, Zechar journeyed alone into the silence of the desert. From the vast pebbled *regs* which stretched from end-of-sky to end-of-sky, the *soufis* had gone from the sea of sand. The holy men were no more. Always, after each journey, Zechar would return to the welcoming arms of Rhissa, and to the tent of Moussa ag Hamadi. They were hopeful, but his words were ever the same. "We are alone."

As a boy, Zechar had learned from his mother's teachings. As a man, he found no one to guide him in the reaches of his faith. His steps were the first upon the new ground of this unseen belief.

No priest had bound his eyes, and mouth, and ears, with words of someone else's thoughts. He was the truth of his own vision. To that, and to the seed of faith which surrounded and nourished him in the wasteland of this desert, Zechar owed his life and devotion.

Slowly, the vision of truth became words. The words came to him in the listening silence of his mind, and he heard the promise spoken of his future.

After one such visit to the Sahara, Zechar came home to his wife with the words, "We must leave this place. I was born beneath the omen of a shooting star. The time has come to find the people the Earth has forgotten and bring them together to become a great nation."

Rhissa beheld her husband's face and knew that *he* was the mystic, the man Zechar had gone to the Sahara to find. In the purifying light of the desert, he had become the holy one. But to leave the land . . .

"I will go with you this moment if you say it," she told him, "but my father is old. To leave him here alone would be his death. And the sheep, goats, and camels . . . who will drive them to the well and draw up water to ease their thirst? Must we leave them to die, when they have given us life?"

"You would go with me now and leave them all behind?" Zechar asked her.

"Yes." Rhissa's eyes met his with this truth.

Zechar took her into his embrace. "You are the wife who was forged in the same furnace of my soul. Your words are wisdom. Always, I will listen to you. Your father is old, as you say, but he is strong. We will bring him with us." He smiled at her look of happiness.

"And the sheep?"

Now he laughed, and the day was blessed with the sound of his laughter. "And the sheep," he agreed, knowing he would forbid this woman he loved nothing she would ever ask of him. "And the camels, and the goats," he added, "and all who will follow after us."

"Is it Allah who has told you to do this, my husband?"

"No. The god of your father has not spoken to me. Only the land has spoken," he told her. "We are the ancient people, born again. The land, the water, the sky . . . the animals on the seeded ground . . . they are my gods. And man, too," he said, "for we are children of the same Earth."

Rhissa's eyes were troubled by his words. "If not Allah, then who do we worship?"

Zechar took his wife by the hand and led her outside the tent. The sun was low in the sky, a hard light of white-gold, burning their eyes to stare into it.

"When man worships one god, be it Allah or any other, he is held bound by that faith, like a cage around his soul. I will have no cages on my soul," Zechar said to Rhissa. "Nor will I lead any of mine into the ways of such a belief.

"My faith is a freedom to see the holiness in all things. My belief is in the water and sky, the rock and the sand. There is spirit in you, and in me. There is spirit in the living earth, and in all that grows from it.

"For too long, we have turned away from that voice which spoke clearly to us so long ago. For too long, we have kept our spirits caged, like captured birds not free to fly. The faith we will hold is here before our eyes," he said to her, spreading his arms out to encompass the Earth, "and here, too." He closed his arms around her, bringing her into the warmth of his love.

Rhissa lingered in this new belief, ancient as the land they stood upon. In her heart, she feared her husband's words. Could they cast aside the names of God that man had come to know? To call upon? Her husband's ideas were simple, and therefore dangerous. Would her father come with them? Putting aside his belief in Allah? Would other men?

Was it right to go back to the beginnings of man's faith? Was that forgetting all that man had learned, and all that God had offered? With a troubled heart, she waited for her father to return. What would Moussa ag Hamadi say to his son-in-law's return to the faith of the first desert nomads? Had they become no better than infidels and unbelievers?

Rhissa worked at the hand loom in her father's tent, and in the hours of waiting for his return, found her fear.

"Are you a dog that you cannot see that there is something mightier than you?" Hamadi threw the contents of the glass of tea into the sand. "That rock will not bring you into Paradise." His voice was loud and angry. "Sand cannot hear your cry or be merciful to your prayers. Only Allah can do this. Only Allah!"

"If that is so," said Zechar, "then it was this same Allah who allowed the people of the Earth to die. Where is their mercy? Where is their faith?"

Hamadi's face was red with fury. "What manner of man have I given my daughter to? Would you go back to the beginning? To seeing a power in trees, and earth, and water? That was man's first tests of faith," Hamadi said, "his infancy. We have come so far."

"It was man's first faith, because the truth was in it," said Zechar. "Since then, we have grown away from our beginnings, but we have come no closer to the truth."

"This is truth? This talk of spirit being within us, within the earth, and sky, and rivers? This is your truth?"

"I see by a new light, Father. My belief is as old as man's first sight of the world, and as new as my own acceptance of that sight. We are all of God. The earth and man are of one nature. I will not part myself from it, or call myself above this land—not even for you. I am a child of the earth, Father. And I have returned home."

In the end, Moussa ag Hamadi left the Sahara with his daughter Rhissa and her husband Zechar. Hamadi was too old to remain alone in the desert. He rode on the back of the camel, across the desert sand and into the mountains of Morocco, remembering a time when the name of Allah was called upon five times a day, and the winds of the Sahara carried the plaintive cry of the faithful to the ears of the Holy One, above.

His grief was unending. "I have lived too long," said Hamadi to his only child.

As if in answer to his lament, the next day the camel stumbled going along the face of a ravine, and Hamadi fell to his death in the canyon below.

They buried Rhissa's father in the soft land below the foothill. His grave looked out over the sea of sand. They did not mark the gravesite, but faced it toward the east, where the sun rises and each man's life begins.

With the dawn, Rhissa prayed that her father's life might begin again. She faced east and cried out to the God her father called Allah, that Moussa ag Hamadi might also find his way home.

In the next days, Zechar and Rhissa drove the herds before them to the green valleys at the base of the mountains. Here, they left the sheep and goats. Here, they left the camels, too, and began the climb on foot. For two days, they struggled up the high passes and into the gray heart of the Atlas range.

Rhissa was silent much of the way. Her thoughts lingered on that place within the lonely valley, a narrow unmarked grave, facing east. She walked beside this man she called husband, but her mind saw nothing of the green trees and the rock face of the mountain. Her mind was remembering another place, a red tent on the desert sand. Her mother and sisters, their voices high in sweet laughter. Her brothers, boys with eyes like wells of black oil.

All dead. And her father, among the rest.

On the third day since beginning their climb into

291

the mountains, they crossed the Upper Dadès River into the High Atlas range, and came to the village of Ait Attig. The walled city loomed before them, a blind stretch of rock and stone, holding its secrets within.

Rhissa felt the emptiness of the village, and knew before they entered the gate that no one living would be found within the stilled breath of Ait Attig.

Zechar led the way through the narrow pathways between the pressed-earth houses. Rhissa had never seen such houses, or such a village with high walls like an ancient fortress. She felt a lingering whisper of the people who had lived here brush against her, like a ghostly finger on her soul. It frightened her. The empty village frightened her. The circular walls like a gaping mouth, frightened her, too.

Nothing moved in Ait Attig, not dogs, not birds of the air, not a shallow wind. Nothing moved, but the spirits of the dead.

Rhissa stopped a few steps away from Zechar's house and would go no farther. "Find your mother," she told him. "I will not meet the grandmother of my children in this way."

"Grandmother?" His eyes were a question.

"I carry a child," she told him. "To see a long-unburied corpse could mark the infant. I will wait for you here."

"You speak as if my mother—"

"Go," she urged him, saying nothing more of what was so clear to her. Zechar would know it soon enough. "Find your mother."

He found the body of Itto M'Hand laid out upon the wood-frame bed. Her arms were crossed neatly, and she wore her finest robe and headdress, as if someone had straightened and dressed her body for burial. Only, she had been alone. Waiting for her son to return.

A sound of the living broke from the silence of Ait Attig. It was a cry of mourning that lifted above the village walls and rose to the blue-black mountains and sapphire plains of the hovering sky.

Chapter Thirty-five

It was Prophet who led Seth and Jonathan to Biosphere Seven. It would be weeks before Sagamore would be well enough to walk, and the man called Brad McGhee had once been as much a part of this place as the one called Josiah Gray Wolf. They went on foot up the steep trail, climbing the broken shelf of land to the higher mesa at the crest of the hill.

Darkness still held the sky in that hidden time before morning. The whispers of dawn were rose-colored fingers piercing the smooth overlay of gray-black sleep. The stars faded, drawing back into that place where no one saw, their glimmer muted by the rising sun.

"The people inside the sphere," asked Seth, "how can they stand to be closed in forever? I would leave, if I were one of them. I would escape, like my father did."

"Some have left," said Prophet. "You know about Cameron and Sidra."

"At least, they took the chance," said Seth. "Even if I had known I would die like Cameron did, I would have done it. I would have broken free."

"They're afraid," said Jonathan.

"No," Prophet corrected him. "That isn't it. The ones who were most afraid did leave. Like you, Seth, they felt trapped and frightened. And they escaped . . . Maggie Adair, Mike York, and now Cameron . . . escaped to their deaths."

Prophet stopped just below the crest of the hill. "The ones who stayed—my wife among them— haven't stayed within the dome because of fear. You'd be wrong to believe that."

"Your wife's in the biosphere?" Seth faced Prophet with a stare of disbelief. "All these years, you've been out here and she's inside?"

"Shut up, Seth!" Jonathan's voice was sharp-edged with anger.

"No, it's all right. I understand how he feels," said Prophet. "It's seemed wrong to me, too, over the years."

He wondered how to explain it to them. "From the beginning, my wife, Jessica Nathan, was the leader of the biosphere team. The others looked to her for guidance and decisions. They trusted her, and she held them together in a kind of colony. When the virus came, it was her strength and will that kept them from splintering apart."

"But, why stay inside that glass shell?" asked Seth. "For what?"

"At first, the people in Biosphere Seven suspected that they were the only humans left alive in the world. They were the race of man. Human life became more precious. Every birth mattered; every death counted. They were all that was left. Because of that, they made the decision to live . . . to go on . . . to build another world

295

within the sphere."

The sun hallowed the morning sky, and the radiance of another dawn broke over the land. Prophet led them the last few steps to the top of the hill. "Come," he said, "see what we're talking about."

They followed him, climbing over the crumbling ledge of the mesa. They stood with their backs to the night, their eyes staring into a crown of gold-white morning. And at the center, the shimmering crystal, the five hundred acres of the glass-domed city, Biosphere Seven.

Prophet heard the breath catch in Seth's throat. "I didn't think . . . no one said it was so big."

"Can we go closer?" asked Jonathan. "I want to see how the glass is held together."

"We'll go as close as you want," said Prophet. "You can put your hand on its side and touch it."

He led them across the high desert tableland. Sunlight sparkled on the diamond panes of glass and the morning light played over it as they approached, coloring the sky above and around the sphere in a kaleidoscope of brilliant hues.

"I never thought it would be like this," said Seth.

"No," Prophet said. "I'm sure you didn't."

They moved around the outside of the sphere, leaning close and peering in at the rain forest and the agricultural wing, at the waterfall and the savannah. Prophet showed them the sea, and told them how Piper Robinson had given her life to save the biosphere from the forced entry of Jordan Talbot Exeter.

"It's so fragile. Anyone could break in and destroy them," said Seth.

"Yes." Prophet turned to him. "Their lives are at risk everyday. Of the six biospheres around the world, only one besides this one remains intact. The seals have been breached in all the others."

"And the people?" asked Jonathan.

Prophet looked away. "No one knows. The virus . . . it might be that some lived."

"Look! I can see someone inside," Seth called to them. His face was pressed against the glass, his hands shading the glare from his eyes. "See! There's a woman near the water. Over there."

Prophet looked at the place where Seth pointed. He watched for a moment, then drew back from the glass and started to walk away. "It's time to go back," he said.

"But, did you see her? Who was she?" asked Seth.

"That was Jessica Nathan, my wife."

They walked in crowded silence across the scarred tableland of the mesa. Above them, a raven flashed its wings against the canopy of morning light, and faded into waking day.

25 December, 2018: Our twenty-first Christmas Day in the sphere. Outside, winter lies in thick, white cold on the floor of the desert. Here, we are warm and safe.

Oh, God—can I go on? Can I continue to lead these people, feeling as I do? Each day I think of opening the emergency exit and walking out. Each day I think of my son, Cameron, buried on the Texas desert. And I wonder, how many more days will we go on? How many more Christmases will we celebrate within these walls?

Cameron's death has brought me to my knees. I am no longer strong. The families here need a leader who has the knowledge and wisdom to guide them in the years ahead. My feeling is, it should be one of the biosphere-born. They are the first generation of this second Eden. Their lives are of more value than those of the original team who brought human life to this replication of Earth.

Trinity Adair is such a one. If I die in the birth of my child, let this journal be my legacy to the world of Biosphere Seven, and my support for Trinity, the first of our children, to lead the families beneath this dome.

Jessica printed the pages of the journal and put them with the others in the drawer of her desk. This was the only record of their days, their lives. Is it for anyone but myself, she wondered. Who will read it?

She rose from the chair, feeling the weight of this pregnancy pull at her strength. Her body was awkward, a lumbering, unsteady block. She felt foolish. And old. To have a child at fifty-two! To bring an infant into a world of so much desperate longing and sorrow . . .

Should have been stopped. The thought was there, more and more. She had become like Diana, a danger to the lives within the sphere. She had risked them all by bringing in this child. *Was Di-*

ana right? Had it been as much for herself, having Brad's child, as for the people in the biosphere? Where was the truth?

Christmas Day. The children knew so little about the celebrations of Old Earth. Why had they kept this holiday and marked it with a small party every year? Because it marks the day of our entry into this world, she realized. It was the door to Pandora's Box they had opened and entered, but had never come back through.

Jessica recalled the words of Maggie's Bible. It was one of the many books she had kept beside her and read throughout the years. The words of Genesis had burned into her mind.

"The Lord God put him out of the Garden of Eden, to till the ground from which he was taken. He drove out the man; and at the east of the Garden of Eden placed a cherubim and the flaming sword which turned every way, to guard the way to the tree of life."

Such a sword kept them back, and prevented their return to the life they had once known. A cherubim . . . she liked the thought. It was a better image than a deadly virus. A cherubim with a flaming sword.

Again, the soft scratching at his door.

The night was a cored-dark that held the men, women, and children of Biosphere Seven in a hushed half-life that was the blind-awakening of dreams. The hours of Christmas Day with its feast, and Christmas night with its presents and merrymaking, were over. Even the children's riotous voices were stilled at last by exhaustion, and the sweet calm of sleep.

Yet, Trinity had been awake, waiting. Knowing she would come to him. Again.

He padded barefoot across the floor, opened the door and pulled her into the room against him, closing the door with a soft push. He kissed her before speaking a word. And she said nothing, demanded nothing, only offered herself to him — wholly, completely.

"You're beautiful," he said. "So beautiful." Against his palm he felt the fast pulse at her throat, the warmth of her smooth skin under his hands.

She let him touch her, allowed the heat of his kisses against her neck, against her thighs. Let the thin robe drop to the floor, never stopping him. And loved him . . . loved him when his mouth found her, when his lips brushed and eased the aching of her breasts.

At first, he was gentle, his hands stroking her skin until it burned with need. And then she reached out to him, wanting more, and the gentleness died. She lay back, a weight against his arm, the tight press of his body lowering her to the floor. And he rose over her like the fire within.

The sounds she heard were little cries, an unknown voice within her world of silence. Rising with him in this heat of pleasure. Soft sounds of yearning and need and want.

"Oh, God. Oh, God," he said, not yielding to the high, sweet cries . . . but held by the fierce grip of her legs wrapped around him and the hard press of her hands against his back.

She lay beneath him, moving like the flame of fire within them both. He watched the words, a whispered passion spoken only by the look in her eyes. His arm slipped under her back and lifted her closer . . . her body moving with his, and his within hers, unconscious of thought. Only need. His mouth was open on the tangle of hair against her ear . . . his hands beneath the soft flesh of her hips . . . the rounded calfs of her legs tight across his back.

He felt and knew the trembling of her need, and when she cried out, he smothered the sound with his kiss, his fingers woven in the furrows of her hair. Holding her, his mouth pressed tightly against hers, holding her until he was with her in that place her body always brought him to. . . .

And broke from all the boundaries of his life, free.

In the quiet that followed, Trinity lay beside this woman, and bending near, kissed the soft corner of her smile.

Cassi was Trinity's secret.

Jessica had been awake and restless at four in the morning. The baby wouldn't rest, so neither could she. It kicked and turned, making sleep impossible. She'd been walking down the hall of the north wing of the habitat, her mind on the prospect of childbirth in the coming weeks, when she saw Cassandra Hunt step out into the hallway from Trinity's quarters.

Standing very still in the shadows of the distance, Jessica watched as Trinity pulled Cassi close

301

to him and kissed her, before the girl turned and hurried away.

She waited until she was sure Cassi was gone, then walked quickly in the opposite direction back toward her own apartment. The question of what she should do about Trinity and Cassi needed thinking through before she spoke to Trinity. *If* she spoke to him. The truth was, she wasn't sure this was any of her business.

She had known that Sidra and Cameron had been in love and hadn't done anything about them. She hadn't felt that it was her right to tell them how to live their lives. Was whatever was happening between Trinity and Cassi so different?

She wanted to believe that it wasn't. Wanted to.

But, it was.

As far as anyone could tell, Cassandra Hunt had the mind of a child. A child who would never grow up. That was why Trinity was keeping this relationship with Cassi a secret from everyone, and why that secret could be so harmful.

Who was looking out for Cassi, now that Diana was gone? The question disturbed Jessica far more than anything else, for the lack of a ready answer meant she'd lost touch with her own people. For that matter, where were Diana's other two daughters? Up until now, she'd assumed that each girl had gone to live with her father, but now she realized that wasn't possible; Mike York was dead, and he'd been Alix's father. Who was Lara's? She didn't know.

Jessica had always believed that Cassi's father was Griffin Llewellyn. He was the man Diana had been living with when Cassi was conceived. But,

302

Jessica reminded herself, Diana had slept with each man in the biosphere, including Quinn, and any one of the men might have fathered Diana's first child.

What does it matter? — Jessica worried the thought — as long as it wasn't Mike York. She tried to remember. Had Diana already been pregnant before Mike left the biosphere? Was it possible that Trinity and Cassi could be half-brother and sister?

She made up her mind to check on all three of Diana's daughters, to find out where they were living, and which of the men believed himself to be Cassi's father.

And then, she'd think of what to say to Trinity. The secret he shared with Cassi would have to stop. It was wrong. She'd have to make him understand. And Cassi . . . that was the harder part. The girl with eyes like blind doves — who would make her understand?

After a sleepless night of worry, Jessica decided; she wouldn't confront Trinity about this until after her baby was born. The pregnancy was difficult enough. She had too many strikes against her already, without adding more. She was an older mother, the pregnancy had been a result of artificial insemination, and the fact that the baby she carried was the child of an Outsider — all of that was stress enough.

Yes, waiting until the child was born was surely the best way. *I'll be stronger then,* she reasoned. *I'll know what to do.* In the meantime, she was determined to find out everything she could about Cassi, and her younger sisters.

A nagging sense of foreboding came at Jessica like a chill wind in the night. Diana had always been a danger. Could Diana's daughter be anything less?

Cassandra Hunt was more her mother's child than either of Diana's other daughters. She was not childlike in her thinking—as people wrongly assumed—or simple. She was deliberate, methodical, and willing to wait for what she wanted. And what she wanted was Trinity.

Pity was the thing that had brought them together—and then sex. From the very first, it had been that. She remembered the day of her mother's death. She had gone to Trinity's room late that night, waited until the others were asleep, and used the pity he'd felt for her to find a way into his arms. Once there, she'd never left.

At first, he'd acted as if he believed he was only comforting a child. She'd let him believe it, knowing he'd soon understand that she wasn't a child. That she'd never really been a child, not the way he thought of children. After the first few nights, comfort stopped being part of their experience.

Comfort had never been a part of it for her.

Cassi came to his room because Trinity was what she wanted. If she had been able to put her thoughts into words, she might have said it was for sex, for that was the feeling she understood the clearest. The way he made her feel when she was with him, that was why she came to him each night, and why she'd made him want her.

But it was something else, too.

Cassi had been jealous of Sidra, of the way Trinity felt about the woman. She'd been jealous, too, of the close friendship he'd had with Cameron. She wanted to be his only love, his only friendship. Now that both Cameron and Sidra were gone, there was no one to stand in her way. It didn't matter to Cassi that Cameron was dead. She had never had any feelings for him. To her, Sidra was dead, too, or might as well be, living with the Outsiders beyond the walls of the dome.

She didn't hate Sidra. Hate wasn't a feeling Cassi understood. She had room for only one emotion, and that was her own desire. Other people didn't matter. Her mother hadn't mattered. Her sisters didn't, either. The biosphere was nothing to her, even though she understood it better than anyone else. She could have gone through her whole life, and never bothered with all of them.

But, she would have done anything to get Trinity for herself. Anything. If that had meant . . . but nothing like that had been necessary. Sidra had left the biosphere on her own.

Now, everything was perfect. Trinity wanted her, needed her. And Cassi would be very sure, nothing would ever keep them apart again. Nothing.

Chapter Thirty-six

Zechar and his wife stayed in the house of his mother until the spring, when the mountain snow melt flooded the green valleys, and Rhissa gave birth to their child.

The infant, a son they named Moussa after Rhissa's father, was strong and fair-skinned, like Zechar. When Rhissa brought the newborn to her breast, she laughed when she saw how light he was compared to her much darker coloring.

"He is a white lamb from a dark ewe," she said, smiling. "He is his father again, this one, and no part of the mother who bore him."

When the spring turned into the first warm days of summer, they left the mountain valley and returned to the foothills and the camels they had left to graze on the sweet pasture. From there, they began their journey, first north to the Mediterranean Sea, then east along the coastal caravan routes across Morocco, through Algeria, to Carthage in Tunisia. They didn't know the names of the empty cities they passed through, only that there was water and food in these places.

When they stopped in Carthage, Moussa was eight months old.

In these first months of their journey, fifteen followers had joined them. Two were children, born long after the days of the virus. They were alone when Zechar found them, a boy and a girl. Although not of the same family, they were close in age, and had forged an immediate friendship. Rhissa said of them, "Theirs is a bond of youth, for they are the only children among us, except for Moussa."

As more people joined them, their two camels became a caravan: eight more camels, a flock of bleating sheep, and a herd of goats.

"Where are we taking them?" Rhissa asked Zechar. She was already carrying her second child, and the constant days of moving to the rolling gait of a camel was making her sick with nausea. "We must stop and let them rest, or we will lose some of the old, and the youngest." She said nothing of her own discomfort, but let him make his decision on the welfare of the caravan as a whole.

"We will stay here," he said, "until all are rested. The sheep and goats have found good pasture on the grasslands, and the camel will soon give birth to the young she carries. There is time," he said, gazing off into the distance. "Here, we will wait."

"But, where are we going?" asked Rhissa again.

Zechar's eyes, when he turned back to her, were as distant as the lands only he saw in his mind. There was some part of him she did not know, and understood she never would. She would travel with him as his wife and bear his children, but she would never understand the vision that drove him.

"I was born beneath the omen of a shooting star," he said to her. "I follow the path of my birthright. I will gather a nation to me, and begin a people of the reborn world."

"But, where?" she pressed him. "Where are you taking them?"

"To all the lands of the Earth. We will become a people gathered under the strength and wisdom of one man. I will lead them into the dawn of a new world."

The child growing in her womb moved, and for a moment, Rhissa felt as if a veil had come over her eyes, for she could not see. Could he mean what he had said? Her heartbeat was swept into a stream of beating fear.

Like the rocking gait of the camel, she felt herself sway, and then fall. Strong arms lifted her from the ground and carried her to the tent. There, a darkness claimed her. The sun was hidden from her eyes. In the healing shelter of that dark, Rhissa felt the reach of her husband's dream. It had touched her life . . . and would touch the lives of so many others.

The child within her felt curled and twisted, like this new torment of her own fear. Hands resting over that pain, the place where the child grew, she heard her husband's words repeat in her mind. "To all the lands of the Earth."

What legacy would the vision of his birthright sow? The thought was followed by another, and for Rhissa, a worse one. What would be the birthright of the children she bore to Zechar al Maghrib? What would be the birthright of her son, Moussa, and of the little one beneath her heart?

In secret, away from the watchful eyes of her

husband, Rhissa ag Hamadi prayed. With the tender heart of a mother, she prayed not only for herself and her children, but for the living soul of the world. In the whispered plea of the hidden believer, she prayed to the God of her childhood, to the God of her father.

In a secrecy of faith, she spoke her prayer to Allah.

Two other children were born in the same month as Jessica's son. In the Outsider's camp that February, Merry Logan gave birth to another boy, and Crystal Rivers bore her first child at forty-two years old, a girl. No one knew who had fathered the child—or asked. All three mothers had survived the births, and one new life had been added to the biosphere, and two more to the People. That was all that mattered.

The fourteen-hour delivery was Jessica's seventh childbirth. Twice, she had believed she wouldn't live through it. The infant was turned on its side along the narrow opening at the neck of the birth canal. Cathe had reached in and forced a wedged leg and arm out of the way before the baby could be born. Then after, there had been bleeding, much more than usual. That Jessica had lived was a testament to the people within the sphere who nursed her, and by whose determined will, she regained her strength.

Jessica named her son Andrew. Like her other children, he would carry Jessica's last name, and not that of his father. The decision of matrilineal lineage within those families of the biosphere—

rather than the patrilineal lineage of the Outsiders—was chosen because of the multiplicity of fathers in each family grouping. The mother was the only constant in these family units, the link which bound all the children together. Andrew Nathan would therefore carry his mother's family name.

He was an almost silent baby. His every need was attended to before he cried, and the few sounds he made were more often the happy babbling and soft murmuring of language contact with his mother.

At first, Jessica was worried that Andrew didn't cry more often, fearing that this might be a sign of brain damage from a difficult birth. He scored at the highest scale on every intelligence and mobility test either she or Cathe offered, and it soon became apparent to everyone that he was simply a well-content and peaceful child. Few babies were born with a sense of bliss; Andrew was one of these rare occurrences, an innately serene and happy human being.

He was a comfort to Jessica, this small bundle. She made a cloth sling—something she hadn't done with her other children—and carried him with her everywhere she went. Even when he slept, he was against the beat of her heart. And slowly, through this bonding with her new son, she began to heal from the loss of Cameron.

Jessica's family was now Trinity, Roarke, Bram, Meredith, Rachel, and Andrew. And Quinn. She had always thought of Quinn as her space of freedom in this confined world. In his acceptance of the life they had within Biosphere Seven, he was the standing rock from which she drew her strength.

But her courage was her own.

It had been an act of courage to have conceived Andrew in this way, and courage which held her secret now. This son would be more than simply her last child. He was the hope of all of them. If his blood carried his father's immunity . . . If Andrew himself could one day pass this immunity on to others . . . there was a chance that she had purchased their freedom by her suffering in bringing this one into the world, and by the blood of this unique and precious child.

Trinity knew the truth, but kept her secret. Since the day Maggie died, Jessica had acted as a mother to him. He loved her, and she knew he wouldn't betray her. In fact, it was to Trinity that she now turned when any fear arose about Andrew, or what she had done. He was the only one she could confide in about this child. Her relationship with Trinity became less and less one of mother to son, and more and more one of friend to friend.

With Quinn, it was something different. He had never asked who had fathered the child. His only comment about the pregnancy was that she was risking her life. Beyond that, he had seemed not to notice, or care. She wondered at his reaction, or lack of one. The fact was, Cameron's death had nearly destroyed them both.

Jessica's salvation had been this infant. What was Quinn's?

Guilt overwhelmed her. With sudden realization, she knew they had been apart too long. She picked

311

up Andrew and walked with him to the main computer room of Biosphere Seven. Quinn would be there. It was his world. We love each other, she thought. We've been alone, trying to heal the hurt. We should have been together, helping each other.

She pushed open the door of the computer room and walked inside. Quinn's chair was empty, but the room wasn't.

Sound was the first thing she noticed, the remembered sound of his quickening breath against her ear. And the little sounds their bodies made when they . . . She stood just inside the doorway. From there, she could see the two of them—Quinn and Alix—Diana's middle daughter.

Unable to take her next breath, Jessica opened the door, went out, closing it softly after her. She ran down the hall, ran until her lungs were bursting and a fire broke into bright flames across her mind. The heat from that fire consumed her. She was wrapped in it, scorched by the searing pain.

They hadn't seen her.

Slowly, she drew the next breath, and the next, and the next. The images she'd seen stayed with her, before her eyes like a story in a window. She couldn't turn away, but watched and watched again. Quinn with Alix. Alix was still a child, Cassi's younger sister. How old? Surely, just a young girl. No, Jessica remembered, Alix was only one year younger than Cassi, and Cassi was nineteen. Old enough to be counted as a woman. Quinn's.

She was hurt, a kind of unrelenting torment that burned through her and would not suffer itself to be healed. She'd needed Quinn during all

312

these months, but he had turned instead to some-one else, someone less needy. A raw anger fused to that deep hurt within. If he wanted this girl, then let him have her.

I have my children, she consoled herself. She lifted the warm weight of Andrew to her breast. There were Roarke and Bram, Meredith and Rachel. They still needed her. And so did the bio-sphere. She'd been lost for too long. Now it was time to become a leader again. To bind them to-gether once more.

Our Lady of the Sphere. How odd the nickname seemed now. And yet, she felt a part of those words. She remembered the dream she'd had on her first night in Biosphere Seven. She had been alone in the dream, floating in a clear bubble, ris-ing above Brad and all the others she knew. Rising above the glass walls of the biosphere and the land. She had wanted to go back to them, but she couldn't. Called out their names, but no one heard. In her dream, the distance had grown greater and greater, until she was completely alone. There was no one to hear her cries. And there, she had remained, alone. Our Lady of the Sphere . . .

She held the baby tighter to her and felt the comfort of his small presence. Her children would hold her to the firm ground of this place. They needed her, and wouldn't let her lift away, becom-ing lost. There was a strength in her, she knew. For these children, and for the people of the sphere, she would draw it forth.

Sometimes, Jessica thought of how much easier it would be to become like Cassi, mute to the world. Or like Quinn. To close her eyes to all that was real. But she couldn't. In all that was honest and genuine about herself, she knew that what she felt was a responsibility for all of them. She was the leader. That put her in a separate place, apart from everyone else.

She wouldn't confront Quinn about Alix. It was a choice he had made out of his own loneliness and the pain of losing Cameron. Because she hadn't been there for him.

The outside light faded. She sat in the chair and let the room be swallowed by the healing dark. She had never been afraid of night. Seeded in the dark was the dream of each awakening day.

Only from the dark could life begin again.

Chapter Thirty-seven

Sidra had hoped that she might be carrying Cameron's child. In the weeks following his death, the hurt of missing him had penetrated every moment of her days, the loneliness without him so hard to bear. She had thought a child would be a part of him she could keep, but she had not conceived. Now, she saw that, too, as a loss.

Months passed. Winter had come with its icy winds and the sacral beauty of a desert snow. The fields lay barren. The stalks of corn stood as row after row of dried-brown wraiths, a shadowland of what had once been green and thriving life.

Days of iron-colored skies and air so cold her breath hurt came to this camp by the Ware River, came into the hearts of the People, and held them in winter's unrelenting grip. For Sidra, it was a time of senses as unfeeling as the deadening cold. Her mind, heart, and spirit were held in that barren field, like the stalks of withering corn. Like them, she waited through the blizzard of winter, and the ice-freeze of the life-giving river, until a warm sun came again to ease the People and the land.

With spring, came a hope that fed up from the

reaches of a greening land. And day by day the snow melted, pooling its water into rivers rimmed with ice and crusted hoarfrost . . . until the shell of winter cracked and gave way to the warmth of the sun, and the renewal of life.

In those days of teeming reawakening, Seth came to the small adobe house where Sidra lived with Willow. The house was set well apart from the others of the camp, at the far, outer edge of the village.

Sidra knelt on a woven rug just beyond the open doorway, shaping and cooking wheels of flatbread for the afternoon meal. There would be goat's cheese and chicken, dried herbs to flavor both the cheese and the bread, and a hot broth to warm them.

Seth could see that she hadn't noticed him, intent in her work, and so he was able to look closely at her as he came nearer. Sidra's long, dark hair hung in a loose mantle over her shoulders and down her back. Her arms were slender, leaning in muscled strength, working the ball of spongy dough. He saw her in that moment as a sweetness of life, a curving grace blending with and rising from the earth in gentle beauty.

Seth held Smoke's reins in the loose grip of his fingers, letting the horse trail behind him as he walked, the sound of the stallion's hooves clopping softly along the dirt pathway to the house. The land was wet with glistening light, a pale opalescence shining on budding leaves, and the cool green wash of buffalo grass. And on the woman.

The cry of a black-winged hawk circling above made Sidra lift her head. She looked up and saw

Seth walking toward her, then stood, brushing her hands clean of the dough.

"Nice day," she offered, smiling.

"Too nice a day to be sitting here," he said. "Smoke's been cooped up all winter. He needs to run a bit, stretch his legs, and the countryside's full of color. Come with me for a ride."

She ran a smoothing hand over the horse's neck, and lay her cheek against the velvet warmth of his shoulder muscle. "He's beautiful," she said, the words soft as a sigh.

"You've never ridden on a horse, have you?"

"How could I?"

"No, I guess you couldn't have. Come with me. I know where there's a stretch of wildflowers covering a valley between two hills. I'll show it to you. Days like this one are few. Don't waste it on work."

Her eyes said she was tempted; they were shining as raindrops. For an instant, he thought she would agree. "No," she said, "I can't." She turned away and started back to the house . . . and the dough . . . and the still weight of silence she had held to all these months.

Lifting Sidra off her feet and scooping her into his arms was the bravest thing Seth Katelo had ever done. He walked with her back to the horse, stepped one boot toe into the stirrup, and with one hand gripping the pommel, swung them both into the saddle.

"What are you—"

"You need some time away from here," he insisted, "and we're going."

He nudged his heels into Smoke's flanks, and in

a moment the red-earth houses were out of sight.

The floor of the high desert opened onto spans of white poppy, Indian blanket, and fields of wine cup. A clean smell rose from the wet, knee-high greasewood. Dull brown curls of the resurrection plant had opened with the spring rains and straightened into green shoots reaching for the sun.

A scattering of cows stood cropping the grass on a shelf of broken hill overlooking the river below. Seth dropped the reins. Smoke drew up as they neared the hill, footing his way carefully down the small incline to the basin of rainwater.

Sidra hadn't spoken again.

He came off from the horse and reached up to help her. She put her hands on his shoulders and let him lift her into his arms and down.

"You're not angry?" His hands still circled her waist.

She stood a head shorter than he, green eyes staring at him like the blowing diamondbacks of leaves in a high canopy of trees above them. "No, I'm not angry. And you were right. I did need to get away from the camp. The day is so much softer here . . . the colors of the flowers, and this pool beside the rock. Oh," she sighed. "I feel like it's the first time I've taken a deep breath in so long. Look, can you see the red and yellow paint-brush flowers? My mother used to point out one or two growing near the biosphere. She loved them, and the primroses."

"You must miss your family, and everyone from the sphere." He sat on the grassy slope at the rim of the basin. "I know how I feel about my family back home," he admitted. "It must be hard for you, sometimes."

She sat beside him, her long legs dangling over the shimmering plane of the water. Her eyes didn't look at him as she spoke. They stared into the distance, as if watching something only she could see. "I never thought I'd be alone. I came here to be with Cameron, but that's over now."

"You loved him?" He knew the answer, but asked anyway.

"Yes."

What had he thought she'd say? No? *I've been grieving for months over a man I didn't love.* She'd loved him, Seth knew. Still did.

"What's it like in Montana?"

The words were a doorway to the past. He leaned back onto the pillow of soft earth, closed his eyes, and pictured the land of home. "Close by our house is Mirror Lake, a body of blue water, and behind that are a line of trees that stand against the gray-black mountains. They fold around us, hemming in the valley on three sides. It's like a wide green river, that valley, flowing with grass for bighorn sheep, moose, and cattle."

"Tell me about your family?"

He kept his eyes closed, picturing his mother's face, then his father's, and finally his brother and sisters. The images hurt to remember, but he wanted her to know them. "My mother lives in a land where there were no other women, unless you count my sisters, and they were still little girls when I left. I think it must have been the hardest for her. Our family, alone up there, that was all we children ever knew. But for her, it

319

must have seemed lonely."

He could see again the nights in the tall house, his mother sewing by the light of the banked fire on the chimney grate. She had seemed old to him, even then. Her head was always bowed to some task, her hands always busy.

"And your father?"

The image of John Katelo rose cleanly to Seth's mind, a rounded Inuit face and a stocky build, the same as Jonathan's. "My father is a man who left a house of death, crossed a sea in a small skin boat, and journeyed through a land of ice and snow. My father found his way on that journey, his spirit path. Do you understand?" He opened his eyes and looked at her.

She was leaning on one elbow, staring down. "Tell me."

Seth sat up. "He found a peace within himself during that journey. After that, I don't think he ever felt alone."

Seth looked at her. She was crying. Tears as quiet as a gentle rain slid down her face. She lay back, curled against the yielding grass. Her shoulders moving in unsounded sobs.

He laid his hand against her back, felt the trembling and the pain. "It's over," Seth said. "Cameron's dead. It's time to let him go."

With a gentle touch, he rolled her onto her back. Tears hung suspended in the corners of her eyes like water jewels. He brushed them away with his fingers, until her face was clear of them and the sobbing stopped.

And then he kissed her. Gently, gently as a soft breath.

"I'm afraid," said Sidra.

Afraid to love him? Afraid to lose someone she loved again?

He was afraid, too. Afraid that she would never feel about him the way she'd felt about Cameron. That she would push him away and not want him. Never want him.

"You're alive. Let someone prove that to you," he told her. "Let it be me."

He'd never been with a woman—not in this way. Didn't know how to begin . . . all the things he wanted. All the things his heart said were waiting for him. Maybe it was too soon. Maybe she could never feel the way he . . .

She reached up and touched his lips with the tip of her finger. Then slowly, holding him locked within the green-keeping of her eyes, she loosed the ties of her blouse. And the cloth fell away.

He bent his head and kissed the softness of her breasts. No longer afraid.

Jonathan sat beside Sagamore in the wide, center room of the house. Before the two men were cups of brewed herb tea. Elizabeth, Sagamore's wife, laid a plate of bread, cheese, and dried beef jerky on a cloth in the space between them.

"She worries about me, my Beth," said Sagamore. "I must eat at mealtimes, take a nap every afternoon, and never get too cold. She watches me," he said with a smile in his eyes, "to see if I sneeze or cough."

"She watches me, too," said Jonathan, "to see that I don't tire you."

Sagamore nodded. "This is the price you must

pay if you come close to dying. People protect you for the rest of your life."

Jonathan gave a soft laugh and sipped at the hot tea. Sagamore had asked to speak to him, sent someone to call him from the fields where he was working. It would be important, whatever it was. Jonathan held a tight rein on his curiosity and waited for Sagamore to bring the subject up. The subject of Willow.

Willow Gray Wolf and Jonathan had become lovers, almost as soon as she had known that Sagamore would live. Until that time, she had remained by her father's side, caring for his wounds and using her knowledge of healing to save his life. Until she had been certain that Sagamore would live, she'd kept her distance from Jonathan.

Only after it was clear that her father would recover, did she turn to Jonathan. She had been bathing in the river one day, and he'd passed by and seen her in the water. For a moment, he had stood at the edge of the bank and stared. Water beaded on her skin, red-gold in the sunlight. She didn't turn away from his eyes.

But, he turned. He'd walked away from the bank and stood waiting for her by one of the orange trees, his back to the river. He'd heard her steps behind him and knew, but didn't turn around . . . not until she was close. He had made up his mind to tell her how he felt. How he wanted her every moment that she was near him. How he wanted her now.

Her hand touched his arm. When he turned he saw her, standing exactly as she had been in the water.

They had been together ever since.

"You know that of all my children, Willow is the one most like me," said Sagamore. It was the beginning, the reason he had sent for Jonathan.

"Willow is only herself to me," said Jonathan, "and you are you. But I see that she has your courage and your heart. She loves you; I know that."

Sagamore didn't try to put an answer to that thought for a moment, letting what Jonathan had said touch him. He seemed troubled by the words. "You know about the tornado?"

Jonathan nodded. "Willow told me. She almost died."

"Yes, almost. And that since that time, she sees images of what will happen, things no one else sees or knows."

"She told me about Rosalina Santos, about the children playing along the riverbank, the death of Merry Logan's son, and a woman named Natalie Peters. She knows what you think of her, Sagamore. That you fear her for this gift of sight."

"Fear her?" Sagamore stood and walked to the small window in the east wall. He looked out on the fields of corn and barley. "Is that what she thinks?"

"Yes. She says you stopped loving her when you knew what she had become. She says the People whisper when she passes, and that you have forgotten what she once meant to you."

"She's wrong." Sagamore still stood at the window, but turned and faced Jonathan. In the stronger light, Jonathan could see the scars from the wounds given to this man in his struggle with

323

the bear which had almost killed him.

"I don't fear her," said Sagamore. "I'm afraid for her. It's best that she leave the People. They can't understand how she knows the things of their future, and they believe she makes them happen. I don't want to lose my daughter a second time. For her sake, she must go from here."

Jonathan rose and walked to where Sagamore stood. "Let me tell her how you feel. Let me tell her what you've said today."

"No." Sagamore's eyes were dark and unknown seas. "If she understands that I'm protecting her . . . that I'm telling this to you . . . then she would never go. I know that my daughter loves me. I've felt her pain everyday, but I must hold my heart from her and drive her away from me, from this land and the People.

"They call her Spirit Woman," Sagamore said, leaning toward Jonathan. "It's another name for witch. If I die, who will there be to save her from them?"

Now, it was for Jonathan to stare out at the growing fields. He thought of the families she'd known here all her life, her brothers and sisters. Could she leave everything? Everyone?

"I know that you came here for a wife," said Sagamore, meeting Jonathan's eyes. "Now that you have found my daughter, take her back with you, to your home in the north country. You do love her?" he asked.

"Yes, I love her," said Jonathan, with no hesitation. If he was sure of nothing else, he was sure of that.

Sagamore nodded, then put his hand on Jonathan's shoulder. "Willow is the first child born of the People. She is the Earth's new beginning. Before you came to us, there was no place for her. I could do nothing to save my own child. Now, there is a chance. For that, you were sent to us. Take her away, to the life that waits for both of you."

"When I left my family," said Jonathan, "I promised my mother that I would return. She stood before me and made me say the words. I've thought of that, lately. Going home has been in my mind."

Sagamore nodded.

"If Willow will come with me," said Jonathan, "I'll take her home to Mirror Lake, to that green valley beneath the mountains. And there," he added, seeing the pain in Sagamore's eyes, "I'll love and protect her, and she will be my family."

"What of your brother?" asked Sagamore.

"My brother goes with me."

"Will he take—" Sagamore started to ask a question, then stopped, leaving the words left unsaid. He shook his head in answer to Jonathan's curious look. "No," he told him, "I ask nothing more."

That night, Jonathan held Willow in his arms. With his kiss, and with the weight of his body on hers, he kept Sagamore's secret, and his own vow of silence.

If Willow would agree to go with him, they would leave this place. With Seth, they would begin the journey home.

Chapter Thirty-eight

The day began with Andrew crying.

The sound woke Jessica from sleep with a start and brought her running to his cot. Andrew never cried. Something was wrong. She leaned over the tumble of blankets, child, and toys. He was bunched in the middle of the cot, a small, squalling lump.

He's not sick. That had been her first thought, seeing him. His face was red and his dark hair damp against his cheeks and forehead. His mouth was twisted in a grimace of pain, and he was screaming.

It's not the virus. It had been too long. He was two months old! It couldn't be. But Cameron had been outside nearly four months before the sickness claimed him.

She picked Andrew up, trying to comfort him, and walked into the brighter light of the room. His body was hot against hers.

"What's wrong, baby? What's wrong with you? It's all right." But, it wasn't. *He* wasn't all right. He was arching his back and twisting in her arms, his body struggling. And crying. Crying hard.

The infant gown she'd dressed him in for the night was wet through. She untied it and slipped the loose gown over his head and off. The damp garment dropped to the floor.

And she saw his skin . . . beetled with red blisters, angry wheals rising across his abdomen, chest, legs, and neck. On his back. And now that she saw him in the better light, the same red marks rising on the pale skin of his face.

A shaking began in Jessica, weakening her arms, weakening her legs. She almost dropped the child. Instead, her knees buckled and collapsed under her. The floor came up around them, a dark tomb, and in that instant, she felt herself falling into a dim awareness. But Andrew's cries kept her. She held the baby close, pressing his small face against hers. Held him to her for one long moment, until she was strong enough to stand.

Without question, she knew what had to be done.

She deadened her heart and mind to the sound of his cries, dressed him quickly, gathered his blankets and a single toy, and carried her son to the docking chamber.

She'd risked it all, endangered the life of every member of the biosphere. There was still one small chance that they hadn't been exposed to the virus yet. If the contagious period began after the blisters broke out on the body . . . there might still be time to save them. Andrew was lost; she knew that. There was nothing she could do for him. He would die like the others. Like Cameron.

She didn't have any choice.

It was early morning when she pressed the access for the docking chamber door. The interior sliding

327

panels opened readily, the biosphere still sealed by the outer chamber wall.

She ran into the room—moving before her mind could tell her to stop—and put the baby on the floor at the center of the docking chamber. Her son. She bent to kiss him good-bye, but couldn't . . . couldn't. If she looked at Andrew's face again, she'd never be able to leave him here alone.

And she had to leave him. She owed it to all the others. She was responsible for every life in this sphere. By conceiving Andrew, she had endangered them all. And she was the mother of other children, too. She couldn't leave them to be with Andrew.

Her son was dying . . . like Cameron. But she wanted to be with her baby! He needed her. She wanted to throw everything else away . . . to snatch him up into her arms, and go outside with him.

"Help me, God!" she cried, and rushed from the room, abandoning her child.

Her fist hit the wall panel, activating the closure of the inner chamber door, followed by triggering the opening of the outer exit doors. Then carefully, she pressed the lock-sequence code to leave the outer door remaining open.

Jessica slid to the floor, her back pressed against the inner chamber wall, and folded into a wedge, arms tightly embracing her bent knees. The baby's cries went on and on. The room was soundproof, but she heard her son's cries in her mind. She would always hear them. If they survived . . . if the biosphere hadn't been contaminated by the virus . . . she knew, she would hear the sound of those cries until the day she died.

* * *

328

It was Willow who heard the child.

It was early morning. She was awake, lying in quiet stillness next to Jonathan. He was a warmth beside her, and she lingered against his sleeping body, not willing to end this moment. The room was cast in the muted light of dawn, a sweet silence beyond the walls of the house. Not yet, that wakeful hour when the clattering noises of cooking and the shrill of children's voices would come like the full brightness of day.

In this quiet, she heard the cries of the child.

The sound went through her. It wasn't a noise she heard with her ears, but a sound she felt. Knew, even as it happened. She saw a vision of the child in a mist before her eyes. Small and crying. And the door to the biosphere—standing open.

Without waking Jonathan, she dressed quickly, left the house, and ran out of the camp . . . hurrying toward the biosphere.

She climbed the rough land of the hill. The broken ground crumbled and slid beneath her feet. A wide river had carved the valley below the table mesa, the same river that now twisted lazily between the banks of orange and lemon trees. She thought of that long-ago water, of the channel which had formed this land.

What force now formed the land? What acts changed it?

Was the child real? Lying in a room alone, crying. And if the biosphere door was standing open . . . what did that mean?

The hill was steep, and as she crested the top of it, she stopped to draw a deep breath. The sun had risen above the level of the plateau, and shone through the clear glass of the biosphere, making the sphere seem alive and burning with an inner light.

In a place like this one, the virus had been created. In a place like this, the death of mankind had begun.

Slowly, she walked toward the sphere. A dread of it had come over her. She was of the Earth and the People. It was another world: where children were bred for genetics, and not love; where Prophet's wife had remained apart from him, for the good of those in the sphere; where lost ones like Maggie Adair, Mike York, Cameron, and Sidra were given up, and never allowed to return. And my father, too, she thought. The man, Josiah Gray Wolf, had once been a part of this world.

Now, he was a part of hers.

Steadily, she drew closer. At last, she heard the child. The sound of its cries carried over the flatland of the mesa, a wailing from within the heart of the sphere. The infant's cries were real, and she hurried her steps, responding to the human call . . . the voice of life, against the silent walls of glass.

The room where Prophet awoke from sleep was in a house of his own making. It was a small room, narrow and empty of any ornamentation or furnishings, except for a raised platform which served him as a bed. One other room, a living area and place where he could cook his meals, completed his house.

His life was simple as his house. Each day he woke to the silence of these two rooms, and in those few moments before he rose and began the day, he knew he was alone. It was in the morning, when other people awakened beside someone they loved, that Prophet felt the cold reckoning of his life. It was in the morning, every morning, that he thought of dying.

He was fifty-four this year, old for a man of the People. He was the only one of them who had contracted the virus and lived. That singular honor was the reason for his testament to the God who had saved his life. It was the act which led him to prophecy.

He had survived more than other men: the virus, a rattlesnake bite, the loss of his world. But it was the loss of Jessica, the wife of his youth, that was the wound from which he could not heal. He carried the pain of losing her as a constant anguish in every day he lived. And now that they had a child, his son, the torment was worse. Jessica was his first thought every day, his last thought every night.

Prophet stood now and dressed. The sounds of morning began to stir around him: children playing by their mother's doors, women cooking cornmeal cakes and hot mush over the large campfire at the center of the village, and the sloshing feet and loud voices of older boys carrying buckets of water from the river.

It was a usual day, a morning like any other . . . and it would change his life.

He unhooked the metal water bucket—one he'd found in the supply room of the old resource center—from its nail in the wall, walked outside, and started toward the banks of the Ware. He had no one to carry water from the river for him, no one to cook his meals. He was one of the People, but he lived by the measure and strength of his own hand—part of them, but not belonging to anyone.

The valley floor was green with spears of tough

buffalo grass, bitter sedge root, and clumps of colt's foot. Across the riverbank, past the lemon trees, a sea of bluebonnets moved in the slight breeze. Their cuplike petals held moisture from the night, and shimmered in the bright sheen of morning. On this side of the riverbank were the ten-foot-tall bird of paradise plants, with their fluted yellow flowers. They were beautiful to look at, but bore a strong odor when walking close to them, a cross between strong garlic and skunk.

It was the same every spring. Now, the land that for so much of the year was drab and plain, bloomed with color. As though the ground were shouting: *Alive.* Prophet understood. His life was drab and plain as the desert, but inside, he wanted a renewal of spring for himself, to uncover the seeds of brilliant color trapped within him, and show that he was here.

He descended the loose-earth grade in a sideways step, filled the bucket with cool water, and climbed with his burden to the grassy embankment above. Shifting the bucket to his right hand, he started back to camp, thinking about the mundane chore of cooking himself a breakfast of two chicken eggs and a slab of fried bread, to be washed down with two or three cups of hot, sweet tea.

The water sloshed as he walked, spilling over the rim of the bucket and splashing onto his deerhide shoes. *I'm as clumsy as those boys this morning,* he thought, and laughed a little at himself. Now his feet would stay wet most of the day, and if the deerhide rubbed them wrong, they'd be sore tomorrow.

Should have been paying more attention to where I was going.

He looked up, determined to take a better account of his direction, and saw a woman walking out of the desert. She was too far in the distance at first for him to see her face, but as she drew closer, he could see that it was Willow.

She was carrying something in her arms.

He put the bucket by the door of his house and walked out to meet her. He'd gone a good ways outside of camp, and still he couldn't see what it was that she was carrying.

And then he thought he did see. A brown-and-gray blanket, wool taken from the unraveled sweaters of Maggie Adair. Jessica had told him about how she planned to rework the wool to use for the . . . A brown-and-gray blanket.

He felt his heart come alive in his chest, knew the hard pace of its beating, where a moment ago he hadn't been aware of it at all. He stopped walking, and waited. Waited . . .

He was the messenger. He tried to read what was coming, but couldn't. Willow's eyes staring at him . . . a brown-and-gray blanket. She was walking back into camp, from the pathway to the biosphere.

She slowed her steps, closer now, close enough for him to see that the bundle was a wool shawl. And inside, was—

"Your son, Prophet." She held the infant out to him.

He couldn't move. His legs were trembling, and his arms felt too weak to hold a child. He worked hard to put the tangle of his thoughts into words. "Why? Why is he here?"

"His mother put him outside to die."

"To die? Jessica would never do that." He was sure. Jessica loved Andrew.

"Look at your son." Willow unwrapped a corner of the blanket, and showed him. "He has the marks of the virus."

Then Prophet did look. The baby's skin was blistered with red wheals. The virus had claimed this infant, and exposed every life within the biosphere to the same contagion.

"Jessica told me to bring him to you," said Willow, "his father." She stepped closer and pressed the baby's weight into Prophet's arms. "Your son," she said, and stepped back.

The baby had been sleeping, but wakened as he was moved into his father's arms. The dark fringe of lashes lifted and brown eyes looked up at Prophet. Brown eyes like Jessica's.

The significance of what was happening hit Prophet. He was responsible for the life of this child. And now, it would be up to him to watch over the baby's death, too.

"What should I do?" he asked Willow.

"He's your son," she said, her answer a simple truth. "Take him home and love him." She walked away, her back straight as her father's. She was Sagamore's child.

And this small bundle in his arms was Prophet's child. Like him.

"Andrew," he said, and touched one finger to the baby's face.

He had no fear of the virus for himself. It had burned through him once, and he had lived. Looking down into the face of his son, it was hard for Prophet to breathe. Feelings welled into him, burning his throat, his eyes, feelings he had buried for so long.

For however long his son would be allowed with

him, this infant was a gift. It was his connection to other people, to a world he had grown disconnected from. He bent closer and kissed the baby's forehead.

"Thank you," he whispered.

He carried the baby into the camp of the Outsiders. Children were chasing after each other, their voices loud and happy. The women were gathered near the hot stones of the cooking fire, talking with each other, some holding babies on their laps. Prophet passed them, passed all those who were heading for the fields. He didn't stop to speak to any of them, but walked straight to the small house where he lived. The bucket of water still waited by the doorway. He left it where it stood.

Prophet went inside. He looked around and saw no place for a baby. The house—like Prophet himself—was a shell, and empty. Moving through the two bare rooms, he walked to the raised platform bed where he had slept . . . and laid the baby down there.

The day was golden with the warm renewal of spring. His son's tiny hand curled into a fist around Prophet's finger. Never letting go.

"Welcome home, Andrew." The words were tight in his throat. Every part of him was awake with feeling. Alive again, at last. If he was to be given only one day with this child, he would cherish it. He laid his hand on the baby's head and said to him, "Welcome home."

Chapter Thirty-nine

On the day that Prophet was given his son, Andrew did not die. Nor on the next, or the next. With each day, the red marks on the infant's body grew less and less, until by the evening of the third day, they were completely gone. To all observers, he seemed a healthy child.

All the people of camp came to see this child of Prophet's, marveling not only at his birth, but at his survival, if he truly had the virus.

"If it's so, it means the sickness is weaker," said Skeet Hallinger. "If this baby survived it with only a few spots, then maybe it's time for those inside the sphere to come out. Time for them to open the doors and walk free."

A few people agreed with him, but others were quiet, unsure.

"Cameron died." The People looked at Sidra, and no one else made any suggestions about the doors of the biosphere being opened.

In all ways, Prophet tried to care for the child himself. Elizabeth Cunningham offered to help. She brought some of the infant clothes she had made for her seven children, a sling cradle she had woven of knotted wool, in which Andrew might be rocked to sleep, and four glass bottles that had been taken from the resource center long ago, and had once held wine vinegar. The bottles were boiled clean, filled with goat's milk, and each fitted with the finger of a rubber glove.

Prophet used the clothes, but put the sling cradle away, liking to keep the child beside him at night. The bottles of goat's milk became a struggle, growing worse and worse as Andrew fought against accepting first the rubber glove as a nipple, and then the goat's milk itself.

He tried. He hadn't wanted to share Andrew with anyone. He had wanted to care for his son completely by himself. Every few minutes, he offered the baby this makeshift nursing bottle, but after only one or two attempts to nurse from it, Andrew would turn away and cry. The awful thought came: his son hadn't died of the virus, but if something wasn't done soon, he would die of starvation.

In desperation, Prophet turned to the two new mothers of the camp, Crystal Rivers and Merry Logan, begging them to nurse Andrew, too. Crystal Rivers—the woman who had once been a Las Vegas showgirl—had always lived among the People as a loner, apart from everyone else. Now, since her daughter's birth, it was as though she had become one of them at last. While Prophet stood and watched, she sat on a cushion in the corner of her house, opened her blouse and put first one, and then the other infant to her ample breasts.

Andrew nursed until he fell asleep on Crystal's arm, contented and full for the first time since he had come to live with his father.

After that day, a regular routine was established, with Prophet carrying his son five times a day to one of the houses of the two nursing mothers. While he

337

waited as the child was fed, Prophet talked with each of the women, comparing things their children did with what he was observing about Andrew. Did their babies push up on their arms and look around? Could they hold their heads up without support? And had they begun to smile?

Andrew smiled. He smiled and babbled, and made his father's life an unending joy.

One afternoon, two weeks after Andrew had come to him, Prophet was called upon to go with Sagamore to hunt. He was a member of the camp, and had always gone out with the other men when the fresh supply of meat was low.

"Leave the baby with me," offered Elizabeth. "I'll care for him as one of my own until you return."

Prophet hated leaving him, hated the thought that something might happen while he was away, or that he himself might be injured while on the hunt, and unable to come home to this child.

"Elizabeth has given birth to seven babies," Sagamore assured him. "They're all living and well. Stop worrying. The child will be safe with her."

But he did worry. All through the day of the hunt, he wondered if Elizabeth might forget to take Andrew to Crystal and Merry for his feedings. He thought about the young children in Elizabeth's house, and imagined one of them poking the baby in the eyes, or pinching him when Elizabeth wasn't watching. While the men were cutting the venison into portions of meat for each family, he imagined Andrew crying and spotted with blood-red marks.

The hunting party remained out that night, and returned home early the next day, bringing in the bounty of the kill: a wealth of venison from an antlered buck, four skinned rabbits, three quail, and led by a rope around its neck, a Hereford cow whose udders—heavy with milk—were swaying with each step.

Prophet wanted nothing more than to be home, to see that his son was safe, and fed, and well.

But Andrew wasn't well.

When the hunting party returned, Jared Gray Wolf, one of Elizabeth's younger sons, raced through the camp to find Prophet.

"My mother says to come quick. The baby's sick. He's spotted again," said the boy.

And the sense of peace Prophet had known since Andrew came to him, disappeared with those words. Prophet dropped everything where he stood, and ran.

He didn't stop at the curtained doorway, but raced into Sagamore's house. When he saw the child in Elizabeth's arms, his fear became a living terror. Andrew's tiny face was swollen and splotched with red blotches. He was shrieking and twisting in Elizabeth's embrace.

"He was fine only yesterday," she said, her eyes saying she was worried, too, "but then he woke this morning like this. How can it come and go? It can't be the virus. I'm sorry, Prophet. I'm so sorry."

Prophet heard her, but the words were lifted from him into sounds he didn't recognize. All he could think of, all he knew, was that his son was dying. On legs which felt wooden of all feeling, he crossed the room and took Andrew from Elizabeth's arms.

"I tried everything I could think of to comfort him," she said. "I rocked him in the sling cradle. He slept in it all night and seemed fine, until . . ."

Prophet heard nothing else. He walked away, out of this place where the virus had found his son, through the silent eyes of camp, and back to the small house he had made by himself before the People came—in the days when he was alone.

All that day, he sat and held his son, knowing the

child would die. He didn't leave the house, not taking the baby to Crystal or to Merry, but offering bottles of the hated goat's milk, and waiting for the end.

The baby cried all that day. By nightfall, he fell asleep from exhaustion, his hunger uneased. Prophet held him through the night, falling asleep toward dawn with Andrew still cradled in his arms.

By morning, when the baby's crying woke him, the red marks and swelling were gone.

At first, Prophet couldn't believe it. He went out into the morning sunlight, holding the child up to the bright daylight so that he could see the marks clearly. But they were gone.

Crystal sat outside her doorway, feeding her daughter. "How is he?" she asked.

"I don't understand it," Prophet told her. "How can the spots come and go? This morning his skin is clear."

Andrew was crying with hunger.

"Bring him to me," said Crystal.

"But the virus . . ."

"It's not the virus. If it were, or anything else he was going to die of, he would have done so by now. He's starving, poor little thing. Bring him here to me, and stop being a fool about it."

More grateful to this woman than he had ever been in his life for any gift—with the single exception of Andrew himself—Prophet carried his son across the courtyard of camp and laid him in Crystal's arms. A moment later, the baby's fretful cries were stilled, and he was nursing happily.

"No sick child would feed like this," Crystal said. She was smiling, and Prophet felt that smile course through him, lifting the weight of fear.

It was three days later when they knew what had caused the red marks. Prophet laid the baby in the wool sling made by Elizabeth, and by the end of the afternoon nap, Andrew was covered with spots.

Hives! The marks had been an allergic reaction to wool.

When he knew for certain what had caused the marks, Prophet took his son to Biosphere Seven and told Jessica that their child would live.

For Jessica, the days which followed after she had put Andrew outside the wall of the sphere, were clouded and lost to her. At first, she had locked herself away from the others, fearing that she might be contagious, and expose them to the virus.

Quinn reminded her that everyone had been around Andrew. He had held the child, and so had many others, just the day before the baby's rash appeared. If she had been exposed to Andrew's illness during that time, then so had all of them. Confining herself wasn't necessary. After Quinn's explanation, Jessica unlocked the door and agreed to live among them.

But, when she learned that she had put her child outside the dome needlessly, she couldn't find a way to come back to her family, or to the world of the living. She waited for hope to find her.

And it did—in the love of her husband, Quinn.

He was there when she woke up startled in the night, searching for Andrew's small body beside her. She felt Quinn's arms around her, holding her from falling forever into the dark. Through the weeks after, she didn't understand what was wanted from her, but let herself be cared for by his strong hands and by a strength of love that touched even that place where her mind had fled.

By the healing power of his love, he brought her back.

And when she was well again, he came to her in the quiet of the night and asked for her forgiveness. "I turned to Alix after Cameron died, because I couldn't turn to you. The pain of losing him was more than I believed I could stand. I needed someone, Jessica. I needed you . . . but you were pregnant with Brad's child."

"You knew that it was Brad's? Even then?"

He nodded. "It killed me, that you did this secretly. That you still loved him. I couldn't turn to you, after that."

So this was the reason why he'd never asked to know who was the father of the child when she was pregnant. Why he'd ignored her pregnancy as if it hadn't existed. And why he'd turned to another woman's arms.

"I should have been there for you, Quinn." She tried to remember those days, a blending into black that fell away and left her empty.

He shook his head. "You had your own share of hurt."

She nodded. "I couldn't see beyond it. But you were wrong about Brad. That's over. What I was trying to do was save our children, yours and mine. I thought if I could bring a child with immunity to the virus into the biosphere, then maybe we could find a way to pass on that immunity to everyone. I knew that if we didn't do something soon, we'd lose Cameron. I thought that I could set him free." She was crying, tears that filled her heart and overflowed into her eyes and down her cheeks. "What happened with Brad never came between us, Quinn."

He took her hand. "We need only truth between us now, Jessie."

"The truth is," she told him, moving closer and kissing the sharp line of his jaw below his ear, "that I

342

was pulled back into life by your love . . . and I'm never going to let you go."

"If you mean that"—his eyes were questions searching hers for an answer—"then we can find a way to survive everything else."

"I mean it. Always."

They sat that night by the shore of a translucent-green sea. The small perfect waves came in across the wet sand and over their bare toes, touching and blessing both Jessica and Quinn with the living water of their ongoing world.

"It was early spring, just after the snows melted, when Seth and I left our family," Jonathan said to Willow. "Now it's spring again. We've been gone a whole year. It's time for us to go home."

She thought about what he was saying, and what it would mean to her. "When will you leave?"

"In a few days."

A few days!

He touched her bare arm. "Willow, I want you to come with me."

She had known he would ask. And she'd made her decision. She was Spirit Woman. She couldn't leave her father or the People. "My place is here," she told him, "among my family."

"Sidra's coming with us . . . with Seth. Maybe a few others will travel with us, too."

She thought of the young people of camp, and knew that many would welcome the chance to see another way of life besides this one. Like them, she longed to see the places which lay beyond this desert. She longed to see forests, and rivers so swift and deep standing horses could be lost in them.

But she would stay here, for her father, for the People.

"Do you love me?" Jonathan asked. "It's all I want to know."

They stood several feet apart, not touching, but she couldn't pull herself away from him. Couldn't deny her heart. "I think that you are the only man I will ever love," she said, then turned and walked away.

That night, Sagamore came to Willow. His face was stern and his eyes dark with secrets she couldn't see. "Father, I —"

"Go with them when they leave," said Sagamore, stopping her words. "The People fear you, Willow. Your life is not to be among them, but far away from here. Go north with Jonathan and his brother. Find a place for yourself and begin your life there."

"I won't leave you," she cried, stricken by the hard look in his eyes. "You need me."

"I need a witch?" he shouted. "When they leave, be sure you go with them. This is your home no longer."

He left her, and she heard his words again and again through the lonely night. Before dawn, she went to the house where Jonathan slept, and woke him with her answer.

"I'll go with you, to whatever land that you would take me. I have no one. You are my family now."

In the end, there were eight in the group who would go north: Seth and Sidra, Jonathan and Willow, Yuma and Jared Gray Wolf, and the seventeen- and sixteen-year-old brothers, Nolan and Martin Wyse. The Gray Wolf and Wyse brothers had joined the journey in the hopes of finding both adventure, and wives.

344

It was on a day of unclouded sky when they left the encampment of the Outsiders. With them went the two horses—the dance-footed black and the chestnut mare. A foal had been born to the mare early that spring, a colt, and it came with them willingly, running on spindly legs beside its mother.

The People stood outside their houses and watched the children go. Sagamore watched in grieving silence as four of his children left. Human life had reseeded itself upon the Earth, and now was reaching forth . . . beyond the boundaries of Eden.

Chapter Forty

The spring came late in Montana, to the house beside Mirror Lake. Ice floes still clawed at the river, and a sheen of gripping cold held the people, and the land.

John Katelo stepped outside the wooden house he shared with his wife and four children. A wind was blowing from between the pointed backs of the gray-black mountains. There would be more days of hard winter before the sun warmed the land.

Waiting in the heart of the earth were seeds of renewal. Promises of life. Waiting in the heart of the Inuit, John Katelo, were the seeded words of other promises. Each day he came alone to this spot and looked to the south, to that place where he had last seen his sons ride away.

What had become of them? Where were these children made of his own flesh?

He turned back to the wooden house. A curl of white smoke rose from the stone chimney. Salena would be cooking breakfast for Amber, Cross, Lacy, and Noelle. Another day had come, and they would live it, here in the bounty of this land.

Voices whispered on the keening wind, voices of those long gone. Katelo stood for a moment and listened to the sounds whipping through the trees. Above the hard plains of Earth were the stolen memories of man, living in the silvered bands of sky, just beyond their reach.

His memories were all that was left of them, the people of the world, and those few he had known by name: his mother and father, sisters and brothers, the people of Biosphere Four in Siberia, ten-year-old Cody, and the two infant sons who had died in this green valley.

These were the voices John Katelo heard on the wind—some unknown, and some painfully familiar.

Life was a journey begun long before birth and never finished. Katelo's ways and beliefs were those of the Inuit of the north country, in that place of ice and snow. A brother to the spirits of those long dead, he continued for them . . . keeping his peace with the land.

One final time he looked to the south, and dreamed of the day when his sons would come home. Then hearing his wife's voice calling, he walked back into the wooden house beside the water and the woodland copse, and quietly closed the door.

In October, 1992, Pinnacle will publish J.M. Morgan's *Future Eden* the next book in the thrilling *Desert Eden* trilogy. Here's a taste of the adventure yet to come. . . .

Future Eden

by J. M. Morgan

The day of the killing flood was a morning unlike any other. Heavy spring rains had soaked the desert for a week, filling the rivers and narrow creeks to overflowing. The land bubbled like a pot of cooking meal, for the ground could hold no more.

In the camp of the Outsiders, those people living along the Ware River valley of Texas—below the climb to the high mesa and the glass peaks of Biosphere Seven—the sky had seemed to join the earth, for everywhere was a wavering gray. The heavens rippled, the land boiled, and the rivers churned with unleashed fury.

The once peaceful river which ran between the

banks of flanking orange and lemon orchards, now pressed over the lip of the earthen embankments, spilling the uncontrollable surge of water onto the valley plain. The lemon trees washed down river. The orange trees were torn from their roots and joined the swollen flood channel. And the earthen slopes of the Ware crumbled into the mad rumble of the storm's deluge.

And the rains went on, unceasing.

On the seventh morning, the clouds parted. A wedge of red-orange sky revealed itself like a portent from an angry god. Fingerlets of this fire bled into the track of gray above the heads of the men, women, and children of the People, as if burning an opening through the hovering mist and vapor.

"What next?" asked Elizabeth Cunningham. She was standing at the door of her adobe house, the floor a wash of sinking mud, and the constant leak of rainwater through the lodge pole and thatch roof. "How will we live?" she asked. "Our crops are rotting in the fields. The river's taken the fruit trees, and even our houses are falling into the destruction of this constant rain. What else can happen?" she asked, turning to her husband.

The Indian nature of Josiah Gray Wolf wished she hadn't asked it. He was superstitious enough to believe that if you voiced such a question the spirits of the land above and the land below would give you an answer. And it was an answer he was sure they didn't want.

"Come away from the doorway, Beth. It's too cold there." With an arm around her shoulders, he tried to urge her back to the warmth of the fire with him and their children.

Stubbornly, she shook the comfort of his arm from her. "I want to see it." The words seemed bitten off, as if made of thin, brittle glass. "I've lost my family and my home once before. I was numb through that. I thought it was behind us, but it's happening again, isn't it? It's taking away the life we've made here, our home," she said more to the blood-orange break in the sky than to him. "This time, I want to see it. Everything we've struggled to hold together, everything we've worked so hard to build . . . gone."

Josiah went back to the small hearth fire where his four remaining children sat huddled beside the only heat in the damp house—two sons and two daughters: thirteen-year-old Una; Walker, eleven; America—or Merc—nine; and six-year-old Tad. They were the four he had left to him. Four others, his daughters Sidra and Willow, and his sons Yuma and Jared, had gone north nearly a year before, to a colony of survivors living in Montana. The land of this place was less without them. He was less.

"Will the rain stop?" asked Tad. The boy was paler than he should be, thought Josiah.

"The rain always stops," he promised the child.

"Mama said God made it rain once for forty days and forty nights," declared Merc. She was her mother's daughter, a child who loved learning as much as food, and had a memory like a tight-fitting box. Nothing slipped away from her, or was ever forgotten.

"That was a story," said Josiah.

She looked at him doubtfully.

"Like a fairy tale?" Tad's eyes were ringed with worry.

Josiah took the boy on his knee. He could feel the cold living in this child, as if his small body could not hold enough heat to resist it. He rubbed a little warmth into the boy's arms and legs.

"The flood that story speaks of happened a long,

long time ago," he told his son. "At the end of the story, it promises that such a thing will never happen again. You don't need to fear that."

Tad's eyes were gentle again, a sweetness that Josiah felt his own spirit returning to as he grew older. The old and the young were the innocents of life. He had once been what this child was, and was now going back to it, in the fullness of his years. They shared this unity of spirit, he and his youngest child. In that, they comforted one another.

"The color of that sky. I've never seen such a morning," said Elizabeth at the open doorway, her voice sounding like a shudder on the wind. Something loud whipped at the air beyond the four earthen walls of the house. And then, "Oh, God! Oh, dear God. Josiah, look!"

He stood, put the boy down, and moved the few steps to the doorway. A wall of water ten feet high raced behind the already swollen Ware River. It was coming toward them, the heel of its boot slamming into the crumbling embankments and flooding the adjacent valley. Already crushing the first adobe houses.

"Children, run!" he shouted.

But, it was too late to run.